SHIVA'S

Photographs by Stella Snead

Jon and Rumer Godden

PIGEONS

AN EXPERIENCE OF INDIA

Alfred A. Knopf   The Viking Press
New York

CONTENTS

Note: To avoid confusion, no diacritical marks have been used in this book.

PREFACE

A book of photographs usually has a short accompanying text, sometimes only captions; it remains a book of photographs. Books written about places and their people often have photographs as illustrations: they are illustrated books. *Shiva's Pigeons* does not come into either category—perhaps it does not come into a category at all—because it is an attempt to do something more. When, in the boardroom of a publishers' office, we, Jon and Rumer, first met Stella Snead and saw her photographs—some of those patterns that escape most people's eyes, patterns of sand-ripples, shadows, iron rods in a river—they showed the way to what we have always thought a book about India should be, a concept of a whole; this does not mean "comprehensive"—no one could write or photograph a "comprehensive" book about India, not in twenty lifetimes—but whole in the way the rishis[1] saw all life as a whole, a concept in which photographs and writing should balance, neither being dominant but both blending and woven so closely together that to take away one photograph or to let a sentence run over its allotted page would disturb that balanced whole.

---

1. India's ancient sages.

The rishis might have been pleased, but for our publishers the task has been difficult; we suppose they briefed us, but the book soon blotted that out; their patience and non-interference have been benign, especially if it is remembered that when, in the generosity of that boardroom meeting, it was decided to embark on this project, they had not encountered us. Nor had we, Stella, and Jon, with Rumer, encountered one another. Stella probably had no idea then how frustrating it would prove, having to bend her independent vision to meet ours; added to which, she worked in Bombay and New York, which meant continual letter-writing—for this book it could be called "pigeon post." We, Jon and Rumer, dyed-in-the-wool novelists, had not imagined what discipline it would be to follow the "dictation" of the photographs, nor where they would take us. Above all, we had to encounter India, her whom, up to then, we had thought we knew so well.

India is always spoken and written of as "she"; other countries are too, but the Indian "she" has something of the quality of her own great universal Goddess; she is manifold. The great Goddess is the "shakti" or energy—everyday Indians call her the wife—of Shiva;[2] he is her Lord, which is why we have, reverently, we hope, taken his name in the title.

The Goddess has many aspects; so has India. Some of us say she is one of her own eager young professional women, burgeoning with new ideas, new processes in agriculture, industry, education, the sciences, art; she has her troubles, of course, but these are growing pains. Others insist she is that ageless mother, calm and untroubled, whose customs and ways have not altered for thousands of years. Or she is a golden princesss who has awakened after centuries of sleep. A princess? She is a beggar woman, her children starving in filth and rags, her hand outstretched to the world for alms. Which "she" is she? The answer is "all." A reasonable person might object: How can anyone be traditional and progressive, rich and poor, old and young at the same time? India can; her "pairs of opposites" are famous and, though she has the mysterious goddess power of reconciling her contradictions so that they do not clash but, rather, give her a peculiar richness, an added or double meaning, they often make her seem utterly baffling.

For instance, the Hindi word for "yesterday" and "tomorrow" is the same, "kal,"[3] as is the word for the "day before yesterday" and the "day after tomorrow," "parson";[4] the verbs with which they are used make them clear, if one knows the language, but it still seems unnecessarily bewildering; only

---

2. Shiva: third God of the Hindu Trinity.
3. "A" in Sanskrit and Hindi is pronounced almost as "u," so that "kal" sounds almost like the English "cull."
4. "Parson," pronounced "purrsoon," the "r" emphasized.

seems: these two small words, the same but different, are indications of a deep philosophy, the Hindu conception of time.

We Westerners instinctively think that everything, including life, must have a beginning and an end: we are born, we live, grow old, and die, and that is the end of us on earth, but Orientals, as the pandit storyteller says on page 320, believe that life evolves in cycles, a process of gradual change, unceasing transformations, while behind them is the force that never changes, "prakriti"—nature—the implacable "law," a recurring continuity. India is changing, not for the sake of change but because she must—there is no place for stagnation in continuity—but underlying the surge of human movement is the changeless rhythm in which it is held. The Hindu is always aware of eternity; Shiva is the god of death, but death that wakes to resurrection; therefore he is also the god of life.

It is fashionable now for Indian intellectuals to deny that India's life is steeped in religion; they may mean, hopefully, that some of the cults and superstitions are being cleared away, but to our minds a Hindu's religion, whether he is devoted or not, as inextricably governs his life today as it did in the days of Varuna.[5] The most sacred verse in Hindu scripture is the *gayatri*[6] which comes from the *Rig Veda*, so that it is at least three thousand years old; it is still whispered in meditation in the most modern of tenement flats, or chanted raucously over the radio for the bazaar or village to hear, and the words have never changed.

There was not room in a single book to go into the other great religions found in India and, too, they are native to other lands, while Hinduism and its offshoots, the Sikh and Jain religions, belong only to India; most of her millions are Hindu, so we have taken Hinduism as the root of this book, and tried to echo its pervasiveness; it is, too, the essence of India's double or paradoxical thought, which is why it is often misunderstood; its myths that seem fairy tales hold profound truths; truths change and interchange; Hinduism is high philosophy/childish superstition, the grossest erotica/asceticism more extreme than in any other religion; but the differences dissolve; India is a mystical land, and mysticism, instead of dividing things into parts as does the analytical thought from which most of us cannot refrain, integrates them into that related whole.

It seemed to us, then, that in this study of India—though "study" is too scholastic a word—we should follow the pandit's axiom and let the book

5. Varuna was originally the most powerful of the early cosmic gods.
6. A hymn to the sun god.

evolve, with only a thread of a consecutive story, and not be concerned with current affairs that are ephemeral; so there are no politics in it, no judgments, not even opinions, only observations.

The photographs, our mainspring, were not planned but taken in Stella's unique way—here, there, and everywhere—as can be seen by the captions at the end: one moment we are in the Himalayas, next in the deserts of Rajasthan; with a peasant boy, a middle-class girl, a gypsy, a sage, or looking at a water channel or the mottled pattern of an elephant's huge ear. We have not tried to explain the pictures but woven them with what each brought, suggested, or reminded us of, linking them but often wandering, as the pandit's stories do, and sometimes borrowing from the generosity of other writers and poets. Our own writing is fragmentary: few customs are common for the whole of India; one cannot say, "When a Hindu baby is born, such and such is done"; it depends where it is born, to whom, and when. A story told in Kulu would not be true anywhere else; a Punjabi wedding is different from a Bengali one; but because too many footnotes are tiresome, we have let the narrative run, always on the understanding that what it tells is true of some people, at some time, in some part, somewhere in India.

We shall be told we have left out a thousand things; more likely it is a thousand thousand. Inevitably: Kashmir has a lake, Manasbal, with water of the deep luminous green of one of the Emperor Jehangir's emeralds, the colour due to its depth. A fisherman, living on its shores, resolved to plumb the lake. He spent twenty years making a rope, then netted one of its ends to a stone so mighty that his boat could only just float under it; he rowed to the middle of the lake, tipped the stone over the side and let the rope run down, fathom after fathom after fathom. The stone never touched bottom.

Take such a simple little thing as the price of a paper kite in the bazaar. If we, Europeans, go to buy one ourselves, the price will be inflated; send our servant, and the price will be different but still not the right one because, as is the custom, the servant must add his commission or "tea money"; we could ask an Indian friend to buy for us, but a friend of Europeans will almost certainly be westernized and in an upper income bracket, and the price will rise again. The urchin who will fly the kite will come nearer the price, but even then it may vary, depending whether the shopkeeper is mild or bad-tempered, or whether the boy is the first customer of the day—bad luck may come if he does not buy. There is no such thing as the exact price of an Indian kite.

Shiva's Pigeons, then, makes no claim to be more than a conglomeration of glimpses, like one of Udaipur's embroidered patchworks that have little diamonds and rounds of mica mirror stitched into them so that the colours reflect and interreflect; move, and the colour reflections change; another person looks from another angle and sees a different pattern; it does not matter; little human points of view wax or dwindle as the cycles turn. Stella's camera can only tell what it has seen, and we can only try to interpret our pooled experience: what we have seen, heard, touched, smelled, and tasted since our babyhood days, learned since—there was so much to learn—and always remembered because, like the pigeons, our spirits haunt the places we have loved.

J.G.
R.G.

SHIVA'S PIGEONS

Shiva, third god of the Hindu Trinity, once found some of his human followers so exasperating that he turned them into pigeons; they have haunted his shrines and temples ever since, hoping for release.

Indian stories should, properly, begin "In ancient times . . ." as in the West they start "Once upon a time . . ."; but India's are far, far older; among the ruins of one of her old buried cities, small seals were found, indicating that Shiva may have been worshipped there seven thousand years ago.

The legend does not tell when, with his "third eye," he "transformed" those erring human beings, but there are always pigeons roosting and fluttering—and strutting, because pigeons and men are incorrigible—round his holy places; not the same pigeons, of course; those have, aeons ago, been freed from their feathered selves.

All Indians—Moslem, Buddhist, Sikh, Jain, Christian, as well as Hindu—are Shiva's pigeons whether they know it or not, all five hundred million of them, as all people, everywhere, are, even if they have never heard his name. No one can escape him, because he is the god of death, yet death that wakes, because he is also resurrection; in Hindu thought, that—until the soul finally earns its complete release—will mean rebirth, the soul's "changing of garments"; but, even if a man can only believe that his end will be to make potash, fertilizing a fruit tree or a blade of grass, Shiva's resurrection is inescapable too; the transformation of the legend is a glimpse of a mighty pattern.

A fledgling grows and flies; one day it must fall to the ground and die. There will always be others in its place to strut and flutter and fly, not aimlessly—they are in the implacable will of the god—but that particular one is gone.

Where? To become what? Shiva knows.

PART I

When a Hindu baby is born, honey is sometimes put on its tongue so that it will grow up to have a mild disposition, "sweet talk"; in some families, on the fifth day a pen and ink, and a stone or brick from the nearest temple are laid out in the birth room, ready for the Unseen Presence, Brahma, the Creator, first God of the Hindu Trinity, who will come during the day or night and write the baby's karma on its forehead.

At first sight these two "baby" customs seem contradictory: how can a minute human action influence what God's hand will write? But God's will and man's act on different levels, and Hindus know that the little cycle of this new life can and must evolve itself in the greater embrace. Karma, too, is not, as most Westerners believe, fate; it is the baby's genes but, in Hindu thought, more than an inheritance from his parents and ancestors; it is also a legacy from the way he has lived in past lives. By deliberate "choos-

16

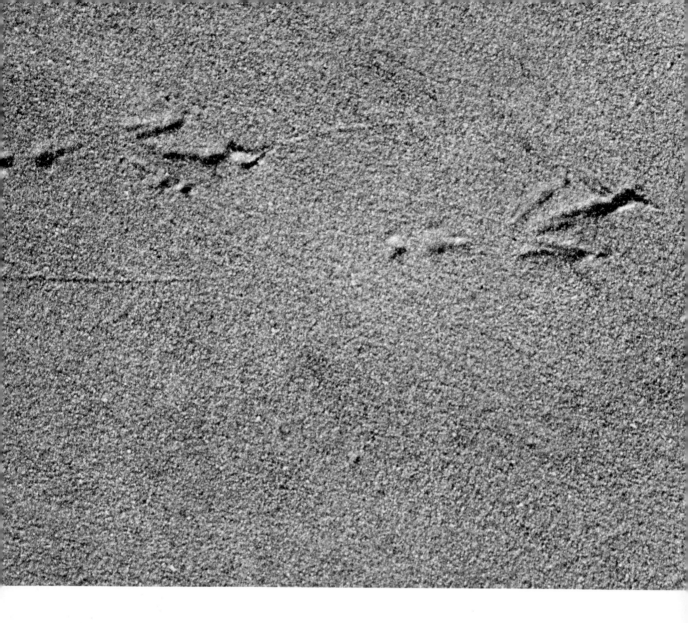

ing"—and discipline—he can alter or free himself even from his genes; indeed he must if he is ever to achieve the goal of all Hindus, release from self and union with God.

Even a baby uses free will; as soon as he can sit up he will be put on a table on which are all kinds of objects: money, books, a pen, tools, scissors, perhaps doctors' instruments, an artist's brush. The one the child seizes or reaches out to touch shows what he may grow up to be.

But his name will be given him, though not by his parents; on the Name-Giving Day, lucky names, sometimes seven of them, are written on different banyan or banana leaves, and a little oil lamp is set near each; the lamp that shines the brightest, most steadfastly, indicates the right one. "Amar," says the priest, "he will be Amar"—which means immortal—and the baby has his name.

Hindu children are often called after gods and goddesses: Narayan, Hari, belong to Vishnu,[1] while Shivnath, Natarajan are Shiva boys' names. Tara is a goddess. Das, which means a slave, can be added to the god name of a boy: Hari-das, Ram-das. Girls are called after the goddess Sita or after Radha, heroines of Hinduism's great religious stories, or are given names of precious stones, flowers, rivers, or certain virtues; Moti, a favourite name for boys as well as girls, means a pearl; a girl may be Kamala, a lotus; Sundari, beautiful; Vimala, pure. It is the pandit who chooses the suitable names and writes them on the leaves, but something even more important than a name is brought to this ceremony—the newborn's horoscope.

In the ancient world astrology dictated the behaviour of countless thousands of human beings; to the majority of Indians it still does; for them there is an auspicious or inauspicious day for everything: marriage, a journey, business deals, a gift, an expensive purchase. Rich men, rajas and princes, used to keep resident astrologers; not many of these household—often hanger-on—astrologers are left, but every town—even an occasional village—has its public astrologer; his fame often goes far and wide. It is he who fixes the dates of all ceremonies and, when somebody falls ill, he is the first person to be consulted, even before the doctor, because the conjunction of the planets can unleash asuric furies, forces of evil and darkness.

1. Vishnu: second God of the Hindu Trinity.

Westernized parents often dismiss horoscopes as superstition. Nirad Chaudhuri, in his *Autobiography of an Unknown Indian*, tells how his grandfather's horoscope predicted that he would meet death by being eaten by a crocodile, so that to the end of his life the grandfather would never go near a river, not even to the village ablutions tank, but took his daily bath sitting on a stool and having buckets of water poured over him. He died peacefully in his own house and the Chaudhuris have eschewed horoscopes ever since; but for most Hindu babies the old faith persists, and Amar's horoscope will be cast from the moment—not the day or hour, the exact moment—of his birth. In the labour room there must be a clock marking the seconds; often it is a huge grandfather clock.

If Amar were a noble or rich baby this casting would take a long time, the astrologer considering the influence of every possible star—and raking in every possible rupee—but for more ordinary people the horoscope will be brought to the Name-Giving ceremony, and from this "name day" the baby will have his stars to guide him.

As he grows up he will hear star stories too. One of these, about the Pole Star, tells of another little boy, Dhruva, a prince, son of the chief wife of his father, the king. The king fell passionately in love with a younger wife, so passionately that he allowed her to persuade him to exile Dhruva and his mother and send them to live in the forest. One day, when the little prince was seven years old, he asked who his father was and his mother told him the sad story. "I will go and see this king," said Dhruva. His mother let him go to the palace, where he found the king alone and climbed into his lap. The king was so delighted to see his son again that he wept and covered Dhruva with kisses. Suddenly the young wife came in and furiously snatched the child away; the king did not dare to protest, and Dhruva was turned out of doors and driven away, back to the forest.

For several days he pondered, then asked his mother, "Is there anyone in the world greater than a king?"

"Yes," said his mother. "Narayan."[2]

"Then his love will be greater than a king's?"

"Yes," said his mother.

"Then I should like him for a father," and the little boy said seriously, "I shall go and find him."

"But he is a god."

"I shall still go and find him."

Dhruva's mother laughed, but that night Dhruva slipped out of bed—the story tells he put on his golden crown—and, small as he was, set out through the forest. He met a tiger: "Are you Narayan?" Dhruva asked, and the tiger, hearing the name, ran away. Dhruva met a bear: "Are you Narayan?"—and the bear too turned and fled. It was the same with all the wild beasts as Dhruva toiled on, day after day, until he met a forest hermit. "Are you Narayan?"

"Indeed no," said the hermit.

"Where *is* Narayan?" asked the desperate child.

"He is where you stand." And the old man took Dhruva into his hut and taught him the stillness into which God can come and, at last, Dhruva was still.

Then the Celestial One bent down and picked his small follower up in his mighty hand. "I shall turn you into a star," said Narayan, "and set you high in the sky so that, among the ever-moving planets, you shall shine for men with the same unchanging steadfastness you have shown on earth."

2. Narayan: another name for Vishnu.

With all their love of stories, Indians have an innate capacity for abstract thought and are aware that man is inextricably linked with cosmic powers. The gods of the old *Vedas* from which Hinduism sprang were nature or cosmic gods, the "Shining Ones," and worshipped long before the present great Hindu Trinity emerged. Pure and invisible, they were such as Varuna, once mightiest of them all, who has become the god of sky and ocean: Surya, the sun god, and his bride Usha, the dawn: Agni, god of fire: and, above all, the warrior Indra, who has ousted Varuna in might and who causes the terrors of rain, thunder, and lightning. These gods are holy still, figuring in the Hindu epics, the *Ramayana* and the *Mahabharata*. When the baby Amar grows up and is married, Agni, purest of all gods, will be present at the wedding, as at all Hindu weddings, in the sacrificial fire or, at least, the flame of a lamp.

This recognition of, and reverence for, the forces of nature, this larger thinking, come perhaps from India's spaciousness; desert people make, for instance, good astronomers.

India's "wise men," as they were called, were renowned before the birth of Christ; when astronomy was almost lost to Europe in the Dark Ages, they were inventing and refining their instruments: astrolabes for measuring the positions of the stars, and gnomons, or sun-dials, which followed the sun's movements with shadows. In 1633 the European Galileo was persecuted for his discovery that the earth moved round the sun; had he been an Indian he would have been honoured; Indian observations and calculations had become more exact and profound, and the pure science of astronomy flourished.

A later star-gazer, and a generous patron of astronomers, was one of the rajas of Jaipur, Maharaja Jai Singh the Second, who lived in the eighteenth century. In Delhi and Benares, Ujjain, Muttra, and in his own capital, Jaipur, he built five observatories, of which the Jantar Manta in the courtyard of the city palace of Jaipur is the jewel, with its collection of giant-sized astronomical instruments, the biggest ever made for observation with the naked eye. These instruments, strange shapes of white, grey, and terra-cotta-pink, made of brass, stone—especially marble—wheels, quadrants, angles, curves, and circles, are dominated by the soaring steps of a giant gnomon mounting ninety feet into the sky and topped by an airy little pavilion.

Perhaps the prince-astronomer sat in his high pavilion after the heat of the day, watching the shadows mark the last seconds and minutes of India's swift twilight before the stars that so fascinated him shone out above.

Sitting, brooding, meditating is a deeply Indian habit.

"What are you doing, Dadaji—grandfather?"

"Sitting and watching my crops grow."

"What are you doing so still, Didi—sister?"

"Sitting . . . saying my japam."

In stillness and a chosen posture she may sit for an hour, even two or three hours, in japam—the repetition over and over again of a holy phrase, perhaps only one word, perhaps simply the name of God: "Ram, Ram, Ram, Ram," perhaps the word "Om,"[3] which releases vibrations and brings another and higher state of consciousness in which "self" has been obliterated from self-consciousness.

Didi's word or holy phrase has been chosen for her by her guru or an esteemed person, and is known to no one else.

3. "Om" is supposed to be made up of the sounds "a," "o," and "u," which signify the Creator, Destroyer, and Preserver, Gods of the Hindu Trinity.

Moslems meditate too. The Mogul emperors, in their gardens in Kashmir, would sit in quietness and harmony, listening to the running water. All Mogul gardens are water gardens, and the water channels in, for instance, Nishat in Kashmir run in marble beds between lawns and groves of chenar trees from one terrace to another. The water flows over slats of fretted stone, carved so that the water makes a thousand tiny splashes, some in knots like tapestry, some in stripes, flowers, diamonds, and each has a different rhythm—water poetry.

Babur, first Mogul emperor of Delhi, kept a diary in which, for all his brilliant conquests in Afghanistan and India, he mourned his native, but lost, state in what is now part of Russian Turkestan; he was homesick for its cool mountains, its valleys of orchards, gardens, and running streams, and longed for its game and fruit, especially its melons. He writes of melons again and again in his memoirs: "a wonderful delicate toothsome melon," "those delicious Ismael Shaiki melons with yellow skins mottled like shagreen." How enticing they must have seemed to Babur in his long campaigns in what he called "the wastes of Hindustan." He soon taught his Indian gardeners to grow melons in the gardens he immediately planted.

Babur was descended from two of the most famous generals of all time, on his father's side from Timur of Samarkand, on his mother's from the ruthless Mongol leader Chingiz Khan, so that it was no wonder he became a royal conqueror—he was nicknamed the Tiger—but he never forgot that sound of running water. This love passed to his successors, the emperors of the House of Timur, known as the Moguls (see table on page 369)

In a dry country water is life; poetry is the essence of life, so that the two, poetry and water, seem to go together.

Poetry has never been prized in the West as it is in the East; in China and Japan practical businessmen used to gather together in different seasons to write poems in praise of snow, of new green bamboo shoots, the flowering of peonies or chrysanthemums, the first cherry blossom; in Persia poets' graves are places of pilgrimage, but only the Moguls linked poetry and water in this unique way. Some of the carved slats are steeply slanted, so that the water runs quickly, some are tilted so that it runs more slowly, and built over the water, above each of these small waterfalls, is a marble dais or throne, big or small, but always solitary; the emperor could choose the throne and water-flow that suited his ear and mood, that tinkled or lulled, accompanying his thoughts or drowning them away.

In Indian thought, to define truth is like trying to catch that running water, hold it in the hand; even in a lifetime, only a few drops can be caught.

A lifetime is such a little span, yet for a Hindu it should hold four aims: first dharma—duty; then artha—wealth-winning, which means practical temporal things like earning money, gaining respect. The third is rati—desire, leading a full, happy sex life; a Hindu knows that to be a balanced person he needs fun and gaiety. Men and women should achieve all these three aims, but no one on earth can tell who has attained the fourth and last, moksha—release, which is not simply death; moksha has to be worked for, and it may need many lives, some as cruel or tormented as, say, that of a leper or a starving beggar child, before a soul deserves to be released at last from its small self.

The rishis[4] of long ago laid down a pattern of four stages of life—another four—that, if men would only consent to live through them, would bring fulfilment and end this perpetual "changing of garments," reincarnation.

The first stage is that of a student who must study and learn as a preparation for life; the next, and usually longest, is living itself, as a "householder"; then, ideally, should come "relinquishment," retiring from the world as preparation for death—death is a part of life; and finally, "sannyasa," the fourth stage of complete detachment.

4. The rishis, priests of the cosmic gods, existed in pre-Vedic times; there were seven famous ones, the "penitents," to whom the *Vedas*, or books of wisdom, were revealed. For centuries these hymns and precepts were thought too sacred to be written and were handed down from generation to generation of priests by word of mouth. They were transcribed about 1000 B.C. There are four, of which the first, the *Rig Veda*, has more than a thousand verses. The word "veda" means wisdom. Legend tells that the seven rishis are still in heaven, shining in the seven stars of the Great Bear.

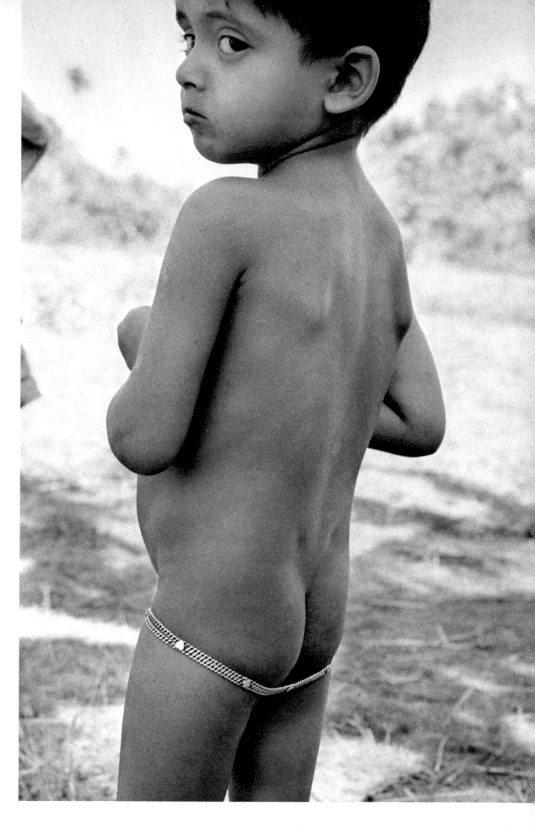

Those ideal four aims, four stages, were laid down for brahmins, but anyone can achieve them, once set on the right path.

This basic Hindu philosophy is simple, clear, yet Hinduism as practised seems the reverse, extraordinarily complicated, a dazzling bewilderment of names—so many, many gods and goddesses: it has been said there are thirty-three crores of them,[5] but, "No, only One," says the pandit and, in reality, there is only One—Brahman[6] the Unknown, Unshown God which lies below, above, around, and in all the rest.

Brahman, of course, is neuter; in writing or speaking of Brahman, "which," not "who," is used, and any attempt to explain the attributes and qualities of this hidden God is bound to fail; after all, if anyone understood God, he would *be* God. To such presumption the vedantic phrase comes back, "Neti neti"—"It is not this, it is not that"—so for the sake of ordinary men and women, Brahman is manifested in gods and goddesses not unlike their human selves. As with human beings, there is now an overpopulation of deities and they have become so interrelated, each with so many meanings, that one simple question may bring a dozen different answers.

"Who is the female counterpart of the God Shiva?"

"She is Parvati/Durga/Kali/Devi/Uma."

And of even one aspect of her, Kali: "The Kali cult is great wisdom/ abominable/very debased/very, very holy."

Again the seeming contradictions are all true in different parts of India, in different cults or sects, but no wonder the outsider, trying to understand, begins to feel that the gods all seem "Neti neti." "Seem" is the right word; one must look deeper than appearances: to the worshipper it is all perfectly clear; as he makes puja to his chosen gods, he is actually practising monotheism because he sees, and worships, through and in them, the one Supreme Being.

The chief manifestation of Brahman is in the mighty Hindu Trinity, Brahma the Creator, Vishnu the Preserver, and Shiva the Destroyer who is also resurrection; each has a feminine counterpart or aspect—to the unintellectual, a goddess wife, but she is more than a wife because she is his shakti, the true role of woman as the force of energy, without which there can be no creation or evolution.

Of the Trinity, Brahma is the one who least lets himself be known by men and nowadays is not often worshipped, but his shakti, Sarasvati, is most popular. She could be called a connoisseur's goddess because she is the goddess of learning, of all the creative arts, and is worshipped by students, musicians, artists, and craftsmen. Her symbols are a white lotus and a peacock. "She who is white like the kunda flower, snow and pearls, clad in pure

---

5. A crore: ten million.
6. Brahman: not to be confused with Brahma, the Creator, first God of the Hindu Trinity; nor with brahmin, the highest caste.

white garments. She whose hand is adorned by the staff of the precious vina."[7]

Vishnu rouses himself only when the universe is threatened by evil; then he comes down to earth as an avatar in one of his nine incarnations. He has been a man-lion, a dwarf; he came as Prince Rama, as Krishna, as the Buddha. His tenth incarnation is still to come when, once again, he will preserve the world. Meanwhile he sleeps on the coils of the many-headed serpent Ananta, who is Eternity, while beautiful Lakshmi, the darling Goddess of Good Fortune, whose symbols are an owl and a cowrie, crouches by his side, pressing his feet as a good Hindu wife should.

Shiva, third of the Trinity, is yet the oldest God and may have been worshipped long before the *Vedas* were written. As he owns no palace, he camps with his family on Mount Kailas in the Himalayas. His consort is the most powerful and puzzling of all goddesses, Parvati/Durga/Kali/Devi/Uma, Mother of the Universe.

To the uninitiated, the Mother can seem dreadful, hideous, and terrifying; this is because, like nature and all cosmic powers, she is implacable. The Swami[8] Ramakrishna spent his young life as one of her priests, tending her in her aspect of Kali.

> The basalt image of the Mother, dressed in gorgeous gold brocade, stands on the prostrate white marble body of Her divine consort, Shiva. . . . On the feet of the goddess are anklets of gold; she wears necklaces of gold and pearls, a golden garland of human heads, and a girdle of human arms. . . . She herself has four arms; the lower left hand holds a severed human head and the upper grips a blood-stained sabre. One right hand offers boons to Her children; the other allays their fear.
>
> The majesty of Her posture can hardly be described. It combines the terror of destruction with the reassurance of motherly tenderness, for She is the cosmic power, the totality of the universe, a glorious harmony of the "pairs of opposites." She deals out death, as She creates and preserves. She has three eyes, the third being the eye of Divine Wisdom; they strike dismay into the wicked, yet pour out affection for Her devotees. She is Prakriti, the procreatrix, nature, the destroyer, the creator. Nay, She is something greater and deeper still for those who have eyes to see.[9]

Ramakrishna indeed had "eyes to see" and went on to become the spiritual genius of nineteenth-century Hinduism.

7. Vina: a stringed instrument (pronounced "veena").
8. Swami: title of a Hindu religious teacher.
9. *Ramakrishna: Prophet of New India* translated by Swami Nikhilananda.

Hindu teachers and sages have tried again and again down the centuries to purify Hinduism, explode some of the myths and cults; only the un-learned, they taught, think of the gods as distinct—but most Hindus are unlearned and insist on the comfort of separating them into personalities. Worshippers tend to fall into three groups: the Vaishnavas, devoted to Vishnu; the Shaivas, who follow Shiva; the Shaktas, who are devotees of the Great Mother. It does not matter; "The paths men take on all sides lead to me," says *The Song of God*. "Howsoever men approach me do I welcome them."[10]

Even if his parents were not orthodox, religion would still be woven, willy-nilly, into Amar's life; Hinduism will condition his thinking; he cannot help being familiar with the gods because he will see them everywhere, from sacred images to cinema posters; he will be brought up on his grand-mother's stories from the religious epics, and they will be in the songs and music he hears, the plays and films he sees; religious festivals will give colour and excitement to his year.

While he is still a baby, he will probably be allotted two particular gods or goddesses; later he will choose a private or personal third, perhaps the god of his own name, but the two he is given are likely to be the god of his village or nearest temple and his family or household god.

In a tenement flat in the city, in a palace, over the courtyard door of a village hut, on a ledge in a shop, there will be a special place or niche for the household god. It may be only a gaudy picture or an emblem of Vishnu or an image of his consort, Lakshmi; frequently it is what seems to western eyes a hideously strange god, Ganesha, with an elephant's head.

Ganesha is the son of the Lord Shiva and has an elephant's head simply because, in her pride over her newborn son, his mother asked the planet Saturn to look at him, quite forgetting the force of planetary powers; Saturn looked—and the child's head turned to ashes. Shiva, in his panic to find a new head for his son, took the first he could see and fitted it onto the baby; it happened to be an elephant's head.

To Hindus this natural, or supernatural, explanation holds seeds of deep philosophy; to them Ganesha is not malformed—the gods do not disdain creatures. Far from it: Vishnu has visited earth as, among other creatures, a tortoise, a boar, and a fish when he saved the sage and law-giver Manu from the deluge;[11] Hanuman, the monkey, is a powerful god. Animals and birds are often "vehicles" of the gods. As for Ganesha, an elephant is the epitome of wisdom, and so the child grew up to be the God of Success, Prudence,

10. *The Song of God*, or *The Celestial Song*, is the *Bhagavad Gita*, part of the *Mahabharata*.
11. Like Jews, Hindus have the story of the Flood.

and Right Judgment, a most suitable god for, say, a moneylender's office, where he is often to be found on a shelf decorated with cut-out paper and an offering of marigolds. It can be seen at once if any office or shop has gone bankrupt: Ganesha is turned upside down.

But some have gone beyond the need for specific gods. "I absolve you from puja—explicit worship," a mother may say to a spiritual and matured daughter, and there are others to whom all is illusion, "maya" created by ignorance; to them the object of life is the realization of the real, the true, self, the Atman which is immortal.

In this body, in this town of Spirit, there is a little house shaped like a lotus and in that house there is a little space. . . . There is as much in that little space within the heart as there is in the whole world outside. Heaven, earth, fire, wind, sun, moon, lightning, stars; whatever is and whatever is not, everything is there. . . . What lies in that space does not decay when the body decays, nor does it fall when the body falls. That space is the home of Spirit. Every desire is there. Self is there, beyond decay and death; sin and sorrow; hunger and thirst; His aim truth; His will truth.[12]

We are shadows until we can find that inner self . . . but in India sunlight is strong—so are shadows; if the shadow of a low or outcaste person falls on the food of an orthodox brahmin, he cannot eat it; the food is contaminated.

12. From the *Chhandogya Upanishad*.

But this strict Hinduism is only for a few. Most Indians, though they worship gods and goddesses and hold to many beliefs, are not subject to taboos; they eat meat—but not beef—marry at the same age as Westerners; many do not go to temples at all; if they are shadows, the shadows are alive, and each shows who this individual is, where in this vast continent of a country he comes from, what language he speaks. He may be a jawan, a Jat soldier

from the Punjab; a plump Marwari merchant; a turbaned Sikh taxi-driver with a heavy beard; a Parsee banker, cultivated, literary, probably speaking several European languages; a coolie woman in her thin cotton sari, sweeping the road with a twig broom. It may be her sophisticated society sister in a sari of fine gold-shot silk, or a Rajasthani woman carrying a basket on her head with unthinking ease . . . . . .

. . . . or an aboriginal boy. . . .

. . . Supposing I became a champa[13] flower . . . and grew on a branch high up on that tree . . . would you know me, mother?

When after your bath, with wet hair spread on your shoulders, you walked through the shadow of the champa tree to the little court where you say your prayers, you would notice the scent of the flower, but not know that it came from me. . . .

When after the midday meal you sat at the window reading *Ramayana*, and the tree's shadow fell over your hair and your lap I should fling my . . . little shadow on to the page of your book . . . where you were reading, but would you guess it was the tiny shadow of your . . . child?

When in the evening you went to the cowshed with the lighted lamp in your hand, I should suddenly drop on to the earth . . . and be me.[14] . . .

13. The champa tree grows in many parts of India, the trees making strong beautiful shapes when their smooth barked branches are bare; they put out the chiselled flowers called "temple flowers," white or ruby red, with a scent that is heavy, heady—and unforgettable.
14. Rabindrinath Tagore, *The Crescent Moon*.

That young woman of the poem might be Amar's mother, a caste Hindu, orthodox and educated; if she were not, she would not have been reading the *Ramayana*, a wonderfully stirring and exciting story-poem; nor would she have been through the purification of the bath, washing herself from head to foot while still wearing her muslin sari, facing the sun, soaking herself with pourings of water, bathing by intention in the holy Ganges, mother of all rivers. Then she would have put on a clean sari, brushed and oiled her long blue-black hair, twisted it into a knot, perhaps with a flower, and, last of all, touched her forehead with a paste of sandalwood and vermilion to make the small exquisite tikka mark.[15] Then, only then, would she have gone to pray.

The courtyard would most likely be of earth and earth-walled, baked by the sun to paleness, probably with a tulsi[16] tree in a pot, or a "worship stone," black for Vishnu, white for Shiva, many-coloured for the great Goddess.

A rich house will have a puja room, where the family gods are kept; this is seldom, like a chapel, built somewhere quiet, apart, and equipped to match the riches and taste of the house; for the less rich it is casual, probably an alcove, perhaps near the kitchen, with a straw mat on which to sit for meditation. It will have a brass pot for ablutions and a low stool-table to hold a tray for the morning or evening offerings of flower petals, slices of coconut and fruit, bits of sugar cane. There will be sticks of incense and a casket or shelf for miniature images of the various personal gods; but, no matter where it is, she will pray—to Shasti, Goddess of Children, or Vishnu perhaps, in his incarnation as Krishna, but Krishna as Gopal, himself as a child, for another son.

15. The tikka mark is the round vermilion mark painted with delicate care on the centre of the forehead with a brush dipped in a paste made with vermilion; nowadays it is often used merely as a beauty spot, but it has a deeper significance as a symbol of the third eye of wisdom. A dancer, making up for *Bharata Natyam*, the classical dance before a god, may pray, "Lord, in my vanity, let me think of Thee."
16. Tulsi: *Ocimum sanctum*, basil is sacred.

An Indian wife and mother keeps the life of her household in her hand.

There is an old story of a Mogul king who visited a part of his realm where he had never been before and found the people living in dark caves. He was horrified at the gloom and ordered every family to be given lamps and oil to light them. Five years later he came again and found the caves still in darkness; the lamps had been broken and forgotten; the oil had run out. The king, though annoyed, gave new lamps, more oil, but in another five years, when he came back, the caves were as dark as ever. This happened five times, and at last, in despair, the king asked his vizier for an explanation. "Ah," said the vizier, who was a wise old man, "you gave the lamps to the men; you should have given them to the women."

The king followed the vizier's advice, and the caves have been lit, the lamps kept burning ever since.

The hands of Indian women are seldom still; slim, brown, long-fingered, they are so supple that, pressing the fingers together, they are able to slide through the hoop of a bangle, sometimes of coloured glass, impossibly small for western hands; Indian women are so deft that the fragile glass does not break as the busy hands cook the food, scour the cooking pots with sand or ashes; sweep, spin, draw water from the village well or pump, thresh the grain and winnow it, or dabble for long hours in the mud of rice fields as they transplant tufts of young green rice from the seedbeds. The air of any village is alive with a soft clinking of those glass, silver, or bone bangles, worn as many as twenty to an arm above the seemingly fragile but wiry wrists.

> How charming are the women's songs as they husk the winter rice;
> a music interspersed with sound of bracelets
> that knock together on round arms swinging
> with the bright and smoothly rising pounder;
> and accompanied by the drone of hum hum
> breaking from the sharply heaving breasts.[17]

The women make decorative patterns on mud walls by dipping hands into a sort of whitewash and slapping palm and spread fingers on courtyard and hut walls, making handprints.

It is, too, the village women's task to collect the cow dung that, instead of enriching the fields, is burnt to ignite and eke out fuel; coal, charcoal, even wood, cost paise that cannot be spared. The dung is kneaded into flat round cakes, which are slapped on the walls with an open palm so that each pat, as it dries in the sun, bears a handprint. In the evening, pungent blue dung smoke rises from every cooking fire, spreads between the houses, and drifts out into the fields where the children are driving the cattle home.

17. *Characterization* by Yogesvara, translated by Daniel H. H. Ingalls.

That a woman's hands should plaster dung on walls seems pitiful beyond comprehension to western minds, no matter how lowly the hands, but there are other handprints, proud aristocratic ones, that tell an even more poignant story. In faded vermilion, they can be seen inside the gateways of old palaces and on the sides of the "death pavilions," the carved, pillared and roofed "chettries" raised in memory of princes or noblemen; these prints were made by the hands of wives and concubines who threw themselves—or were thrown—onto the funeral pyres of their husbands. No one who has seen them can forget those hands; a few are children's—child brides of only seven or even five years old but old enough to be a sati.[18]

Outside India the sati, as she was called, has always been looked on as a victim, and it is true that the practice led to unwilling women being thrown into the fire; yet voluntary sati came not from weakness but from strength, in the spirit of the crucifixion, a woman's ultimate sacrifice for the redemption of her husband's soul.

On the earthly side, she would probably have said she had no wish to go on living without her husband, be left "empty-souled"; and this feeling remains. A Hindu woman may be a scold, a shrew, having the failings that come from generations of seclusion, love of tittle-tattle, slyness, deceit, yet from the moment when, at her wedding, she makes her first shy namaskar to her bridegroom, almost invariably she will be dedicated to her husband, love, honour, and serve him.

18. Sati was prohibited by law long, long ago, but voluntary cases have recurred from time to time; the last time in public was in 1963 in Jodhpur, when the crowd was so huge that neither police nor soldiers dared intervene in what was a deeply religious act.

Namaskar is the traditional Indian greeting; both hands are joined to-gether, fingers to fingers, palm to palm, and raised to the level of the chest to greet equals, to the forehead or above the head for especially revered people or gods. Disciples greet their gurus and, often, children their fathers and mothers, by bending down and with both hands touching, or "taking the dust" of, their feet.

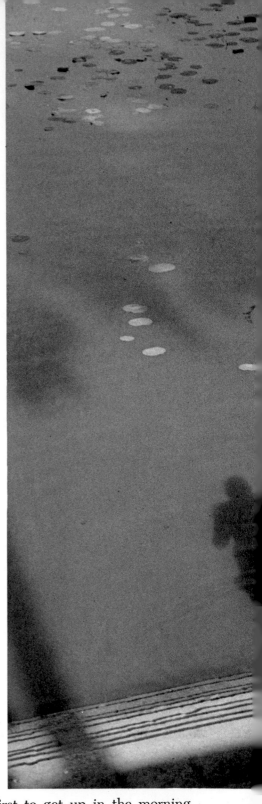

Maji, the wife and mother, is probably first to get up in the morning. Early mornings in India seem more perfect than morning anywhere else; it is not only the freshness before the heat, the colours muted by the soft light, the sparkle of dew; morning is the time for cleansing and prayer.

Often Maji will have made her morning puja before she reverently wakes her husband for his ablutions and prayers; if they live in a village, he will probably bathe in the village tank or pool, but if there is a river near he will go to the river.

A lazy woman, a slugabed, will be despised by her neighbours—and her servants if she has any; servants expect their mistress to watch their work, even scold and harry them. In return, she must see that they are cared for, fed and clothed as part of her family. She guards the keys of the storeroom and cupboards, never trusting them to anyone, and keeps the bunch on a silver tasselled chain attached to her waist or, in a humble household, knotted into a corner of her sari. In the country, or in a town where the cowman comes every day to her door, she must keep a sharp eye on the cow or cows being milked to make sure water is not added to the milk, which is anyway thin; the calves stand by on unsteady legs and wear muslin muzzles to prevent them helping themselves to the milk which is rightfully theirs.

She will watch over the cooking if she does not do it herself. There is a strange idea in the West that household life in the East is simple, whereas Indian dishes, especially curries, take hours to prepare; for a good curry all the ingredients must be fresh, the spices freshly ground.

Beds are not "made" in the western sense; every morning all the bedding must be taken up and hung out to air; even in the rains, quilts, pillows, and sheets appear on balconies and verandas; then each set is rolled up and put away. Rooms are swept, often with a broom of soft grasses, mats shaken. The courtyards and verandas must be washed, most likely with cow dung added to the water, and, if it is a festival day, the floor or a wall may be ornamented with rangoli—patterns made by a hand dribbling a mixture of rice flour and water, preferably Ganges water, through the fingers; the flour is often coloured.

In late summer there is a gay and happy festival called Raksha Bandhan, which came from the gallantry of the Rajputs towards their women but has now spread over India. "Raksha" means protection, and "bandhan" a tie; so girls tie a bracelet, a rakhi made of scarlet silk with gold tassels, round the wrist of a chosen brother, cousin, or friend. It is an honour to be chosen, and the boy or young man must give a present in return and promise help and protection if ever these are needed. There is a great deal of badinage, teasing and laughing. It is the girls and women, too, of a bride's family who meet her young bridegroom with songs and music when he arrives with all pomp for the wedding; before or after it they are allowed to tease him unmercifully to see how good-tempered and quick-witted he is.

54

A Hindu mother is honoured; her influence is probably far greater than a father's, and in early times India was a true "mother country," a matriarchy. In the south this has never really changed; the Vindhya mountains, which stretch across the land from the Western to the Eastern Ghats, protected it from the northern conquerors who brought with them the idea of the patriarch and initiated the system of caste to keep themselves from intermixing and losing their distinction. This made it necessary for their women to be controlled—women not only fall in love but, inconveniently, wish to marry their lovers. Another reason for sequestering wives and daughters was the constant warfare, in which women were considered prizes of loot. Soon riches and the new social status brought the idea of many wives, hidden as treasure in the andar.[19] This idea of purdah and the subsequent degradation of women is usually blamed on the Moslems, but by law they could not have more than four wives and were allowed these only because so many men were killed in the wars that a surplus of women was left unprotected. When Hindus took to polygamy, they knew no limit: one of the Maharajas of Patiala, for instance, had three hundred wives; wives were literally bought and sold.

Yet the power of the mother remains: Mother India, Mother Ganges, the universal Mother Goddess; and every Hindu knows that women are shakti —that essential force of energy the world cannot do without—so it is not as surprising as it seems that during this century Indian women have emerged from their seclusion into professional and public life.

They have not fought ungracefully for their freedom as western women had to do, but simply soared, often into the highest positions. What European country has had a woman Prime Minister? Yet even in exalted places, Hindu women manage to reconcile business, politics, full-time professions with the grace of femininity and a happy family life.

A Hindu girl can stand alone now at the bus stop, waiting for a public bus to take her to school, college, university, or to work in an office. In some families she is even allowed to go out alone with a young man, perhaps sitting sideways, pillion on the back of a motorbike, wearing goggles and a crash helmet, her arms round his waist, with the end of an ethereal sari streaming out on the wind.

19. Andar: a separate, usually inner part of the house, enclosed for the women.

"Are you so modern that you will be disappointed if it is a son?" That is a quip one can make now to a young Indian father-to-be. "Another little calamity!" friends used to exclaim when still another daughter appeared, but to have a girl baby is not the disappointment it used to be—even that dragon-swallower of money, the dowry, is often waived; all the same it is still for a son that the Indian woman prays, and when one arrives he is adored by his father, almost worshipped by his mother, sisters, and grandmother.

For an orthodox Hindu family, a son is more than a joy, he is a necessity; no one else can perform his father's funeral rites. Amar—be he seven or twenty-seven—must be the one to set the funeral pyre alight and fulfil the ritual if his father is to have any chance of attaining heaven; nor can any of his ancestors stay long in heaven if there is no male to continue the family line.[20]

---

20. The intervals between births are spent partly in heaven, partly in hell, according to the virtue or the villainy of the life just left. The Hindu heaven is Brahma's mythical city behind the Himalayas on the golden mountain of Meru, which is eighty-four thousand leagues high. The sacred River Ganges, which is every river in the world, flows round the city, and nearby is another mountain, Mandara, used as a churning-stick to stir the Sea of Milk and make the foam of ambrosia, necessary to the gods.

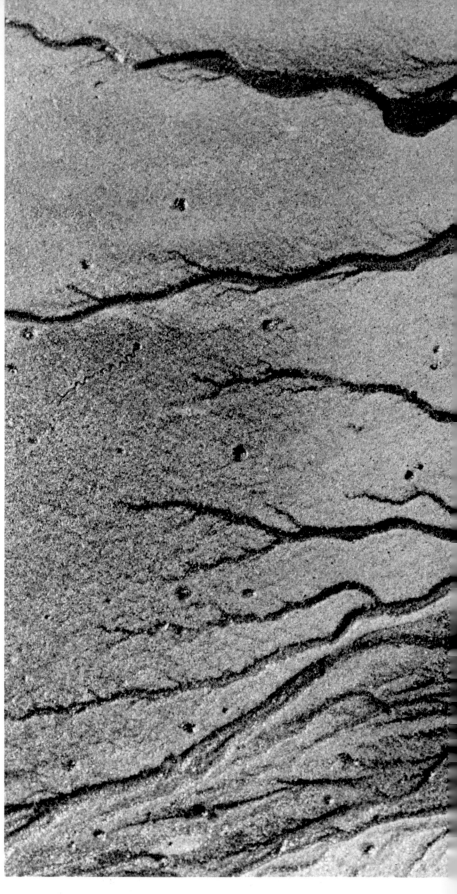

There must be sons, numberless as grains of sand on an infinite seashore.

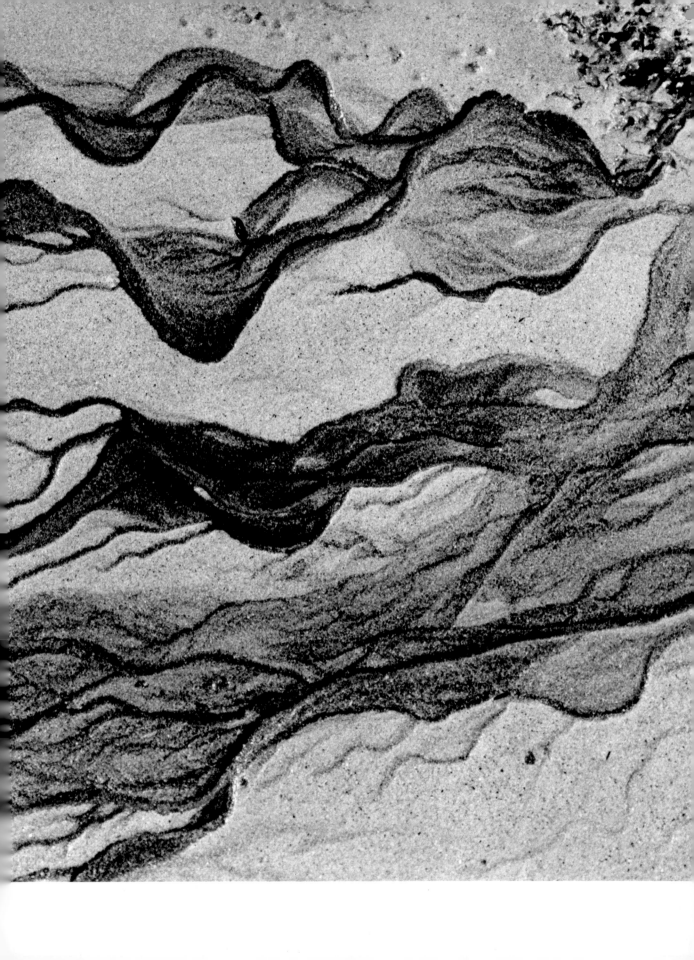

PART II

What the rishis taught three thousand years ago is just as valid for a Hindu today because these wise men were seers and saw a man's life as a whole, a cycle; but before any cycle can begin, there must be initiation, realization of who one is.

A small Hindu boy such as Amar is casteless—in a brahmin's family his father cannot eat with him—and so, when Amar is between seven and ten years old, there comes a day when he will be taken from his familiar nest of women into a grave circle of men; not even his mother or grandmother[1] is allowed, though his mother will be the first person from whom he later will beg symbolic alms. Alone in the middle of the circle Amar will make obeisance to the priest and be initiated, given the threefold sacred thread, the munja, of an upper-caste Hindu; it is worn from the waist diagonally over the naked left shoulder, coming to the waist again; he must remember, when he goes to relieve himself in privy or fields, to loop his thread around his right ear to prevent its coming into contact with his genitals. Certain mantras are said, and then the little boy picks up a bundle and walks in an imaginary journey round the circle, saying good-bye.

"Where are you going?"

"To my guru in Benares." It is for his guru that he pretends to beg money; probably Amar is only going to school, but the ceremony marks his first conception of himself as a Hindu and of his place in the big Indian world.

At school he will learn a little of his land's vast geography, from sea-coasts to Himalayas; of her problems—too many people, too little food—even in Amar's comparatively well-off family he may already have had experience of this; he will have a child's view of her uglinesses—and her beauty; perhaps wake to the fact she has other religions than his own, other, and manifold, customs. For a little while, he himself may feel lost.

. . .

A dot upon the sand,
Myself I cannot find;
For time has angled me
With boundless sky, land, and sea.

My only traces are
Thin smoke puffs in the air
And prints marking my way
That waves will snatch for play.[2]

1. In some parts of South India, though, the opposite is true: the mother has to be present; if one parent is not alive, then an elder brother and his wife will act for the parents, or paternal uncle and his wife. The ceremony has to be in the presence of a couple.
2. *Evening at the Seashore* by Nalin Vilochan Sharma, translated from Hindi by J. Mauch.

As a peninsula, that pear-drop shape so familiar in the atlas, India has a sea-coast that runs for thousands of miles, starting in the west from the bulge of Kutch and Kathiawar, down to Bombay, on past the ancient Christian state of Goa, through the palms and waterways of green Kerala to the toe of India, Cape Cormorin, where three seas meet, the Bay of Bengal, the Indian Ocean, and the Arabian Sea. Turning northwards, the coast runs up past once French Pondicherry, the harbours and beaches of Madras, the famed Coromandel coast, to the mouth of the sacred Godavari River—most of the rivers of the Indian plateau flow towards the east. Then come miles upon miles of sand, fringed with palm and casuarina trees, sands that could be the play-beaches of the world, though only a handful of strangers play there.

The beaches give way to the delta of the Ganges and Brahmaputra Rivers, which flow into the Bay of Bengal; these are the Sunderbans, where, in the low green jungles that come down to the water's edge, crocodiles and tigers abound; then the coast hooks round past Pakistani Chittagong to Burma.

Except in the ports—and around them—India's shores are usually lonely. There are holiday villas and small hotels at Gopalpur or Puri where people come to surf-ride on the large rollers or, at Puri too, gather for the yearly Jagannath festival, but even there the shore is often deserted except for fishermen. The fishing boats put out, the men—like the surfers—wearing pointed wicker helmets to break the crushing force of the waves; when the boats come back, a long line of magnificent men, naked except for their helmets, their gold-brown bodies glistening with wet and salt, haul on a rope, bringing in net after net, or a group, their heads wrapped in wet cloths against the sun, push a heavy boat into the rollers with a slow, undulating chant.

In Madras they sing:

Valai valai	Net, net
Va valai	Come net
Aila sa aila sa.	[rhythmic sounds used when strength is needed].

Vada valai	Come on, you net
Yen padagu	My boat
Yen padagu	My boat.
Aila sa aila sa	
Aila sa aila sa.	

In little inlets and bays the fish are spilt out on the sand, silver on white; a woman bends to sort them and has her finger snapped off by a baby shark she has rashly turned over on its back. There are haggling and teasing and shouting of bids, because the fish is bought on the shore and sent, on ice, to many parts of India; the rest of the catch is dried on the strand, strung up on scaffolding in the sun and wind, tainting the air around. Some of the men have long luxuriant black hair almost to their waists; asked why, they will explain that when it is really long they will sell it and get what to them seems a high price; it goes to the wig factories of Europe and America.

The sea has always brought money; the ships of King Solomon sailed to India, and Arab dhows carried on a trade with her long before the galleys of the Romans came from Rome's Egyptian and Arabian colonies to India's western coasts. South India's pearls and ivory, precious stones, spices, silks, India muslins, rice, and indigo were in great demand, but there was an exchange: wine, gold, and especially horses were brought from Europe and Arabia; if Indian beryls were used for fashionable cameos in Rome, Roman mercenaries were employed by southern rajas to guard their palaces.

Early in the first century A.D., Saint Thomas the Apostle arrived at Taxila, just northwest of what is nowadays Rawalpindi. Saint Thomas, who with Barnabas was sent to preach to the East, was received at the court of Gondophares, a king whom some believe to have been Gaspar, one of the three Wise Men who journeyed to Bethlehem. It is known that Saint Thomas sailed down the western coast and founded churches in Malabar, but the new religion was fiercely opposed when the Apostle crossed to the east coast, and he was martyred at Mylapore near Madras; a cathedral dedicated to him still stands on a hill outside the town. It was to Saint Thomas's shrine that King Alfred is said to have sent Sighelm the Saxon nearly eight hundred years later. Certainly it was from India that several of the Christian church's best-known customs and ideals came: the revering of relics, asceticism, and the Buddhist rosary and halo. The Portuguese brought them back to India, and with them the splendour and pomp—and the intolerance—of their version of Catholic Christianity; the Inquisition was in force, and all temple worship was forbidden. A gentler, kinder Christianity was to come; Christian missionaries have done wonders for India, hard pioneer work in education, agriculture, and medicine; the people still respect, often love, them, work for and with them, but out of five hundred and fifty million Indians, only about eight and a half million are Christians.

Of the Portuguese conquests, Goa still has more Catholics than any other province and, though annexed now by India, is in spirit still Portuguese; the Portuguese were followed by the French, the Dutch, and, more important, the English, but all of them came first as traders. In 1612, for instance, one

Robert Couverte wrote "A true and almost incredible report of an Englishman that, in the East Indies, travelled by land through many unknown kingdoms, with a discovery of an Emperor called The Great Mogul." The Emperor was Jehangir. The book, with its old paper and long s's, is difficult to read but it is full of surprise and vivid touches:

> The Mogul had great state and as much pomp as may be desired for princely pleasure. He had brought before him every day 50 elephants clad in clothe of gold and silver, whereof some fight one another and some with wild horses and cannot be parted save with raquets of fire made like hoops, the flame thrust in their faces. Also the King has deere, ramms, lyons, leopards and horses that fight with alligators and crocodiles.
>
> Every stranger must present the King with some present be it ever so small, which he will not refuse, and I gave him a present, a small whistle of gold weighing almost an ounce, set with sparks of rubies, which he tooke and whistled therewith almost an hour.
>
> There are bazaars every day of the week. All things to be bought and sold there at a reasonable rate—a hen is twopence, a turkey sixpence, also a good store of fruit as lymmons, oranges, apricocks . . . but with their grapes they make no wines because their laws forbid it. But there were raisins, as great and faire as raisins of Damascus, with a store of clothe of golde, velvets and silks.

Having viewed and seen this great and rich country of Agra with the pleasures and commodities thereof, he left.

It is likely, though, that Amar has never seen the sea; distances are so tremendous in India that few of her millions ever do, unless they make one of the arduous pilgrimages to a sea temple or sacred sea-place, such as Rameswaram in southernmost India, where Rama, seventh incarnation of Vishnu and hero of the epic *Ramayana,* launched his attack on the Demon King of Lanka. The Demon had stolen Rama's faithful wife, Sita, and immured her in his palace at Lanka—ancient Ceylon. Rama's monkey allies helped him to build a bridge[3] between Lanka and Rameswaram.

> . . . while the monkeys were building the bridge a small squirrel took pebbles in its mouth and brought them to the workers: "These are to help in building the bridge to Lanka so that blessed Rama may bring back his wife. I must do my share of the work."
>
> "You, what?" cried a monkey. . . .
>
> "I am helping to build the bridge, sir," replied the squirrel. "Look, I

3. Gift and art shops all over India sell small replicas of this bridge carved in ivory or ebony, or modelled in silver or brass, an arch made of monkeys holding on to each other's tails.

am carrying the small pebbles that with your rocks will help to form the bridge."

The monkey burst into a mighty roar of laughter. By this time a crowd of monkeys had collected and the first monkey roared out, "Did you hear that? The squirrel says she's building a bridge with her pebbles! Hai! Hai! I've never heard anything so funny in my life."

The other monkeys thought it was a good joke too. They held their sides and laughed. When they could laugh no more they said to the squirrel: "Here, little creature. Do you think Rama is in need of your pebbles? He commands the largest army in the Seven Worlds, and for him we carry whole mountains with their granite and rock. He does not want your little pebbles."

The squirrel said, "I cannot carry mountains or rocks. God has only given me strength to carry my pebbles. I cannot do more, but this I will do, for my heart weeps for the sorrowing Rama, and what I can do to help, I will."

The monkeys said, "Enough of your foolishness, little one. We have no time for play and for the likes of you. Go home to your nest in the trees and let us get on with our work."

But the squirrel would not go. Again and again the monkeys picked her up and put her down out of the way, and again and again she returned, with her pebbles. Then the monkeys were angry and threatened to throw her into the sea.

Still the squirrel said, "But I want to help too."

Then an angry monkey picked up the little squirrel and flung her away. But she, crying the name of Rama, fell into his hands, where he stood.

And Rama held the little squirrel close to him and said to the monkeys, "Despise not the weak and the small, for according to each man's strength will he serve. And to me what matters is not how great the strength and service, but how great the love and devotion. This little squirrel with her pebbles has love in her heart that would move the earth and the heavens by its strength and power."

And he chid them for their pride. But the squirrel he held close to him and said: "Little one, your devotion has touched my heart. Be blessed then by me whom you have loved and served." So saying, he stroked the little squirrel's furry back. And as he put her down all who had crowded round saw upon the brown fur the three white lines that were the marks of Sri Rama's fingers.

And ever since then the Indian squirrel has carried the three white stripes on its back.[4]

4. *Ancient Tales of India* retold by Shanta Rameshwar Rad—one of the folktales that have grown, as it were, on the fringe of the *Ramayana*.

The temple at Rameswaram is surrounded by a pillared corridor three thousand feet long, the pillars making avenues leading to the sanctuary and giving vista after vista of columned halls. All day they are thronged with pilgrims, as are the other huge temples of the south but, as the coast runs north, the shores return to loneliness. At night they are deserted, though there are still signs and sounds of humans: a drum throbs from a stilt-hut village behind the palms, and, perhaps, from the low hills behind, a procession of men will come carrying red chests slung on poles, marriage chests for a fisherman's wedding. A twinkling light shines from a shrine built on the shore among the casuarina trees, and a garland of marigolds, thrown by a sea-worshipper, washes back and forth in the waves.

Hindus worship the sea, as they worship the rivers, and with equal cause; it is from the sea that the monsoon comes—the rain-laden wind without which the harvest would fail as it failed the poor peasants Rukmani and her husband Nathan in their small-holding in southern India, a thatched mud hut of two rooms and a grain store, a vegetable patch, a rice field, and a small orchard.

. . . That year the rains failed. A week went by, two. We stared at the cruel sky, calm, blue, indifferent to our need. We threw ourselves on the earth and we prayed. I took a pumpkin and a few grains of rice to my Goddess, and I wept at her feet. I thought she looked at me with compassion and I went away comforted, but no rain came.

. . . Each day the level of the water dropped and the heads of the paddy hung lower. The river had shrunk to a trickle, the well was as dry as a bone. Before long the shoots of the paddy were tipped with brown; even as we watched the stain spread like some terrible disease, choking out the green that meant life to us.

Harvesting time, and nothing to reap. The paddy had taken all our labour and lay now before us in faded, useless heaps.

Sivaji [the overseer] came to collect his master's dues and his face fell when he saw how much was lost, for he was a good man and he felt for us.

"There is nothing this year," Nathan said to him. "Not even gleanings, for the grain was but little advanced."

"You have had the land," Sivaji said, "for which you have contracted to pay: so much money, so much rice. These are just dues, I must have them. Would you have me return empty-handed?" . . .

Nathan went into the hut and I followed. A few mud pots and two brass vessels, the tin trunk I had brought with me as a bride, the two

shirts my eldest sons had left behind, two ollocks[5] of dal[6] and a handful of dried chillies left over from better times; these we put together
to sell.

"Rather these should go," said Nathan, "than that the land should be
taken from us. . . ." He stared awhile at what we had to sell and at last
he said, choking: "The bullocks must go. Otherwise we shall not have
enough." . . .

The drought continued until we lost count of the time. Day after
day the pitiless sun blazed down, scorching whatever still struggled to
grow and baking the earth hard until at last it split and great irregular
fissures gaped in the land. Plants died and the grasses rotted, cattle
and sheep crept to the river that was no more and perished there for
lack of water, lizards and squirrels lay prone and gasping in the blister-
ing sunlight. . . .

Then, after the heat had endured for days and days, and our hopes
had shrivelled with the paddy—too late to do any good—then we saw
the storm clouds gathering, and before long the rain came lashing
down, making up in fury for the long drought and giving the grateful
land as much as it could suck and more. But in us there was nothing
left—no joy, no call for joy. It had come too late.[7]

As such stricken peasants often do, Rukmani and Nathan went to the city,
where, as with thousands of others, there was nothing for them. Put down
for a moment, their bundles were stolen; Rukmani had their few pieces of
silver tied carefully in a corner of her sari and tucked into her waist knot,
but light fingers untied the knot and robbed her as she slept. In any big
Indian city, destitutes crowd the temples waiting for the priests to dis-
tribute the god-food offerings, but newcomers must be driven off or there
will not be enough to give even an ounce of rice, a dab of dal to those who
are there already. Families beg in the streets, cook—if they have anything
to cook—on tiny fires made of leaves, twigs, dung in the gutter, and sleep
on the pavements.

5. An ollock is about a pound in weight.
6. Dal is a species of lentil.
7. From *Nectar in a Sieve* by Kamala Markananda.

On the night pavement
they lie,
soft exclamation points
to the gutter,
wrapped in thin grey cloth,
not in disarray
but correct, circumspect,
in place, as if to say
"This is where we are
in the cycle of existence.
We lie with grace
in our believing sleep."

And yet, who knows?
It could be
that round the dreams
of Kali, Krishna
in that mild, brown-bodied
sleep, there curls the smoke
of a violent anger
ten centuries deep.[8]

8. "The Street Sleepers"
   by Lillian Morrison.

But there will seldom be anger; intense suffering often brings instead a peculiar dignity. All over India a multitude of men, women—and children— quietly accept homelessness, near-starvation, ostracism, dirt, disease, work that would be too hard for animals; they even accept cruelty. Babies can be sold, hired out as assets for begging; sometimes their soft limbs are distorted by bending and tying. Indians love children, as the beggars know only too well, and these little creatures wake such pity as they lie in the wooden carts that they conjure paise from the most meagre purse as, "Ma, Ma, paise doh—give money for my poor son," whines the pseudo-mother. The passers- by, though they give money, seem philosophical about such abuses, but it is not that; they know that the road each soul must travel cannot be changed: the law of karma—cause and effect—is implacable: he who does evil de- serves evil; he must be cleansed by sorrow and pain, and, paradoxically, these victims in their helplessness may be far nearer moksha than the white- dressed Hindu gentleman who bestows paise or the lady in her immaculate sari who quickly averts her eyes. Endurance gives strength.

There are too many people. "I have twenty mouths to feed," the hard-working little tailor cries in despair. "Twenty mouths! Not one of them my own."

Every year the government makes family-planning awards for outstanding services by doctors, nurses, and social workers in this field but, to try to avoid the faking of statistics, the doctors were warned that, in judging the success of their work, its quality would far outweigh quantity; too many cases listed probably meant that some were fictitious or not dealt with properly, and so sterilizations were limited to twenty a day. One doctor, trying in his clinic to follow these instructions faithfully, was faced by a mob of angry women; they had come to be sterilized, and sterilized they would be, and "in typically submissive Indian womanhood manner," as he said afterwards, they locked him in his office until he agreed to do them all—and lose all chance of winning a five-thousand-rupee award.

Men, too, are offering themselves for sterilization, or being persuaded, bribed, to it. Women, even in the villages, are often pathetically anxious to learn birth control, if only by the simple bead or rosary method—but not all women. "What next?" say indignant grandmothers, mothers, aunts. "It is against life." Newly-weds usually want to start a family—and at once; marriage without a baby seems a reproach, from husband to wife, or wife to husband, and one baby will not do, even two; life is so uncertain for a child in India that a quiverful is desirable—besides, the very act of begetting is holy.

"The woman is the fire," says the *Chandogya Upanishad*. "Her womb is the fuel. The invitation of a man is the smoke. The door is the flame: the entering the ember: the pleasure the spark. In this fire the Gods find the offering. From this offering springs the child." The *Chandogya Upanishad*, attached to the *Sama Veda*, is a book of the highest mystical teaching.

Westerners have taken such books, books about the sex act—the *Kama Sutra* is one—and treated them as pornography, but to the Hindu there is no such thing; he is not ashamed of sex; it is as holy as life; the female yoni, a round hole, and the lingam or phallus that fits it are carved over and over again in stone (see page 257) and wood in temples and shrines for worship. "I am the lust that procreates," says the young god Krishna in the *Bhagavad Gita,* one of the most beautiful books ever written. "Let me be many that creation may be. . . ."

And creation proliferates,[9] not simply souls but bodies with those mouths that so torment the little tailor—stomachs that need to be filled. Even in a good year there are too many to share, and there will be famine if the monsoon fails.

The monsoon gives its name to a whole season; gathering force far out in the oceans, it divides when it hits India and Ceylon about the middle of June; deluging the green south, it streams up the Western Ghats as far as Bombay and, meeting the coast hills, largely expends itself before spreading out on the Deccan and the arid, gasping central plateau. In Delhi it may be as much as a month later, because it whirls round and across Ceylon, flows over the sea to Burma, and, doubling back on itself, turns a great cartwheel and streams westward, then northward over the rice fields of Bengal, up over the northern plains, until it meets the barrier of the Himalayas.

9. India is said to have five hundred and fifty million people now. "Next year there will be twelve million more: that twelve will quickly become twenty-four million: in this last minute, while we have been talking, twenty-five more Indian babies have been born." These statistics beat into brains and hearts until, for many people, a panic sets in that prevents India from being seen except as a vast ant-heap—of starving ants.

The ranges of the Himalayas, the great peaks, stretch across the width of northern India from farthest east to farthest west: Everest, Kanchenjunga, Kabru, Siniolchu, Simboo, Pandim, Chomalhari, and countless others, some over twenty thousand feet, some nearer thirty, all eternally capped with snow.

Somewhere, floating behind and among them, is the legendary Mount Kailas, and Lake Mansarovar, out of which Lord Vishnu emerged on the back of the many-headed serpent. This is the mythical universe of the Hindus; seven is the most important mystical number, so this universe has seven continents or coils, surrounded by their seven seas; of these our world is the innermost, and the only one where there are sorrow and hunger and weariness, where men must work to achieve release.

In summer the nearer peaks are a pellucid blue, white-streaked with snow; the giants, such as towering Kanchenjunga, are always glittering white, sometimes with a blizzard blowing off them that, in the distance, looks like a harmless puff of icing sugar blowing into the sky; the wind that blows is iced too, even in summer, gently iced, like an iced drink.

In the early hours of the morning, well before dawn, a cavalcade of ponies may set out from Darjeeling—thickset, thick-necked, small Bhutia ponies, not unlike the palfreys of the Middle Ages; each has an attendant syce or groom who runs behind if the rider can ride, or holds the pony's bridle for a novice; hooves clatter over the stones of the winding rocky way, but voices are instinctively hushed in the darkness because it seems strange to be up and riding at this time. Nowadays parties can go by car or by bus to Tiger Hill, using the lower or motor road—cars are not allowed in the upper town of Darjeeling itself; the levels are too steep—but the romantic way is to ride along this meandering path above the tea gardens and patches of bamboo, jungle, and deodar forest, and come out on the high plateau of Tiger Hill just at dawn.

From Tiger Hill the distant snow cap of Everest looks small because it is so far away, but in the pale glimmer of the first daylight all that can be seen of any range is a faint outline in a sea of cloud. Then the sun rises, not, it seems, from the horizon but from the earth itself and, if this is a lucky morning, the light will pick out one peak after the other; Everest catches the first fire. It is a shock to find how high the eye must look up in the sky to

see them; at first they are pale shapes of white; then, as the sun grows
stronger, they turn from pink to red, to gold—true gold, not yellow—the
marvel that is called "the flowering of the snows."

People travel literally from the ends of the earth to see it, even though it
does not always happen; too often the peaks are hidden in cloud, but if they

do flower it is a never-forgotten spell. The colours slowly fade to yellow, to pink, to a tinge of pink, then white, and it is over. The servant from the rest house calls that breakfast is ready; there is a welcome smell of coffee and sausages—Indian sausages come out of tins—a more pungent smell is the pony men's rancid-butter tea.

Just below Tiger Hill the high town of Ghoom seems perpetually shrouded in swirling mists; cloud lies on the bazaar, fills the houses, and makes the many-roofed Buddhist monastery, Ghoom Gonpa, look as if it were lifted on a bed of cloud.

Siddhartha Gautama, the Buddha, son of a king in Nepal, was born within sight of the Himalayan foothills over five hundred years before

Christ. Thousands of Hindus broke the precepts of the brahmins to follow
him, drawn by the sweetness, the reasonableness of the Way he taught, the
eightfold Path of right views: high aims; right speech; upright conduct; a
harmless livelihood; perseverance in well-doing; intellectual activity—in
Buddhist teaching ignorance and sloth are worse than sins, they are blas-
phemy—finally comes right rapture.

One of the greatest converts to Buddhism, some three hundred years later, was the Emperor Asoka, who had been a conqueror, one of a line of powerful emperors, strong rulers but as ruthless and cruel as they were luxurious; after his conversion Asoka became humble, gentle, and frugal in his personal life. He devoted his riches to building Buddhist monasteries and colleges all through his empire, which stretched from the Bay of Bengal to the Hindu Kush, and from Kashmir to Mysore. For the common people he ordered rules of conduct to be engraved on stone pillars; a few are still extant. Asoka's reign was a blessed one for India, with complete religious tolerance, and charity even for slaves, animals, and birds.

Buddhism is the most peaceable of religions; no one has ever been tortured, put to death, oppressed, or—perhaps worst of all—ostracized, in Buddha's name. It is this that, in modern times, has drawn the lowest castes, sudras or sub-castes of sudras, and particularly the untouchables.

> He who is Blessing passed by my hut,
> passed me, the barber.
> I ran and He turned, waited
> for me, the barber!
> I said, "May I speak to you, Lord?"
> He said, "Yes."
> 'Yes' to *me*, the barber!
> I said, "Can your Peace be for a person like me?"
> He said, "Yes."
> His Peace for *me*, the barber!
> I said, "May I follow you, Lord?"
> He said, "Yes,"
> to me, the barber!
> I said, "May I stay close to you, Lord?"
> He said, "You may,"
> close to *me*, the poor barber![10]

These outcaste converts were led by a passionate reformer, Doctor Ambedkar, who had been an untouchable himself. Buddhism had almost vanished from India, the land where it began, stamped out by the renaissance of brahmin teachings under the Gupta emperors and the relentless crusade against the newer religion by the Hindu philosopher Shankaracharya, who, before he died in 800 A.D., had brought Hindus back to the wisdom of the *Vedas*. Doctor Ambedkar, though, must have had something of his divine Master's spark; after his own and his tribe's conversion, and

---

10. *Chant du Barbier. Morceau de littérature bouddhiste ancienne.* Translated by R. G.

especially after his funeral, more than eleven hundred years later than Shankaracharya's, there was an almost mass resurgence and hundreds of thousands of his "low-borns" became Buddhists.

In the dim interior of the monastery hall, the monks, shaven-headed, in their maroon robes, sit cross-legged on the floor. There is a smell of incense, of butter lamps burning; a deep-tuned gong sounds gently as the ritual is chanted for Evening Prayer:

May there be peace and happiness in the world.
May the crops be bountiful and may the Teaching of the Buddha ever
more widely unfold.

The chanting is interspersed by murmured mantras; sometimes the mantras trail away into silence and the only sound is of wooden beads moving.

"Om mani padme hum."[11] Om, the jewel, is in the lotus. "Om mani padme hum."

The words are cut into rock faces and boulders in the mountains bordering Tibet, and printed hundreds of times on the prayer flags that flutter from long poles above villages and on hillsides; they are written over and over again on scrolls encased in the small prayer-wheels carried by monks or travelling lamas who spin them as they walk; sometimes wheels as large as drums are put in mountain streams so that the rushing water can turn them endlessly.

Mendungs—low stone walls—carved with "Om mani padme hum" are built beside mountain tracks and along the trade routes of the northeastern passes; as soon as the snow melted in the short summer of the high Himalayas, mule-trains used to come to India from Tibet with the sound of bells and the crack of the muleteers' whips; it is reverent to pass a mendung on the right-hand side, and even the mules, untaught, used to swerve out of their way to do this.

The muleteers were tall and broad-shouldered with clear brown skins through which the red showed in lips and cheeks, so that they looked astonishingly lusty. Tibetan women, if they are pale, often smear their cheeks with pig's blood.

The bells are silent now; the mule trains no longer come. Hundreds and thousands of Tibetans are refugees, their monasteries empty of lamas.

11. "Om," among the old brahmins, was the equivalent of the name of God. When anyone says "Ouch!" in pain, he is really crying out to God. The jewel is the utterer's soul, while the lotus which appears over and over again in eastern theology is the symbol of universal being. Its petals that fall are compared to the stripping away, seven times, of the layers of selfhood in which the soul is wrapped.

These strange buildings, often perched like enormous birds' nests on the flanks of the mountains, were not simply retreats for monks but places of high learning. As once upon a time with the *Vedas*, much of the wisdom was not written but stored in individual memories. "When a Buddhist community wanted an extract from the scriptures they would borrow a learned monk as one borrows a book from the library."[12] But, written or taught, it was vital knowledge—the world will never know what it has lost.

The Dalai Lama lives and works and hopes in the mountains above Dharamsala, a hill station in India where new lamasaries and nunneries have been, and are being, built, with schools for young lamas who can begin their monastic lives at five or seven years old. The lay refugees live, and do what work they can find, in the foothills of the Himalayas, where, even at five or six thousand feet, they are as out of their natural element as would be one of their own yaks—"It is so hot," "The heat!" "Oh, for an ice wind"—but they have not forgotten how to laugh.

12. From *India: A Short Cultural History* by H. G. Rawlinson.

Buddhist stories are usually dry; they have a point and make it slyly. One of them tells how two monks, an old and a young one, were journeying back to their monastery when they came to a river; at the ford the water had swollen to waist height, and a young woman was standing in distress on the bank because she dared not cross. The old monk ignored her and went straight into the water, but the young one immediately offered her his broad back and carried her safely over the ford, set her down on the farther bank, and went blithely on to catch up with his brother. The old monk at once began to scold. "Your eyes should have been looking down; you should not even have seen her, let alone talk to her, let alone *touch* her!" The scolding went on and on until they reached the monastery gate. "I shall go straight to the abbot," said the shocked old monk. "I shall tell him you carried a woman over the ford. You cannot deny it."

"I do not deny it," said the young monk, but added, "I carried her over the ford, but you have carried her all the way here."

Hill women are often beautiful enough to tempt anyone; some of the tribes are dark-skinned, but others have complexions like a white-heart cherry.

To these northeast ranges of the Himalayas come collectors of butter-flies and flowers, trekking up from the mountain kingdoms of Nepal and Sikkim. Here the white wild orchids grow in festoons from trees, there are rhododendron forests and, in the far uplands, alpine flowers—the blue Himalayan poppy, primula, edelweiss. There is always the hope of finding some new rare specimen; six hundred species of orchids have been discovered. It is from Nepal too that the mountaineering expeditions usu-ally start, the famous climbings of Everest and Kanchenjunga; the para-phernalia come from Europe or America, but local sherpas—porters—are recruited. Everything is highly scientific, but the elaboration dwindles to minuteness when the tiny human effort reaches the white "moon world" of silent peaks and glaciers, where the ice-fall face looms against the sky, daunting in its solitude.

And people come with no high purpose and make no effort, come because they are weary in mind and body and need the healing peace of mountains, rushing streams, and sun-filtered forest. They are ordinary travellers.

"The lock of error shuts the gate," says the poet Kabir.[13] "Open it with the key of love." For people who come to India that gate is often shut, simply through prejudice, through believing clichés, giving way to the little fears that so many visitors bring to India. These clichés and fears may be true, but there are always surprises, rewards, for minds that are open and friendly—another side of the coin, of the rupee, the humble paisa.

A young man in the valley of Kulu runs out with a basket of cherries to greet a lady visitor whom his friend Khaliq, the pony-man guide, has brought. Schooled in tourist shibboleths, she does not exclaim at the size and colour of the cherries but instead asks suspiciously, "How much?"

The young Kulu, in his red velvet braided hat and homespun woollen coat to which the winter smell of woodsmoke, hookah smoke, and a little of onions clings, seems nonplussed, but at last, "Five rupees," he says, as if the sum came out of the air.

Over and over again foreign visitors have been told they must bargain in India and, "Five rupees!" the lady says in simulated indignation. "Five! Far, far too much."

"Give three."

His smile is disarming, but the old phrases have been beaten in: "They will cheat you if they can," "Never give what they ask," "One must always bargain in India; they expect it," "They don't understand anything else," "You must show you are not a gullible tourist," and "One rupee," the lady says firmly. "Not a paisa more."

The smile grows less disarming. "Take."

The basket changes hands, but the smile has gone. "I should have paid fifteen paise," she says to Khaliq. "Probably he is really delighted."

Then why has the smile disappeared? "They expect you to haggle in India." True, true, but not always.

"You see, he wanted to give them to you," says Khaliq, the pony-man.

13. Kabir, called the Weaver, was a mystic whose poems and teachings are the essence of understanding love, of toleration. Born about 1440, he was at once the child of Allah and of Ram because, without changing his religion, he became a disciple of the Hindu ascetic Ramananda. After Kabir's death, it is told that his Moslem and Hindu disciples disputed for the possession of his body, which the Moslems wanted to bury, the Hindus to burn. As they argued, Kabir himself appeared before them and told them to lift up the shroud and look at what lay underneath; in place of the corpse was a heap of flowers, half of which were buried by the Moslems at Maghar and half carried by the Hindus to Benares to be burned.

It seems strange to think of cherries in India, of blossom, cherry, peach, apple, and pear, but as the ranges of the Himalayas stretch westward the valleys grow more lush; from Kulu and its neighbour Kangra, valley of songs, fruit, especially Kulu apples, goes all over India.

A story is told of one of the Mogul emperors graciously deciding to build a summer palace in the Kangra valley, a graciousness that frightened the people because a palace with its court meant extortion. Emperors are not easily prevented but, with splendid presence of mind, the local raja hastily collected all the women he could find who had goitre of the neck, once only

too common in those hills; when the emperor arrived with his queens to choose the site, the raja presented these women as their future maidservants.

"What is the matter with them?" asked the emperor. "What are those hideous lumps?"

"Fruits of Kangra," the raja answered sweetly. The queens recoiled in horrified dismay, the emperor went far more quickly than he had come, and the valley was left in peace—but the Moguls were not to be deflected from Kashmir.

Indians say that no one who has loved Kashmir can be quite whole again; there is a quality that steals the heart in the beauty of this "pearl of Hind," as the poets call it, a pearl of water and flowers; the water comes from the glaciers on the far snow-peaks and runs through high alps and valleys, through forests and down rapids till it falls to the vale floor and flows into lakes which give the vale its extraordinary fertility; "pearl," though, seems the wrong jewel: a zircon or emerald would be more fitting.

The Moguls knew how to prize their jewel—especially Jehangir. From the heat of the Delhi summers he would make the long trek up the old mountain route from the Punjab, staying, with his queen and, perhaps, a thousand courtiers, soldiers, and servants, at the Mogul serais[14] built along the way; though these were only resting places, perhaps only for one night, they had their courtyards—an inner one for the women—their arched rooms, audience chamber, pavilions, bath-houses. Most are in ruins, but the Mogul serai at Rajauri is still used as a rest-house.

It was on one of these treks that Jehangir died, at Chingaz, in sight of the snows; his heart and intestines were buried there, the rest of his body taken to Lahore, but he left beauty behind him; everywhere he went, he and his queen, Nur Jehan, Light of the World—and light of his eyes—planted their water-poetry gardens: in Kashmir, the cherry garden of Shalimar, the rose garden of Nishat.

Nur Jehan discovered accidentally how to make attar of roses. One festival night, in Agra, to please her emperor she ordered the water channels of the Anguri Bagh—the grape garden—of the fort to be filled with roses.

14. Serai: a building for travellers, a caravanserai, or the old equivalent of a motel.

During the heat of the night the petals decayed, and in the morning an oil was floating on the water; skimmed off, it distilled the true fragrance of a rose.

Roses, like bulbuls and precious carpets, seem to conjure up Persia rather than India but, though Persian influence is strong in India's arts and crafts, Indian workmen—skilled artists, in their own right, of extraordinary deftness and patience—soon surpassed their imported teachers in painting, inlay and filigree work, weaving and design; chintzes do not seem Indian, but India was where they originally came from, as well as muslins, gauzes, silks, and brocade.

Kashmir's crafts are perhaps finest of all, far, far removed from any peasant art. Kashmir makes delicate chainstitch carpets, walnut wood carved and polished to a satin finish by sandalwood powder rubbed in with an agate stone; her handwoven wool—paschmina—is spun from goatbeard hair, and her silks have the subtle colours of vegetable dyes; Kashmiri embroidered shawls can truly go through a ring, and her papier-mâché was painted with gold leaf, the paints ground from semi-precious stones, lapis lazuli, cornelian, amethyst; but these treasures are becoming difficult to find. "What can we do?" ask the merchants, Suffering Moses, Dishonest John, Subhana the Worst—derogatory names they like to give themselves. "Tourists won't pay the prices," and cheap substitutes are sold. The vale once attracted summer "residents," chiefly English; now it has a stream of tourists from every part of the world. Even the raja's palace on the Dal Lake is a hotel, and he lives in a country house.

He is a politician and Minister of Congress now, not raja, and is Hindu, though most Kashmiris are Moslems.

The faith of Islam is the antithesis of Hinduism; it does not try to give personality to God or make a cult of His aspects or saints, and so has no images—no priests, either, only wise men and teachers.

There is one God, Allah, and Mahomet was His prophet: one scripture, the Koran. Mahomet laid down simple rules for health and discipline: to prevent the eating of carrion, the throat of an animal for meat must be cut while it is alive, so that the blood flows; a Moslem will offer a prayer asking forgiveness as he makes the cut, and this is not hypocrisy; in Mahomet's desert land the only other food was dates. Anything to do with the pig is unclean: Asian pigs can be carriers of an incurable disease. Before each prayer time, ablutions must be made, a discipline in country where real effort was needed to get water—and a little would not do; hands and arms had to be washed up to the elbow, feet and legs to the knee.

Even before the cocks crow comes the call from the minaret, the dawn call to prayer, though nowadays often it is not in the muezzin's voice but in a broadcast recording. No matter where a Moslem is—in a shop or a street, his own home, a mosque—his mat or prayer rug must be unrolled five times a day, his face turned towards Mecca, and he must pray, standing, bending, kneeling, touching his forehead to the ground.

No faith could be more sensible, more manly, but, though many Moslem women love their religion, it relegates them to a position that can be ignominious. Few of them, even when upper-class and educated, take any part in public life or have a profession; some, when they go out of the house, still wear the borkha, which covers them from head to foot, leaving only a narrow lattice for the eyes. Poor Moslem women are still too often simply chattels, particularly in Kashmir.

As well as hunting and fishing, all the fine arts of Kashmir, the skills, including lucrative domestic service and the pleasant task of guarding ripe fruit trees, belong to Moslem men; hewing wood, digging the land, fetching weed out of the lakes to manure the fields, carrying loads, are women's work. Few women can read or even sew; their hands are too hard and rough. It seems strange that, among such fertility, Kashmiri peasants should be so poor—though compared to the poverty in the plains they seem well fed. They do not often go hungry, but there is not enough land to go round, the men are lazy, exploitation is rife—the proverb says a Kashmiri will sell his brother's skin for two paise—and there is the long, long winter.

From December till April an icy greyness grips the vale. In the tall wooden houses of the villages, cows, goats, and ponies are fastened into the lower rooms to be safe from hungry leopards; the warmth rising from the midden is a primitive means of central heating and takes the chill off the upper rooms; but in the boats, where whole families live, there is no midden and the walls are thin wood or mats. The men, wrapped in warm shawls, sit hugging their firepots;[15] they talk and smoke and call for more tea; the wives or daughters, whose pherans—loose gowns—are only cotton, whose legs and feet are bare except for straw sandals, bring in the steaming samovar—samovars are used by everyone in Kashmir for making salt tea, which is pink in colour and strong—then the women go back to their perpetual work, fetching, carrying, cooking, scouring, tending the animals, poling the heavy boats.

Kashmiri winters are called the Time of the Three Sisters, Forty Days' Death, then Twenty, and then Ten; the last Sister is the fiercest because then the people are weak. The sound of shuffling feet, of digging, of the maulvi's voice chanting prayers, comes all day from the graveyard, where

15. In winter every Kashmiri man, woman, or child carries a wicker container holding a small earthenware pot filled with hot charcoal; it is held under the loose clothes against the stomach, making everyone look pregnant, and is wonderfully warming, comforting—and dangerous: children upset the pots as they play so that the live coals spill down their thighs and legs; there are often terrible burns.

the ground is so frozen that the graves are shallow, built up into mounds. There is probably only one coffin to a village; the corpse is tilted out and covered simply with earth, marked with a stone, but irises are planted on the graves; in Kashmir irises are symbols of money.

Both as flowers and as money they blossom in the spring—Kashmir's "soul-enchanting spring," as Jehangir called it. Visitors begin to come, bringing their rupees, and irises burst into flower on the graves, where often the bones burst out as well from a too shallow burial. Irises mix with red tulips and mustard on soft earth-and-thatch rooftops and cover the hillsides. On the lake, the curious floating gardens, islands of water weed, are planted with vegetables and melons.

The time of pink and white fruit blossom, the small wild candy-pink-and-white-striped tulips, gives way to the purple of Persian lilac, the blue of flax. Birds that appear in embroideries and painted papier-mâché haunt the orchards, lakes, and gardens: bulbuls, kingfishers, hoopoes, long-tailed birds of paradise. Soon lotus honey will be made from flowers that cover the lakes; lotus leaves, flat, round, and silver-green, are often large enough for a child to sit on. Lotus hearts are fried for eating.

There are speedboats on the lake, and water skiing, but the shikaras, Kashmir's own small boats, are still used for work or as water taxis across the Dal Lake and over the Jhelum River. There are plain humble shikaras for carrying loads of wood, vegetables, firewood, cattle, or for fishing—a man standing motionless on the prow with a spear while his wife gently paddles the boat along; these are rough boats, weatherbeaten, but the merchants sit on Persian rugs in their jewel or carpet shikaras; confectioners keep their cakes and sweets in scarlet boxes, which, like the flower boats laden to the gunwales with roses, lilacs, ranunculuses, lilies of the valley, send reflections in streamers of colour across the water. Taxi shikaras have names like *Whoopee, Fairy Land, Water Beetle, Pin-up Girl,* and are gay with canopies embroidered in scarlet or yellow, and cushioned seats; a team of four, six, even eight men, with their long-handled heart-shaped paddles flashing in and out of the water, sends the boat speeding along to a chanted rhythm.

Even for women, spring brings a little freshness: Kashmiri working women change their clothes once a year, in spring; they may even have new pherans in pink, mustard-yellow, emerald-green, lined with white that soon

goes grey. The lake shores, the river banks, the flights of stone steps leading to the water in the city, resound with shrieks and sobs and splashings; the children, little Subhan and Taji, are having their once-a-year bath. Taji's plaits will be undone, probably ten or fifteen narrow plaits under the small skullcap all little Kashmiri girls wear, and her hair combed and searched for lice.

As spring goes on the nomad bakriwals—goat people—come swinging through Srinagar, Kashmir's water-city capital, on their way to summer their flocks on the high mountain pastures; when the snow melts these are rich in grazing and flowers. Clan by clan the bakriwals pass with their long-haired, long-horned goats bred for fine wool, their buffaloes, sheep, and pack ponies. Bakriwal men carry nothing except a favourite child, a lamb, or a kid, but the women are laden, iron cooking pots in nets on their heads, babies in their veils; the children, ragged, brown, handsome, run free with the fierce thick-coated dogs. These nomad people are Moslem but they look Hebraic, with fine bold features, and are often hook-nosed; many of their names are biblical: Yusuf, Ezekiel, Ibrahim, Davood—perhaps it is true that one of the lost tribes of Israel wandered into Kashmir. The men prize their women as they do their mares and she-buffaloes, for spirit and endurance and the number of children they breed. Babies are often born on the march, the mother, with an older woman as midwife, resting for an hour perhaps while the baby is washed in an ice-stream; then they catch up with the rest.

At night camp is made, the black tents are pitched beside a stream, fires are lit under a boulder or fir tree, samovars unpacked. Moving on again at dawn, the bakriwals climb higher and higher, sometimes carrying the herds, except the sure-footed goats, up a steep funnel of rock; even ponies have to be carried; eleven men will bring a buffalo up on their heads until, through silent forests of fir and pine, the flowery meadow or alp is reached where, the autumn before, the clan left huts made of huge logs and turf. The flocks graze on the rich grass all summer, moving still higher as the months pass, until they come almost to the tree line above which nothing grows, not even juniper, which, with the buffalo dung, makes the smoky nomad fires. The world is all tumbled rock; the marmots, from the mouths of their burrows, echo the goatboys' whistles, and the snow shines against a sky that is deep, pure Kashmir blue.

When the birches turn golden on the mountainsides and the call of the great Himalayan stag, so seldom seen, resounds across the valleys, the bakriwals will batten down their huts against the coming snow and, taking up their belongings, will slowly, by easy stages because of the buffalo calves, the kids, and the foals, make their way down to the vale or the plains of Poonch.

As mountains go, the Himalayas are young and, geologists believe, still growing.

Along the line of their foothills is what is known as a fault, a thousand-mile-long crack in the crust of the earth, which is the cause of the earthquakes that have shaken the foothills several times in the last hundred years. The Goddess of Earthquakes lives at Jwala Mukhi, on the road from Kangra to the Kulu valley, where jets of inflammable gas rise from a cleft and are worshipped as sacred fire coming from her mouth. She has proved a munificent goddess; oil is being found near her clefts—perhaps Akbar the Great, as tolerant as the poet Kabir, showed foresight when he presented her with a golden umbrella. A Moslem to honour a Hindu goddess! An earthquake is called a "zil-zila" and, in the last big one that shook the valley and was felt through the whole northwest, though the goddess's temple was destroyed, her image was unharmed. The zil-zila was so dreadful "that," said the priests, "the earth seemed to swing and tremble, but came back to rest."

Kabir says:

Between the poles of the conscious and the unconscious, there has the
 mind made a swing:
Thereon hang all beings and all worlds, and that swing never ceases its
 sway.
Millions of beings are there: the sun and the moon in their courses are
 there:
Millions of ages pass, and the swing goes on.
All swing! the sky and the earth and the air and the water . . .

The snowy peaks of the Himalayas look down from their heights; below them the plains of India spread like a coloured map marked by silver threads—huge rivers—from the foothills into the hazy distance.

PART III

For a Hindu to enter the stage of "student" does not necessarily imply going to college or university; the "student" may be learning a trade, probably a hereditary one, but it is now that, ideally, a boy or young man, especially if he is upper-caste, should "go into the forest," away from the shelter of his home; it used to be that he went to his teacher's ashram; in ancient days it was often to the actual forest, where he had to live on his wits and learn to know nature and her creatures, treating them with recognition, with respect, and without fear.

At first he may feel cut adrift, lost as that small boy on the seashore felt lost, but this is from a growing awareness; even if he is the love and pride of his family, Amar, for instance, begins to realize that "he is a lonely being . . . as a material entity only an insignificant bundle of atoms in a vast, frightening, impersonal universe . . . yet he feels he is more than this. He is conscious of a spark within himself. . . ."[1] He is eager to take up causes— modern students are not as selfish as their forerunners—and a young Indian grows in thoughtfulness as he learns something of his country's wonders, of the ups and downs of her complicated history, her long vicissitudes, and the pressure of her modern ones of overcrowded cities and, still, countless, countless backward villages. The separations of caste may rouse him to indignation or he may, equally indignantly, fight to keep them. He has to learn what he thinks and needs: nowadays his "going out into the forest" is a going out into the jungle of the world—but he can go much farther.

Air India, the national airline, has a flying carpet as its symbol and there is a magical quality in what flying has brought to India; other countries have opened up their natural beauty, their palaces, their ruins of ancient civilization, but in India these have an added quality, fabulosity—there is such a word. Her wonders are fabulous in a way not found in other lands: for instance, that flowering of the snows. Between Delhi and Agra there is a

1. From *Mysticism* by F. C. Happold.

natural bird sanctuary, a huge jheel or swamp-lake, set in yellow mustard fields and wheat fields deeply green; the trees are coated with lime, bird droppings. As the sun goes down, the birds fly in from the Jumna River, where they have been feeding: skeins of wild geese honking their lonely cry; wild duck; big white and black birds called painted storks; egrets; flamingos, pink as the sunset clouds. The air is full of the sound of wings, thousands of them, while the water reflects the sunset colours; there is an unearthly beauty in the stark white trees, and the fields grow deeper yellow and green; no other green glows as those fields can—they are like the fabulous emeralds that are still cut and polished in the little back streets of Jaipur.

It seems fabulous too, going out snake-catching in the early dawn near Calcutta, watching the snake-charmers at work, burly, bearded men, quick with hands and fingers, who carry their cobras coiled down in flat baskets hung at each end of a light bamboo yoke on the shoulders; the charmers wear heavy orange turbans, and each has a pipe made from a gourd, like a single bagpipe, with a strange high note; it is the vibrations that charm the snake, not the sound—a snake has no ears.

In the Wild Life Sanctuary of Periyar in southern India, cars are not used as in other game reserves; instead small open boats, quiet except for ripples left when the motor is silenced, glide by a bank where bison graze, and can float to within twenty yards of an elephant herd crossing the water. The bulls go first—all but the chief, who stays on the bank to see the cows and their calves safely in, the babies swimming beside their mothers, trunks lifted like infant periscopes. Sometimes a very young baby is taken between two cows, their sides holding it up; sometimes an obstreperous youngster will not go into the water and the old bull has to smack it soundly with his trunk.

Even the tourist-trodden sights keep this fabulosity, whether they are Hindu, Moslem, Rajput, or older, far, far older.

The prehistoric city of Mohen-jo-daro may go back to 3000 B.C.; its remains were found in 1922; the buildings are of burnt brick set in mortar, streets wide, laid out to a spacious plan; houses have bathrooms, there are house and street drains, the gutters are all of pottery, while the public bath is of a pattern that would rival swimming pools of today.

The earliest of the Ajanta and Ellora Caves, hewn out of the hills near Aurangabad, date from the second century B.C., and the Elephanta Caves, away on their island in Bombay Harbour, from the ninth century A.D.; their great carved figures have a calm that nothing, not even tourists, can disturb.

There is Udaipur and its lake: the architectural perfection of the Palace of Winds at Jaipur, built high so that the pampered maharaja could catch the breezes as he slept: there is the honey-gold colour of the Street of Carvings at Jaisalmer in remote Rajasthan, where every face of every house is so intricately carved that it looks like embroidery. Jodhpur's rugged fort stands hundreds of feet above the surrounding hills and plain: with its old palaces, courtyards, jewel house, barracks, stables, elephant lines, and Gate of Victory, it gives some idea of how impregnable those Rajput kings could make their citadels—unless they ran out of water.

The Mogul Fort at Agra is a courtly contrast; below its walls a giant enclosure was used for elephant and tiger fights, and among the myriad courts is a pachisi board, a chequered marble floor where the "pieces"— dancing girls or courtiers—were moved in the game, which is more like backgammon than chess; on the high terrace above, outside the Hall of Public Audiences, is the emperor's white marble throne and, opposite, a small black one for his jester; here too is the lovely little mosque rightly called "the Pearl," its emptiness glimmering with a milky lustre.

Floating in a country boat down the Ganges in Benares'[2] early morning brings a strange sense of wonder and of peace, as if the spirit were temporarily out of the body. The sun strikes the top of the old buildings and slowly filters down over huddled houses and alleyways until it reaches the river bank, the countless bathing steps, and turns the giant palm-leaf umbrellas orange in the new light. To Hindus, Benares is the most hallowed place on earth, and the air is filled with splashing and chantings from the pilgrims' prayers and cleansings in the sacred waters. Flowers—marigolds, garlands of jasmine, rose petals—float by and, as the boat draws near the smoke of the burning ghats, the smell of burning flesh mingling with incense, the guide says quietly, "I will tell you when you should put your cameras down." When he gives the signal the most avid tourist reverently obeys.

The guide may be Amar, a true student now at university and, like hundreds of his chronically poor fellow students, trying to help to pay his board

2. Benares is now called Varanasi.

and fees by working; this is not easy for an Indian: he cannot, like his American counterparts, do menial work, waiting at table, helping in the kitchen, because in India this would be unfitting; besides, inevitably, he would put someone more needy out of work. He can only hope to do some tutoring or translating or, luckiest of all, be appointed a government guide where, besides wages, there are tips, sometimes surprisingly meagre, occasionally munificent, and Amar, whether in western clothes or shirt and dhoti,[3] is careful to be impeccably clean and polite. "What perfect manners . . . so gentle and sweet," say his charges . . . but the night before he may easily have been in a demonstration or a real riot. For all their bantering cynical talk among themselves, Indian students are idealistic, anxious to take up cudgels, and, because they are more responsive, are even more easily inflamed than their western contemporaries; they are, too, extraordinarily gifted in distorting a story!

3. Dhoti: men wear a straight piece of cloth, usually fine white muslin, about five yards long, draped round the waist, then drawn between the legs and tucked into the waist again so that it falls in folds. Worn with a loose flowing shirt, it is exceedingly graceful.

When that genius of a film director, Jean Renoir, was making a picture not far from Calcutta, there was a night scene of Diwali, the Feast of Lights, in which a procession of women extras brought their lamps to put before a shrine: each woman wore a sari with its pallu—loose end—drawn over her head in reverence so that she was almost veiled, but two words had gone to Calcutta: "night," "women"—the American-sponsored company was shooting a night scene with Indian women. In an hour, the rumour had grown to "shooting a night scene with naked Indian women," and the students, several hundred of them, decided to march.

The set, built on the edge of the river, was of a bazaar, crowded with extras and flimsily built. The first warnings were sounds like a far-away roaring; feet make no noise on sand; these were voices. Then the outlying stalls and flimsy huts were overturned; in a moment they were on fire. The women fled—fortunately there was a real bazaar near—but the crew was left, a handful of Westerners and perhaps thirty Indians. The valuable Technicolor cameras were whipped into fireproof locked boxes; the English technicians were armed, but the Indian crews begged for no retaliation; "That would be fatal," they said. Europeans and Americans were "please not to speak or move," but to stay in the centre while the Indian crew stood round them.

As the march, lit now by flames and torches, came on, the noise rose to a tumult and the students started throwing sand; sand sounds harmless but it can be blinding, choking, and it stings; but the Indians stood unmoved, their hands joined in namaskar; they still made namaskar when the first rank reached them and began hitting them across the faces with lathis,[4] but to hit someone who stands quietly and unmoved is nonplussing. The lathis faltered; the sand began to stop, the noise to ebb, and when Renoir, huge, calm, benign, mounted the boxes to speak, the students were still—hundreds of upturned young faces and dark heads on a sea of white-clad shoulders.

Indian sympathy can be kindled as quickly as Indian anger, and before the night was out the students had rebuilt much of the set and, allowed by the wise Renoir, sat around it till daylight, watching the scene being shot.

The company was lucky; even though the first ranks paused, those behind who could not see might have pressed them on; the mood was ugly, even dangerous, and riots have often ended in real arson and murder. A mob of Bengali students recently threw an unpopular professor under a train. Yet

4. Lathi: a light stave, usually used by the police.

demonstrations can take a typically Indian or inconsequential turn: a tremendous rally of the People's Party was held not long ago in Delhi, to which students from universities far around were to march and meet there in force. One contingent set out with flags and banners, the young men wearing their orange caps, but Agra is only one hundred and twenty-five miles from Delhi, so, on their way, they decided to make a little detour and see the Taj Mahal; its beauty so stunned them that they forgot why they were marching and never reached the rally.

Perhaps they were sensible. Taj means a crown, and this shrine, built by Shah Jehan, son of Jehangir, as a tomb for his queen, is the most beautiful building in the world. Even in daylight, surrounded by coaches, cars, tongas, touts, hawkers, throngs of people, and litter, the symmetry of its dome and four minarets soars into the sky just as in life the emperor and his queen, Mumtaz-Mahal, Pride of the Palace, were above everyday people. Seen at dawn, always the witching hour in India, the marble, like the Himalayan snows, catches the flush of the sunrise; by moonlight, its whiteness glimmers. Carved marble screens throw fretted shadows, delicate as bamboo shadowings, round the inmost chamber; the inlays of jade, jasper, agate, and cornelian are iridescent; true to Moslem precepts, they are of flowers—one small flower may have eighty-seven pieces—flower buds, leaves, wreaths, and scrolls; no human or animal, or even bird, face must intrude on the soft gloom of this chamber above the vault where the royal lovers lie side by side but, "If there is a minaret and a monkey, and you want people's attention," Amar complains, "they always look at the monkey." Amar, as he leads his trail of Americans or Germans or Scandinavians or, quite often nowadays, fellow Indians over the lawns of the fort or down marble paths edged with cosmos flowers, is proud of what he is doing. Temptations for Indian students are as many, or more, as for students anywhere else; drugs are ridiculously cheap, yet few young Indians become addicts. Dropouts from the universities of America and England roam the streets of Delhi in the balmy winter of the plains; they have a colony at Goa, but the students do not envy them; in fact, the average Indian regards them with contemptuous pity—and pities their countries more. "Has America, has *Britain* come to this?" Though, like most modern Indians, Amar longs to go to the West, he can be intensely national and, "Don't they care about their heritage?" he asks with genuine bewilderment.

India's is as old as it is rich, a conglomeration of races, language, cultures, the rise and fall of dynasties, emperors and kings (see table on page 369), conquests and defeats, battle after battle after battle.

It would seem natural to think that the immense ranges of the Himalayas have always made a boundary for northern India and so protected her but, from earliest times, their mountain passes, such as the Khyber and the Kurram, were busy thoroughfares for trade, traffic, and troops, and again and again in her changing history northwest India has been one country with Kabul—modern Afghanistan—and the states beyond. The river Indus used to be a far more formidable barrier and it is in the Indus Valley that the wonderfully laid out cities of Mohen-jo-daro and Harappa have been discovered. No one knows what happened to their people; some think they were easily conquered by the Aryans—neither of the cities was walled—while other historians say that the Aryans,[5] when they came, found no big cities, only barbaric tribes.

Nor does anyone really know exactly who those Aryans were; only that in the centuries between 2000 and 1500 B.C. there was a restlessness, an overflowing amongst the peoples of southernmost Europe and Asia Minor; the old civilizations of Crete, Minos, Troy were broken by the Aryan Greeks, and the Vedic Aryans came through the mountain passes into India, perhaps first as raiders but later as settlers, agriculturists in their new land. They were distinctively fair-skinned, fine-featured, and this led to the establishment of caste to keep themselves apart from the people they called barbaric—the Sanskrit word for caste is "varna," meaning colour and texture, refinement. They drove the Dravidian-speaking natives to the south, contemptuously calling these darker-complexioned people "dasyu"—slaves; Hindus below the dividing line of the Vindhya mountains still differ from the northern Indians and are proud of the distinction; they claim they have an older, far more rich culture; certainly the arts of South India, especially music and dance, are sublime.

A few of the tribes would not be driven but took refuge in wild country, hills and jungles; these were probably the aboriginals—the Todas of the Nilgiris, the Gonds of Madhya Pradesh, and the Santals of Bengal are three of these tribes; they have kept themselves mysteriously untouched for more than thirty centuries and are quite different from the people round them, even from each other. To marry outside the tribe is to be outlawed. They call themselves "children of the forest" or "of the soil," and are often hunters of unthinking courage; armed only with a bow, arrows, and knife, they will track a tiger on foot. Their looks are distinctive too; often they have flat noses, thick lips that mark them off from the Aryan, and their skins are sometimes ebony-dark (see the picture of an aboriginal boy on pages 40–41).

5. Though these early conquerors are loosely called "Aryans," there was no such ethnic stock. Aryans were people who spoke Aryan languages, from Sanskrit to Greek, Teutonic, and Celtic.

The idea that fairness is, above everything, desirable still persists: "Wanted, a fair-skinned educated girl for young Government-intended graduate," runs a typical advertisement for a bride—brides and bridegrooms are openly advertised for in the newspapers. "Fair-skinned, knows music and knitting . . ."

There has always been a flow of peoples in and out of the northern regions. Alexander took the Punjab and the Indus Valley in the fourth century A.D. and left them to a friendly mixture of Greek and Hindu kings. Arabs and hordes from central Asia, especially the White Huns, came deep into India, as did the ruthless Mongols; the heat of the Indian plains drove most of them back to the higher lands of Central Asia. They came, plundered, and went away but left their influences—especially the Greeks and Persians. Even those who stayed were not absorbed as invaders have always been absorbed by the Chinese; perhaps this was because no one can become a caste Hindu in the way he could turn Moslem or Buddhist or Christian by being converted; a convert to Hinduism has to start as an untouchable and, though he will be within the fold of Hinduism, it is only by rebirth, perhaps hundreds of rebirths, that he can achieve caste.

India, too, is so vast that, until she was unified under the British, newcomers never penetrated the whole; the first Mogul emperors, for instance, had not even heard of the wonderful southern kingdom of Vijayanagar.

The earlier Moslems spilled over, as it were, from Central Asia and the poor lands of Kabul; they too came first as raiders, then established their dynasties, last of which was the Mogul; the two religions, though, kept as distinct as they are now. There were persecutions: the first Moslem conqueror, Mahmud of Ghazni, was called "the image-breaker" because of the temples and gods he overthrew. Akbar the Great had the dream of a reconciled religion but, like his dream of a perfect city, rose-red Fatehpur Sikri, it ended in ruin. India settled for coexistence and, though there are still Hindu-Moslem riots, coexistence is what she has now; there are more than sixty million Moslems in India.

Alexander took nearly a year to sail the armada he collected on the Jhelum River down the Indus to the sea, but he, of course, fought battles on the way and founded a city. When Babur had established his rule in the "warm land," as he called India, and had decided to stay in Agra, he sent for his queens and children from Kabul; one of these children, a small daughter, Gulbadan—Rose-body—"close to his heart," tells in her memoirs how she travelled with the chief queen's entourage; she was six when they left Kabul, seven when she reached the approach to Agra and beheld her father, the Padishah[6]—the ladies had been five months on the way; to fly

---

6. Babur had given himself this title, "Padishah," "Ruler of Kings," or Emperor, long before it came true; it must have been one of his moments of vision—or what seemed to his harassed army sheer cockiness.

from Kabul to Agra now takes an hour and forty minutes, with a change and slight wait at Delhi.

Planes are still called "hawai-jahaz"—wind-ships—by the common people, and this magical travelling is obviously best for anyone with enough money; some surprising passengers seem to have the fare: a family, carrying endless bundles, baskets, and pots—there seems no limit to the hand luggage allowed in an Indian plane—comes down the steps from a silver Caravelle and goes off in a bullock cart; a sannyasa—holy man—perhaps naked except for a loincloth, sits next to a cabinet minister "London returned," visiting his small home town. The minister will be greeted by officials and hung with garlands while, as the speeches are made, his children, who have come to meet him, stand in a decorous row on the edge of the crowd and run in one by one to bend and touch their father's feet with folded hands; he takes not the slightest notice of them—until he goes home, when there will be a carnival of joy—but the holy man may be received by a multitude.

Yet as more and more Indians take to planes, more and more Westerners, especially young ones, are going back to the ancient ways of Indian travel.

"Are you the two who are going up the Ganges in a country boat?" the assistant at the High Commissioner's office asks wearily. "Or crossing India on a camel? . . . by bullock cart? . . . on foot?" Or, more frequently, "On the way to Swami Shivananda's ashram?" while travel agents advertise "Nomad expeditions for young mixed groups . . . penetrating the interior to observe the Kochi Nomads in the pastures of Hindu Kush," or "Join the annual pilgrimage to the holy cave of Amarnath." The assistant's weariness is because these trips so often bring troubles. Western stomachs and bowels are easily infected with dysentery or typhoid; people who do not understand about sun get sunstroke, get heat stroke; they lose their money and themselves, become stranded. Though to travel in India in any of these ways, to go among the people, is no longer a pioneer achievement, it is still a hard one because everyday life in eastern countries for most of the people is hard. Indians are sweetly hospitable—it is amazing how they will allow strangers to sponge on them—but they cannot give what they do not possess.

Amar, when he leaves university, will swiftly learn how hard it is for most people to make even an adequate living in India. A teacher, though he may have graduated with honours, is poorly paid all his life; a clerk in an office or bank starts at between three hundred and fifty to four hundred rupees a month; even as a senior he will seldom rise to more than eight hundred—about forty-four pounds sterling or a little over a hundred dollars—for everything.

Factories pay even unskilled labour as much as two hundred and fifty rupees a month, but factory work is privileged, even for women. Poorer-class women, though, find it harder than do men to make enough rupees to exist; prices rise all the time, which is why, in fair employment, dearness allowances are paid. Indian women work in coal mines, mica and gold mines, though nowadays only above ground; in the mines their wage is likely to be around five rupees a day, but for women working on roads or buildings—"women of the dust"—the highest wage is three rupees; they are truly women of the dust because they work in dust and dirt from morning till night and the road-workers often sleep in camps by the sides of the roads. It is the women who pull the rollers, break the stones and carry them in baskets on their heads, bear iron ladles of cement and, with sweat and panting, carry enormously heavy loads.

There are still the traditional beasts of burden, camels, donkeys—and ponies, those small, rough little beasts known as tattu that, for all their blue bead necklaces, have mouths of iron and uncertain tempers; mules are more valuable because they can go anywhere a man can, scrambling like cats up the narrowest rough, steep tracks—and there is always the bullock cart.

A tribe, the Lohars, iron-workers, once of Rajasthan, live always in their handsome wooden bullock carts that are studded with brass inlays and nails, the wheels carved with signs of the zodiac. The carts creak from village to village as the Lohars ply their hereditary trade, making of fine tools. They wander because, in the sixteenth century, their Raja, Pratap Singh, was defeated by the Moslems, and the tribe made a vow that its people would never live in Rajasthan until Pratap Singh was king again. Four centuries later they still hold to it!

But bullocks, all animals, must eat, often more steadily and better than human beings, and that costs money; the cheapest labour is still man: men, women, even children, an endless supply.

A family may not be able to afford a bullock cart, but where work is to be done, there will be baskets; large and small, deep and shallow, closely woven of cane or flexible strips of bamboo or palm leaves. Large flat baskets, a cross between an umbrella and a hat, are a protection against the heavy rains; deep baskets, called kiltas, are covered with hide and have lids that can be locked; stores and provisions are carried in them on journeys. Toppas—baskets open on one side, used in the hills—have a seat fixed halfway with a platform for the feet, and are used on strong backs to carry the old and sick. Children of rich people take their airings in a toppa instead of a perambulator, their ayah walking beside the coolie carrier. Pony panniers are loosely woven baskets, and in the tea gardens, which are not so much gardens as large estates, the pickers, who are usually women, carry baskets on their backs as, in their white headscarves and long cotton skirts, they move between the closely planted bushes that have been pruned into dark green table shapes, sometimes thinly shaded by feathery-branched trees.

Tea bushes have flowers a little like camellias, small, white, waxy, with golden centres. If left to itself, a tea bush grows into quite a large tree. Tea was introduced into India and Ceylon from China, but later it was found growing wild in Assam; now it is cultivated in terraces on the slopes of the lower Himalayas below Darjeeling, and in Kangra, and along the hills of southern India, and in flat gardens on the plains of Assam.

Just as there are noted vineyards, some hillsides grow notable teas. The height where tea grows, the soil, shade, sunlight, rain, the week in which it is picked, first flush, second, or third, can make a difference to its quality. There is a story that a young planter thought he would shade his bushes with almond trees; his tea tasted of almonds.

The plucking of the new leaves—"two leaves and a bud" was the ideal hopefully held out by the manager—begins in early summer; baskets, filled with incredible speed, are weighed before the leaf is sent down to the factory, and the pickers are paid accordingly; now and then a flat and unobtrusive rock is found under the green heap.

Each tea estate has its own factory where the leaves are fermented, rolled, fired, graded, and packed. The well-known square tea boxes, lined with tinfoil and stamped with the garden's name, are carried to the nearest

131

main road, often many miles away, by ponies, men, or boys; a large box of leaf, which weighs forty-five kilograms, makes a full load for a boy.

Where there is work, there will, too, always be bamboo. When an Indian touches a bamboo he makes beauty. He understands exactly how to work with it; the plants with their pointed leaves and green and yellow colour make innumerable things: houses of bamboo lathes covered with clay; the water-lifting poles for wells; scaffolding; fine little bridges; a mast for a country boat and the wicker cowls for the boats' living quarters; the slats of fishing nets, and needles for making the nets themselves; bows and arrows, the bowstring made of twisted fibres of bamboo; drinking cups and liquor flasks; water pipes; spoons; scalpels; and baskets.

Bamboo is as strong as a man, as yielding as a woman, as simple as a child, and, in the country, it costs nothing.

Bamboos grow in a tope or grove, but the tea gardens were carved out of real forest, cleared by human labour. The encampments of the wood-burners—their charcoal is indispensable for braziers and homely mud ovens—are found deep in the forests, discovered by the pall of blue smoke from their fires. When these men, and women, go into the forest to cut wood, they may meet a bear in the hills and, in the jungles of the plain, come across a tiger's kill.

Hill people and jungle-dwellers are careless of their trees, but down in the plains, during the long, dry, baking summers, the smallest tree is prized. Shade is precious; in the *Vedas* there is a promise: "He who plants a tree will have his reward." Several trees are sacred; these often have medicinal powers—and their own legends.

The asoka, which means "sorrowless," is dedicated to Kama, god of love; legend says that it will break into its orange-scarlet flowers only if touched by a beautiful woman, and in the courts of the Rajput kings the loveliest of the princesses was chosen to kick the trunk gently with her gold-ankleted foot.

Mangoes are evergreen and are planted in groves and along roads because of their thick shade. Their fruit is luscious and their dark leaves, strung into garlands, decorate all religious occasions.

The neem is graceful and feminine, giving a shade that is always cool. She is sometimes married with full ceremony to her male counterpart, the pipul, but in her own right the neem is so refreshing and healing that her leaves are strewn round the sleeping mat of a sick child.

A banyan is tall and gives a spreading shade as the myriad roots it puts down snake along the ground until they multiply into other trunks that send roots down into the earth in their turn. Where a banyan and a pipul grow side by side so that their branches intertwine is an especially holy place; it suggests the growing together of body and spirit.

In the shade of the village pipul, the panchayat meets, a council of five elected wise men or "elders"—though nowadays some of them may be young; they settle, or try to settle, village quarrels and behaviour, and the government gives them a budget to use as they think best: to buy better seed, dig a well, build a school for girls, or revive a village craft.

It is under the pipul tree, too, that the village "club"—but for men only—gathers in the evening to smoke, gossip . . .

How much?
How much
did it cost?
Did it pay?
Was it worth?

Two paise
a seer
on the price
of rice!
Ram! What has come over the earth!

Advice
—given twice—
that young Anil should be married.
Anil . . .

Once we were young.
Aie! The urge was strong!
Tharuk's Nitu has given birth
at last to the son she carried.

Biris glow and are stubbed out on the ground.
From a hut across the fields comes a drum's soft dub-dub sound.
Fireflies begin to flicker in the pipul tree.
A boy brings bowls of tea.

How much
did it cost?
Did it pay?
Was it worth?

But nowadays it may not be to gossip, but to listen to the village radio.

As the great jet planes cross India there is nothing to be seen of the land by day but a hazy brownness; by night there is something commonplace in other countries but, in India, new, cluster after cluster of lights, villages with electricity. Things are changing even in the villages; they used to be self-contained little republics, each with its own panchayat, its common pasture land, islands in a sea of crops, numerous as stars in the sky, although long, dusty miles apart. Radio has helped to break the isolation; a set blares in almost every village—blares is the right word. For one thing it has to be shared among many people; also radio is good, therefore it is good to have as much of it and as loud as possible; Indian ears seem impervious to noise.

Foreign affairs are discussed now—and foreign does not mean, as it used to, "outside the village," the iniquities of Congress, of government taxes, government seed; it means America, Russia, China; no one can pronounce more firmly now about the policies of these countries than a village elder. Soon there will be television: as the pylons and poles stretch farther and farther across the land, bringing electricity, television must follow.

For years, on the walls of every village, there have been government propaganda posters: vaccination, told as a strip cartoon: Mother shrieks, "Cruel doctor, scratching blood from my baby's arm!" while, in the next picture, she has its ears and nose pierced; there is a crocodile head snapping up a small man with its cruel teeth—the crocodile of litigation, to which Indians are so tempted—but some of this welfare has become fact; babies are vaccinated now—though they still have, of course, to have their ears pierced, jewellery is valuable and must be properly anchored—men and women are slowly learning about family planning; more and more children can read and write. A van bumps its way over the dirt road between the fields, bringing a medical squad to spray tanks and swamps against mosquitoes. In the fields themselves there may be a new tractor, and every tractor brings change, willy-nilly a new vision.

Fields around an Indian village are small and tend to grow smaller because land is not left to the eldest son but divided among all the sons; often it is owned by a landlord who rents the land out to be cultivated, field by field, each by one man, who, to help irrigation, carefully builds mud walls around his field, further closing it off. A tractor needs space in which to work and turn; the mud walls must break down, the farmers must amalgamate, cooperate—all those modern words. . . .

Indians, though, have a way of imbuing even a machine with personality. A peasant, as much yoked to the soil as are his bullocks, can appreciate the marvel of a tractor's power; it seems godlike to him, an opulent god machine among the wooden ploughs and clumsy harrows. All mechanization is marvellous and so, in India, tractors, buses, trucks are offered worship with garlands and daubs of ochre; they often wear jewellery.

But these changes are not coming overnight, nor in a year, nor twenty years—perhaps not even in a hundred. India is too big for that, and there are many, many villages where the men listen, discuss, nod or shake their heads, and go on exactly as they did before; and for all the new laws against discrimination, the villages still have families who are bound and classed by their traditional occupations and have to live in separated enclaves: enclaves of cobblers, tanners, weavers; a single one of a barber, or a washerman or woman. In a large village there will be at least one butcher's shop with half-flayed bleeding carcasses of goats and sheep hanging on hooks; no brahmin will go near it, but most Indians are lower-caste or casteless and eat meat when they can get it—as long as it is not beef.

Though the word for caste is that Sanskrit "varna"—colour—to a Hindu caste is not what it seems, and would be in other countries, human discrimination against humans; a man's varna is, again, the result of his behaviour in the lives he has lived before and so is part of the inexorable journey.

Brahmins, first and highest of the four main castes, sprang from Brahma's head and were intended as people who had been refined until they were capable of dealing with things of the spirit, a class of men who would devote themselves to study, expounding the sacred laws, acting as teachers, doing no paid work but supported by the rest of the community. Brahmins have had to become more practical now; they work not only as priests in the temples, but as lawyers, teachers, office workers, and even do manual work; a brahmin household has to have a brahmin cook, and a gardener is often a brahmin, living apart from other servants in a hut of his own. He must keep apart because brahmins are so fanatically clean that they avoid contact with anyone of the outside world because he may pollute them. Oddly enough, other Indians do not resent brahmins but look up to them.

The kshatriyas came from Brahma's shoulders, and so they bear the load of authority; they were the princes—no brahmin can be a king—and warrior defenders; now those who have kept their positions are army generals, admirals, air marshals, political leaders, heads of state or of business houses. A kshatriya is free from taboos—in warfare he could not observe them—and his caste is the one most open to change, most easily westernized; eating meat and drinking alcohol, physical contact such as shaking hands, do not offend him.

Only a "twice-born" of the three higher castes is allowed to wear the sacred thread, and the last of these, the vaisyas, came from Brahma's thighs and are traders, merchants, bankers, religiously orthodox and as strict as they are rich. They give enormous sums to priests and temples and have huge, elaborate houses filled not so much with western furniture as with western curiosities: one merchant, with a garden house near Calcutta, had a thousand clocks in his main rooms so that the whole house was filled with tickings and chimings. Their children go to school, but the women, though they can be learned, prefer to be sequestered.

The sudras, by far the largest caste, were fittingly born from Brahma's feet; to Hindus, feet are not only lowly but impolite; to sit with the feet pointing at anyone, or touching them, is almost an insult; the greatest reverence that can be shown to a man or woman is to stoop and take the dust of their feet—like the children at the airport with their father the cabinet minister. Sudras, though, have often shown a sturdy independence; they

have become rajas and kings, but, as no man is supposed to change the trade handed down to him by his father, most sudras live and die as artisans, peasants, often soldiers. Once upon a time, if a sudden calamity wiped out all the village washerwomen, no one else would do their work and a washerwoman would have to be begged from a neighbour village.

"Panch" means five, and the panchamas—the fifth division of Hindu India—are the outcastes, "untouchable" because their touch was unspeakable pollution; they were once almost unseeable too—even their shadows could defile.

In the villages perhaps a whole field separates them and their trades from the other villagers; yet even they are separated from the lowest outcastes of all, who will remove—and eat—carrion and carry night soil to the fields. No outcaste was allowed to use the village well or go into the temple; in communities that had hospitals for sick animals and birds—brahmins were often very kind to animals—there was no help in illness for the panchamas; no doctor would treat them.

Buddha was against caste: "Not by birth does one become a brahmin," he wrote. "By actions alone one becomes a brahmin." Nearly two thousand years later Guru Nanak, the founder of the Sikh religion, denounced caste too. "Evil-mindedness is the low-caste woman; cruelty is the butcher's wife; a slanderous heart the sweeper woman; wrath the pariah woman. What availeth it to have drawn lines around thy cooking-place, when these four sit with thee?" But it was not until Gandhiji[7] came and called the untouchables "harijan"—children of God—that India listened or, at least, began to listen.

Gandhiji was born a vaisya, but caste—or man-made rule—was not strong enough to hold Mahatma Gandhi; Mahatma means "great-souled." His parents, though Hindu, were followers of the Jain belief that ahimsa—hurting nothing and no one—was of paramount importance, a belief Gandhiji followed all his life. His weapons were passive resistance, civil disobedience, fasts, and prayer—methods that left the authorities literally disarmed: no one can go on firing on people who lie down, row after row on

7. Jawaharlal Nehru wrote: "I have seen some extraordinary explanations of this 'ji' in books and articles by English writers. Some have imagined that it is a term of endearment—Gandhiji meaning 'dear little Gandhi'! This is perfectly absurd and shows colossal ignorance of Indian life. 'Ji' is one of the commonest additions to a name in India being applied indiscriminately to all kinds of people, men, women, boys, girls and children. It conveys an idea of respect, something equivalent to Mr., Mrs., or Miss. Hindustani is rich in courtly phrases and prefixes and suffixes to names and honorific titles. 'Ji' is the simplest of these and the least formal. . . ." (*Jawaharlal Nehru, an Autobiography.*)

the ground; as the rioting students on the film set found, it becomes futile to hit with a lathi someone who stands in quiet dignity, taking the blows while making namaskar.

The simplicity of the tools Gandhiji used for defence made it possible for every Indian, man, woman, and child, to join in: in 1930, for instance, he decided that the Salt Act, by which salt was taxed, should be disobeyed; salt in every household should be homemade from sea-water, and he himself led the march to the sea, against which the authorities were helpless: no police or army can arrest millions of people. It was the same with the boycott of imported English cloth. "We shall spin and weave our own," said Gandhi and again led the way, spinning every day on his small hand charka; it became a mark of honour among Indians to wear homespun cotton.

Gandhi was put in prison, but that only spread his fame so that he came out more powerful than ever; silenced, his silence was more eloquent than words. The thin, dark little figure, light as a bird in his loincloth and shawl, steel spectacles perched on his nose, was feared by the government as much as he was adored by the people.

Gandhiji's death was a martyr's: he was shot by one of his own country-men, of his own faith, as he came out of the house where he was staying to lead the evening prayers—and it did not end his teaching or his spirit. "What is all this snivelling about?" Mrs. Sarojini Naidu asked when she arrived at the house of mourning. She—poet, politician, and patriot—was one of the Mahatma's oldest friends. "Would you rather he had died of old age or indigestion? This was the only death grand enough to hold him." Gandhiji's charka is on Independent India's white, green, and yellow flag, and the law protects the untouchables now. Too often it is still only the law; the old segregation goes on, but legally no one can refuse a panchama entry to a temple or force him to use a separate well. He is a harijan—child of God.

Perhaps, in a way, he has always been a child of God—as any Indian is—and, even though he does the lowliest humdrum tasks, he treats his work almost as a dedication, which is one reason why he never hurries. God is not only in the temple; He is in hands and hearts and the things of earth, stone, wood, iron; and so, like the farmer with his tractor, a mechanic will worship his tools on certain days, laying flowers before them, saying prayers. Why not? A worker's tools are his best friends, his means to creation, even though it may be in the most prosaic way.

And life is not all toil; even in the ordinary working day there are lulls; it is good, when the sun is hot, to set down the loads for a time and sit in the shade of a tree to rest, to smoke, or talk, that endless Indian talk; or just to sit and dream or, perhaps, like the gopis, the cowherd girls of long ago, to hear above the chatter and laughter the irresistible sound of Krishna's flute.

Besides being the unvanquished god-warrior and statesman, Krishna, eighth incarnation of Vishnu, is the ideal child, youth, and lover, mischievous, playful, teasing, disarming, and sensual. The call of his flute draws all mankind—or all womankind. As a child, to save him from a demon king, he was hidden away among the cowherds on the banks of the River Jumna and as he grew up all the milkmaids—gopis—fell in love with him. He grew to an enchanted manhood and used to play his flute in the woods; the gopis, when they heard it, would go out and look for him. They could never find him but he gave them a promise that he would dance with them in the month of Kartik—October/November. At last the autumn came, when the heat and rain were finished, and on the night of the full moon Krishna went towards the forest, playing his flute.

The gopis left their husbands and, following the sound, found him, but his loveliness made them stand abashed under the trees. Then Krishna called them; the forest was transformed into a golden terrace on the river bank, the trees hung with wreaths and garlands, and the humble gopis found themselves dressed in robes and jewels. Lutes and cymbals began to play while the young god stood amongst them "like a moon in a starry sky." He multiplied himself so that he danced with each one in the Rasa Lila dance; they grew so intoxicated with love that they lost all shame and Krishna vanished, taking only Radha—his best-loved gopi—with him.

Why are there so many Krishna stories? The world of reality is full of pain; men and women, even children, are as cruel to one another as if they were caught in a cycle of cruelty from which there is no escape, except to Krishna's world of fun and love; there, for a few moments, they play, find solace, comfort—and it is not all make-believe, because Krishna is divine as well as human love; his flute is the aspiration that draws men and women on and on, the search of the soul for God. Radha is the prototype of that human soul.

152

It was by no accident that all-wise Vishnu chose, for this, his eighth sojourn on earth, to be brought up as a cowherd; the Hindu worship of the cow goes back to more ancient bull-worship, and every part of a cow is holy, from her horns to her milk, urine, and dung—all of her except her mouth, because she once told a lie. Brahma and Shiva had an argument and the cow was called in as a witness to certain happenings that Brahma wished to prove. Thinking to please the Creator, she told a lie, but Shiva, in his wily cross-examination, found her out and cursed her mouth, which has been foul ever since.

The Rajasthani peasant sings:

Give a son to my wife
And a daughter to my buffalo. . . . .

She-buffaloes and cows are riches—a poor man's riches. Where there is enough milk the family will be healthy: milk can be sold to help pay taxes, and a cow can be used for ploughing, though oxen are better. A tractor, of course, is better still, but for most that is still a dream, and a cow or she-buffalo comes first on the list of peasant necessities. Then, if his village has that marvel electricity—the Hindi word for it is bijli, lightning; if his field is near at hand, well cultivated, and there are a strong cart, baskets and tools; if the house roof and its mud walls do not leak, and the strings on the bed are well knit; if there are a few good cooking pans, a banana tree in the courtyard so that there will be plenty of plates to eat off, a clay oven, sleeping mats, a quilt or two, a little cloth, and some bangles, even if only glass ones for the wife and daughter; if there can, now and then, be small extras to eke out the daily rice or wheat-flour, chapatis and vegetables: a little jaggery—molasses—some curd or ghee, dal, a few chillis; if now and again a man can have a small bowl of arrack or toddy and a biri to smoke, his friends to gossip with, he is content. His needs are simple, yet there are always those "ifs." It takes so much toil to win so little and if, again, his village still has no pumped well and the monsoon fails, or the cow dies or there are too many small mouths to feed . . . if food has to be bought . . .

Righteous men, to gain merit, feed ants with fine white sugar, but they are not above selling short-weight wheat and rice or adulterated flour.

. . .
Silently stand some children of the poor,
And shyly, hungry eyes half-turned aside,
Observe the eater through the open door.[8]

8. *The Subhasitaratnakosa.*

Above all a peasant needs a good wife. "May my wife be a wise woman who keeps the seed ready for the fields," sings a villager in Uttar Pradesh. "Let me hear my wife's bangles as she grinds the corn," says his brother in the Kangra valley.

At midday she will come to him in the fields, where she has probably been working too until it was time for her to go in to do the cooking; now, balanced on her head, will be a pot, perhaps two, one of freshly cooked food, the other of cooling buttermilk. It is she who fetches the family water.

Few Indian villages have running water in their houses, any more than they have sewage pipes; everyone goes out into the fields to relieve himself, carrying a brass lota for water with which to clean his private parts with the left hand, which is never used for eating or for offering anything to anyone. Household water may come from the village well or a tank or, nowadays, an unromantic but far more cleanly village tap piped to an electrically pumped well; but well or tank or pipe, it is the heart of the village, although it may be quite a way from some of the houses. The women gather there, sometimes several times a day, and linger a little to talk and laugh, to gossip, then help each other lift the heavy filled pots and balance each on a ring of twisted straw or padded cotton on the head. Water is often carried now in petrol tins, plastic pails, enamel jugs, but these will not balance on the head and women still prefer the old earthenware, copper, or brass pots, sometimes two or three, one on top of the other, sometimes only one spot that seems far too large and heavy; but the slim gold-brown necks are strong, the balance of the taut straight bodies is wonderfully sure, and not a drop will be spilled.

In the hot weather the bhisti—water-seller—his water bag made from the skin of a whole goat and carried slung across his back, is a familiar sight in village and town. Modern hotels hopefully have modern plumbing, shining new baths, basins, lavatories, cisterns, but there is often no water to fill them, and the bhisti has to come; to take water for even the shallowest bath gives a feeling of guilt.

Rajasthan and the Punjab have some lucky districts that are irrigated by canals. If a peasant's fields are in canal country, he may not have to watch the skies for the monsoon, but probably he will have to contend with the machinations of a neighbour who, if he can, will divert the flow to his own fields.

Water is conserved, preserved, reserved against the dry seasons; with infinitely patient, antlike human labour, huge dams and artificial lakes have been made—the lake that holds the white reflections of the Lake Palace of Udaipur is one. The water level of these man-made pools—those tanks—is carefully measured, and they are usually shaded by trees to prevent sun evaporation; a temple tank may be set like an emerald in front of the holy place and reserved for its worshippers. In palaces and rich houses, pools are built slightly above one another, so that, as in the Mogul gardens, water may flow gently from each to the next through channels cut in stone or marble, curves, circles, spirals, to give what the West would never count as luxury, but which in the arid Indian plains is luxury indeed—the sound of running water.

PART IV

To be a "householder"—the second stage of life—means living; now a man must really encounter—and counter—the world; sometimes he feels he has the whole weight of it on his back.

He must, first, find a position or build one up. He should marry—there are few bachelors in India, and a Hindu needs a son; besides, where better can he learn prudence, patience, toleration, self-sacrifice than in marriage and bringing up a family? Often he will find with surprise that his wife can be his gentle leader in all these. He should have, too, a full sex life. Hindus do not understand why virginity is so reverenced in western religion—a vestal virgin is an extraordinary idea to them—and this is the stage of life in which a man like Amar could, and should, enjoy sex, just as he enjoys food, drink, recreation, art. No one can know the meaning of relinquishment, say the rishis, unless he has first experienced; but living, let alone pleasure, has to be earned; politics, economics, intrude and it is now that Amar may have to know the unevenness of life. If he is not well off, he must endure the bitterness of seeing other people's children have what his own must go without, the humiliation, perhaps, of taking, in the hope of promotion, an expensive garland to honour someone he despises; he will see extravagances that offend and jar.

India's rich men, her nobles, rajas, and kings, had subtle refinements of luxury that the West has not even imagined, and words that Amar, as that student guide, used to say so carelessly take on a different meaning now.

"This is the cool hall where the Emperor Shah Jehan made artificial rain, swirlings of spray from three hundred and fifty fountains. See, in those marble niches flowers were put by day, mica lamps by night, so that the falling water flowed over colour."

"This is the emperor's winter bath, which took, for each bath, eight hundred pounds of wood to heat."

"The queen's bath. Its floor is inlaid with myriad tiny fountains that jetted warm rose water."

"The royal children's bath—all of carved marble."

Bathrooms themselves were sometimes walled with hundreds of tiny mirrors so that they sparkled like a thousand diamonds. Did it make any difference to the pleasure of bathing in them, of watching graceful fountains, to know that millions of men depended for their lives—and their children's lives—on a trickle of water and on the rain that the gods will or will not send? That hands grown hard, cracked, and calloused had quarried and polished the marble, carried it on heads or sweating backs? Not a whit. The palaces and mansions, cool courts and garden walks, the windows set in screens, intricately carved, through which queens, princesses, and their maids could watch the amusements of the court, were for the divinely born few.

India now has naya paise—"new money,"[1] the decimal system, to try to reduce differences and to simplify—but the old coinage gave a far better idea of her extremes of life. A crore is ten million, a lakh a hundred thousand rupees. The rupee was split into sixteen annas, an anna into four paise, a paisa into three paise, and below that were still cowries, shell coinage, which could buy a few grains of rice, a spoonful of oil, a leaf or two of sag—a kind of native spinach.

Crores and cowries; rajas and peasantry; the old fabulosity as fabulous as the clothes in which the rajas used to be painted and photographed, not only the high-collared coats of brocade buttoned with diamonds that have become almost familiar, but robes of handwoven silk, stiff with silver and gold, scarves of gold-shot gauze, turbans fantastically wound, tasselled and hung with pearls, though the richest of them all, the Nizam of Hyderabad, usually wore plain white muslin.

1. The government had wondered if the simple peasants would understand the new system; they took to it so quickly that they could short-change a buyer before he had added up the bill!

What is known of India's old dynasties is revealed only in flashes of light between long periods of darkness as names of kingdoms and empires stretch back to the kings of the Vedic Aryans. Two Chinese[2] who travelled in India at the beginning of the fifth and the middle of the seventh centuries have left descriptions of the country and its people, of the vast Indian armies of bowmen, cavalry, and elephants, and of the magnificence of the courts of Chandragupta the Second, of the Gupta era, and of the noble Harsha, Emperor of the Five Indies, which were the Punjab, Kanauj, Bengal, Darbhanga, and Orissa. Harsha was almost equal in stature with Asoka and Akbar.

Ballads tell of the Rajputs, who traced their descent from the sun, moon, and divine fire, and who in chivalry and courage seem to have equalled the knights of medieval Europe, although their continual feuds and clannishness were more like the Highland Scots. If there were no wars, they hunted, but they preferred a war; if no other enemy could be found, they fought with each other, often on the flimsiest pretext; perhaps this aggressiveness lives on in the Indian love of litigation, which is almost a national sport.

The Rajput queens and princesses married whom they chose, went hunting with their men, followed them into battle, and proudly immolated themselves on their husbands' funeral pyres. The princes, though, knew how to manage their women; in their palaces was a room called the anger chamber, where a queen could be shut away until she was brought to reason—but she could also shut herself in and refuse to come out!

Though the Rajputs dissipated their armies in feuds with each other, it was they, alone among the Hindu princes of India, who, for a long time, kept up the struggle against the Moslems; even when many of the proudest and bravest were won over by Akbar's policy of reconciliation and lived more or less at peace within his empire, one of them, Rana Pratap, refused to give in or to compromise and went on with the unequal fight for the rest of his life; but a hero of militant Hindus now is seventeenth-century Sivaji, the Maratha, who rebelled against the Emperor Aurangzeb.

2. Fa Hsieng, who was in India from 401 to 411 A.D., and Hsuan Tsang, the Master of the Law, who came in 630 A.D. to study Buddhism and stayed till 645.

Sivaji's troops were based on fortress hideouts in the rocky hills and jungled valleys of Marasthana, from which they used guerrilla, almost bandit, tactics against the disciplined but unwieldy armies of the emperor; they also burnt up all the grass and grain so that the Moslems' horses and elephants were useless. Sivaji himself seems to have been like quicksilver; seek him there and he was here; seek him here and he was there. It was his rebellion that helped to break up the Mogul empire and bring a Hindu renaissance, and Aurangzeb had to admit that the "mountain rat" had won his domination. Stories about Sivaji are still told and sung in towns and villages; in India's struggle for independence he was held up as an ideal to encourage patriotism among the low and outcastes, because he, a leader-king, was born a sudra; he was, they like to tell, as religious as he was fierce, taking orange—the colour of an ascetic's robe—as the colour of the Maratha national flag; it is the colour now of the People's Party, Rashtrya Sevak Sangh. But Sivaji was ruthless and treacherous. He made a treaty with Aurangzeb's general that the two of them would meet in a tent for parley, without guards, without arms, quite alone. The Moslem general kept his word, but when he came in Sivaji embraced him with hands that were gloved with baghnak—tiger claws—and so killed him. Perhaps it is significant that the People's Party was responsible for Gandhiji's assassination.

Maharaja means "great king," and some of them were great men, but it was a miracle, in old India, that any raja should have emerged temperate and wise; in most their arrogance was as overweening as their extravagance and selfishness. It was not their fault; from the day he was born, a kumar, prince, was taught to think himself entitled to have his own way, no matter what the cost in money or pain. It was a shock when the British government insisted that some of the young princes be given English controllers or tutors—bear-leaders as they were impolitely called—to try to instil a little self-discipline, a proper education into the future rajas. For the controllers it was a delicate, difficult task; what boy will sit at lessons when he can ride, play polo, shoot, speed in cars? How keep him well when he can eat all the sweet things he likes, drink, and, from the age of twelve or thirteen, have women?

The British did not try to curb the grown rajas' extravagances; when Lord Auckland became Governor General in 1834, his sister, Emily Eden, went out from England to stay with him and kept a journal in which she describes some of the splendours:

The first show of the day was Runjeet's[3] private stud. I suppose fifty horses were led past us. The first had emerald trappings, necklaces arranged on its neck and between its ears, and in front of the saddle two enormous emeralds, nearly two inches square, carved all over, and set in gold frames, like little looking-glasses. The crupper was all emeralds, and there were stud-ropes of gold hung on something like a martingale. The young rajah, Heera Singh, said the whole was valued at 37 lakhs but all these valuations are fanciful, as nobody knows the worth of these enormous stones; they are never bought or sold. The next horse was simply attired in diamonds and turquoises, another in pearls, and there was one with trappings of coral and pearl that was very pretty. It reduces European magnificence to a very low pitch.[4]

A bridle and crupper of emeralds seems too foolish to believe, but rajas, like many other wilful overrich men, were given to nonsense: it is nonsense to have coffee cups made of rubies, dining-room furniture of crystal or mother-of-pearl; to have a waxwork bodyguard in full dress which will present arms to the tune of a musical box; to plate a Rolls-Royce with gold or to spend the day playing the children's game of snakes and ladders when dignitaries are waiting. The rajas of Oudh, if other amusements gave out, used to arrange dog weddings with all the panoply of a human one—and far more bawdiness. The rajas did all these things and, in a way, that is what they were there for; Indian peasants are inured to going without bread but they dearly love pageantry and wonders. The crowds that come to watch polo used to keep their applause for His Highness of Jaipur and run to mob him when the game was over—even to touch his boots was enough.

From the time when they drove chariots, the Indian princes have delighted in blood horses.

3. The Sikh Raja, Ranjit Singh, Lion of the Punjab.
4. Emily Eden's diary, *Up the Country.*

Racing, hunting, pig-sticking, above all, polo, are the sports of princes. The present government will not allow horses to be imported, except a few for stud and for the army, so that the quality of the ponies belonging to the Indian international polo players is not as high as it used to be; "country-breds" have distinctive ears with a tell-tale curl to them, but "strings" are still brought to Calcutta and Delhi for the polo season. A "string" is needed; the game is so fast that ideally a pony should be played for only one chukka —seven minutes—but with the denuding of the princes' revenues, taxation, and high prices, most ponies are used for two. All the same, crack players such as Rao Raja Hanut Singh of Jodhpur and his sons are still among the finest polo players in the world.

Only a few rajas are left now; soon there will be none. Before independence there were five hundred and fifty-four states, some huge, some only a few miles square; they have been absorbed into the rest of the country. Their rajas were to be allowed to keep their titles for life and their sons and daughters-in-law were still called "kumar" and "kumari," but that was to be the end; future generations would have no titles—perhaps no riches either; but recently the President, using his special powers under the constitution, took away their titles, and as this book was being written the princes were seeking restoration through the Supreme Court. The ruler of every state, great or small, used to have his secret treasure horde; only he and his vizier —his prime minister, not elected by vote but chosen by the ruler himself— knew where it was hidden, probably in an underground vault of the palace, or away in the jungle. In due time, the eldest kumar would be solemnly let into the secret and perhaps given one priceless piece. There are stories that these treasuries were guarded by cobras, but it is far more likely that the wardens or guardians were a chosen clan of thieves—thieves, after all, should know best how to catch a thief. In India, even thieving can be a hereditary occupation and these guardianships were a privilege strictly kept in the family.

The worldly among the princes moved what they could to other countries in time; some have been allowed to keep their private jewels, but the government confiscated what it could find of the rest. Some princes have chosen exile; others linger on, living still in their states on privy purses or pensions granted them by the first Congress government, but these may be withdrawn. Some have gone into politics; one of the most beautiful of the young maharanis stands as a candidate for her party; when one meets her at a fashionable dinner in Delhi, her figure like a wand in white chiffon, a diamond solitaire large as a hazelnut flashing on her finger, it is unimaginable that she has perhaps spent the day bumping in a Land Rover from village to village, trudging through the dust, speaking from rustic platforms

or in the bazaar through a megaphone. Some of the princes, like Kashmir, who is a doctor of literature, hold high posts in the government, but they have to be hard-working and thoroughly practical; a London court jeweller was asked recently if he could design a collapsible crown that would go in a suitcase.

Palaces are schools now, or museums, or have been turned into luxury hotels, often run by the rajas themselves, but the splendour has not all gone. India is so big that, in the remote states, old powers and ways still hold; a visiting male should not be surprised by the offer of the loan of a dancing girl for the night or a few days—if she is valuable the raja usually wants her back—and in the palaces, particularly if they are deserted, the fabulosity is still strong.

Amber, the old capital of Jaipur, was built on the steep slope of a hill and looks down at its massive reflection in the lake. The palace is a small city of alabaster and mosaic, of honey-coloured marble and glittering jewel and spangle work; there are marble domes and courtyards, airy pavilions opening onto gardens. Doors are of sandalwood inlaid with ivory, and gateways are high, because they were built to let an elephant and its howdah through; there are long lattice-screened galleries, vast audience chambers, and tiny private rooms. Besides the wide main staircase, ramps connect the different levels, up and down which the ladies were transported in miniature rickshaws decorated with mother-of-pearl. The palace elephants had a ramp to themselves leading from the main road below the palace, up which —before motor cars were invented—only they could climb; elephants bring tourists up now, stepping as slowly and majestically as if they still wore their brocaded howdahs.

High on the palace terraces, the maharaja had a private court with a domed pavilion; it is so high that its courtyard seems roofed with stars. On moonlit nights, in the moon's radiance, dancing girls danced there for their lord alone. Now it is empty; there is no music or tinkling of anklet bells; the only noises are plebeian ones coming up from the bazaar below.

The moonlit court, the Sukh Niwas—Hall of Pleasure—the whole palace of Amber seems like a dream, but dreams are more potent than reality; a dream can be bought, particularly in the East.

> From groves of spice,
> O'er fields of rice,
> Athwart the lotus-stream,
> I bring for you,
> Aglint with dew,
> A little lovely dream.
>
> Sweet, shut your eyes,
> The wild fire-flies
> Dance through the fairy neem;
> From the poppy-bole
> For you I stole
> A little lovely dream.

"From the poppy-bole . . ." Sarojini Naidu's[5] lullaby has a sinister undertone which she probably never realized.

---

5. Sarojini Naidu was one of India's few women poets, an enchanting person and an eloquent supporter of Gandhi; she was imprisoned by the British three times, which was ironical when so many of her dearest friends were English; it was Sir Edmund Gosse who persuaded her to tear up her poems of English life and write about her own country.

Opium is made from the oily juice of the seed capsules in the white or pink poppy. Poppy fields are planted in autumn for the spring harvest when, just before the petals fall, the pods are gashed in the evening to let the "white tears" exude and be collected at dawn next day. The juice is simmered over a slow charcoal fire, allowed to dry, and the crust is removed; this is repeated six times; then the pure opium left is smeared on wooden boards with a wooden spatula, dried in the sun, scraped off, and rolled into cakes that fetch a high price. A field of poppies is more valuable to the peasant than a field of grain.

Opium can be a boon as well as a curse; a little will deaden the pangs of hunger and those of pain; ayahs know that a fingertip dipped in opium and given to a baby to suck will hush its crying; those fierce Rajput princes, when not fighting, hunting, or hawking, would sit in the pavilions of their flowering gardens, drinking kusumba, which is opium water—perhaps nothing else would have calmed them and made them sit still.

For a shooting camp to run smoothly, its elephants to be properly cared for, the mahouts must be given a regular supply of the drug to steady nerves and tempers.

If an important guest is invited to a shoot—in the old days it might have been the Viceroy, now it may be a foreign ambassador, a prime minister, or a millionaire tourist—he must at least see, if not shoot, a tiger. To make sure he does, the kill to which the tiger will return, and the drinking holes, may be doctored with opium. Tigers can become opium addicts.

Most of the opium, though, was, and is, exported; the solaces of most Indians—Hindu, Moslem, Sikh, Jain, Parsee, Christian—are more likely to be smoking or chewing tobacco . . . and chewing pān.

An Indian may smoke a clay pipe like the one in the photograph; most men and women enjoy cigarettes, but English or American brands are horridly expensive; the small, exceedingly pungent cheroots called biris are cheap, but the refinement of Indian smoking, cooling and refreshing, is the hookah—hubble-bubble; its polished shell or jar is filled with water, the cup with scented tobacco; as the smoker draws through the tube let into the shell, the hookah makes a deep soothing, gurgling sound, but it is difficult to smoke—old ladies are experts—and when groups of men gather for talk—in women it would be called gossiping—the hookah is passed sociably from mouth to mouth; this disgusts caste Hindus.

Tobacco is often chewed, but more popular is pan, a mixture of spices, lime paste, areca nut, sometimes tobacco, folded up in a betel leaf to make a small wad.

The areca nuts grow in the areca-palm groves, but betel is a vine planted under a canopy of other plants to keep off the sun, or else in the shade of a matting enclosure.

Betel leaves vary: Bengal grows choice pale green, mild leaves, but there are deeper green leaves, tougher and "hot"; people like to mix their own fillings, so that a hostess will offer her box of leaves, smaller boxes of lime paste, nut. These boxes, silver-chased or even gold, are an important part of a bride's trousseau. Betel has a clean, refreshing taste, a little acid, so that the palate puckers, as after eating a sloe. It is the kutha, mixed in with the lime paste, that stains lips, teeth, and saliva brilliant red; spit marks on pavements or bazaar roads make scarlet patches.

Amar, in his work—suppose he has become an architect or a doctor, or is in government service—may have travelled overseas and will certainly have mingled with Westerners and probably have learned to like western drinks, wine and spirits. In India they are not always easy to get; some provinces are "dry" and even visiting foreigners have to apply for "permits"—they used to have to declare themselves "addicts"—and, even when they get a permit, they will find in, for instance, Bombay's renowned Taj Mahal Hotel, that they can drink only in the "permit room," and they cannot offer a drink to a guest unless that guest has a permit too. Prohibition even applies in the air; flying over one of these dry provinces, the stewards lock the alcohol away. At government functions anywhere, even at state banquets, only fruit juices or lemonade are served.

Amar's family are nondrinkers too, officially, but in his baithakhana[6]— the man-of-the-house's sitting-room—his father used often to "slip behind the curtain" to his private store; if his wife saw him a little merry, she would dutifully shut her eyes and mind to it. "But Amar is a boy," she protests.

"Funny kind of boy, with three boys of his own," says Baba.

Baba's surreptitious drink would have been brandy; common people do not have to be surreptitious, "go behind the curtain"; they have no such inhibitions, and hill people often get rollicking on beer made from rice or millet, while the beautiful innocent palms of the plains supply the peasants.

---

6. In big joint-family houses, each grown male would have his own baithakhana.

The palms' long, slender unbranched stems rise perhaps fifty feet high, each crowned by a cluster of gigantic stiff leaves. They are abundant friends: a Tamil poem, "Tala Vilasam," describes more than eight hundred ways in which these trees help men, making them palm-leaf umbrellas and fans, palm-fibre rope, rough palm-leaf writing paper—the ancient Hindu and Buddhist scriptures were written on these palm leaves. Nothing is wasted; mats for roofing and for the floor are made of palm fibre; coconut palms give their great nuts for milk and flavouring; there is palm oil for lighting and cooking and palm molasses or jaggery for sweetening. It is the male palmyra that yields the juice for this molasses, sometimes as much as four or five pints a day from its crushed flowering stalks; as fresh sugary juice it is a harmless sweet drink, but when it ferments it is distilled as arrack, the fiery, potent brandy of peasant India. A "cousin" palm gives even more juice that becomes toddy, but to tap these palms—from a cut that drips into a pot hung from the tree—needs a government license. The villagers will make a sling of cloth or rope that slides up the stem; held in the loop they can walk, almost erect, up the tallest trunk.

Humans are not the only ones whom the palm blesses; a minute bird, the eastern palm-swift, glues its nest to the pleats in the underside of a palm leaf and spends the whole of its little life hawking for insects round its particular tree.

When the explorer and adventurer Vasco da Gama landed in Calicut in 1498, he was asked by his astonished hosts what was his object in coming to India. "For Christians and spices," answered da Gama and might have added, "especially spices"—Europe was crying out for them. Spices used to come from factories in the Levant owned by importers from Venice and Genoa, who brought them in through Kabul, Balkh, and Samarkand; then the Turks captured Constantinople in 1453 and these overland trade routes were cut off. Spices have always been expensive, but when Vasco de Gama eventually reached home, his Indian cargo of cloves, nutmeg, and pepper was priceless—trading in spices was far more profitable than making Christians.

Nowadays the spice-seller comes round with his basket of dried spices carefully displayed in paper or palm-leaf bags; he has cloves, pepper, cardamom, cumin, coriander, to give food zest and pungency, and turmeric to give it colour, the rich red-gold seen in curries.

When people think of Indian food, they probably think of curry; curry and rice and all those accompanying tiny dishes: raita, bhurta, dahi—of which yogurt is the nearest equivalent—salads, chutneys, poppadums—crisp biscuits, thin and light as paper—and Bombay duck, which is not duck but dried fish. Indians do eat a great many curries, sometimes every day, even twice a day, because they are cooling; the Indian idea of "hot" or "cold" food has to do not with its temperature but with its effects. Curry is good, but there is a world of Indian cooking besides, gourmet cooking: it is an education to eat chicken tandoori or to taste the pulaos of the "Persian dinners" given on state occasions by Moslems, especially in Kashmir, when, piled on rice, there are such delicacies as apricots stuffed with mutton, mutton balls stuffed with spices, roast kid, ending with honey rice. A Persian dinner should properly have thirty-six courses; mercifully, these are usually reduced to eighteen, but even so the diners are left uncomfortably replete, grateful for the little bowls of cinnamon tea brought to signal the end, and with only a hazy recollection of the goodness. The favourite meat of the Prophet, though, was camel and it is quite common to see, even in Bengal or the hills where workaday camels are unknown, a solitary beast being walked down during Ramazan to be ready for the feast of Id.

The Emperor Babur, a connoisseur of food, said that camel tasted like tenderest mutton, but most everyday Moslem families make do with a kid fattened up for the festival.

Hindus, even when they are rich, usually live frugally; there are only two real meals a day: one in the morning, the other towards evening or night, with tea or the less expensive buttermilk in the early morning with a little leftover rice or fresh fruit. Women often seem to exist on practically nothing, and it is quite ordinary for a hostess, even a westernized one, while serving her guests with mouth-watering food—she has perhaps even cooked it herself—to excuse herself from eating, saying, "This is my fast day."

If she has not been to the bazaar herself, she will have examined everything her cook—if she has one—or her husband or son has bought that morning, and she will not hesitate to criticize or blame: "Two annas for *that*? Far, far too much. And see, that papaya has a bruise on one side. You shouldn't have taken it." A chicken, carried live and head downwards, will be pronounced stringy, but she will be pleased if the money has been well stretched, if there are fresh prawns perhaps, or a good plump fish.

There is a clean and sterilized supermarket in Delhi now. Calcutta's New Market, where anything, from ivory and gold to cabbages, can be bought, has its long ranges of food shops health-inspected; there, as in most big eastern markets, shops of a kind are grouped together: shoe shops in what is almost a street of shoe-sellers, toys in another, fruit-sellers, confectionery, soda fountains, sports shops, pet shops, curios; but the higgledy-piggledy streets of the ordinary bazaars are unchanged except for the deafening radios and car horns—one or two streets in the cities have restrictions on blowing horns, but in most the driver can make as much noise as he likes.

What is seen in the bazaar depends on the eyes that see it—on eyes, ears, nose, stomach, and mind. To some it is a contamination even to walk through a bazaar; they see the cess in the gutters, where children—and

192

grown men—unconcernedly squat down to relieve themselves; the ground itself is stained where betel nut and cough phlegm have been spat out; there are flies that rise up from litter heaps and settle on the sweets and foodstuffs in the shops. Smells of hot frying mustard oil, garlic, rotting fruit hang in the air with, always, the smell of latrines, of refuse, unwashed sweat from the coolies, of coconut hair oil and sandalwood from the cleanest white-clad babu.[7] There are beggars, perhaps a leper, or a woman with elephantiasis; the children's stomachs are swollen with fever and spleen; even babies can have flyblown eyes. The dogs are pariahs, mangy with outstanding ribs; cats are starving; buffaloes, which are water beasts, pull carts in the sun all day long; birds are hung out in cruelly small cages, and sometimes a mynah is blinded to make it sing.

There seems nothing attractive or picturesque in the bazaar; it is simply sordid and poor, with no products of its own, no muslins or silks or rugs, weaving or ivory. Even the temple is often hideous and cheap, its roof of hammered-out kerosene tins, its gods sometimes large jointed German dolls.

The misery and filth seem too overwhelming for anything else to be seen; they cannot be denied but, as always, there is a balance, and the squalor is only part of the whole; the sun is a good disinfectant, people are more tenacious than they seem, and most of them conjure up, from these conditions, not a precarious but a healthy, often immaculately pure, life—so that, to eyes which can see beyond the dirt and sweat, the bazaar teems with interest and life.

7. Babu is the courteous title for a Hindu gentleman; it came to mean "clerk" in the time of the British and was often used derisively, which is why many Indians have discarded it.

The cloth shops are inviting, with rolls of cloth on shelves open to the street, cottons and prints with patterns and crisp new sari lengths. Two boys walk up the street from the dyers', holding a sari dyed bright pink; stretched between them it will dry in the sun as they walk. Quilt and pillow shops have gay patchwork cushions and scales loaded with fluffed-up cotton. There are jewellers, gold and silversmiths working in filigree; the fronts of some of their shops are barred so that they seem to sit in cages.

In the grain shops, the grain is set out in black wicker baskets, and the sweet-shops cook balls like American popcorn and cubes of sweet paste that are like marshmallows and clear toffee spun in beautifully spiralled rings. There is a shop entirely for kites; a cheap bangle shop devoted to bangles of glass; a secondhand-bottle shop. The sacred bull, almost too fat to walk, helps himself from food shop to food shop as he lumbers along and wears a lovingly netted blue and white bead cap on his hump. Bells ring from the bicycle rickshaws; cars move as slowly as the bullock or buffalo carts because they cannot get through the crowds. In the gutter a barber is shaving the head of a man who must be in mourning; next to him a scribe, his desk on the ground, takes a letter that a ragged old crone anxiously dictates—but the letter-writer will couch it in the elaborate flowery words he loves. Beside him a bead-stringer will be stringing pearls on a loop of gold or scarlet silk. There are shoeshine boys, a monkey man whose dressed-up monkeys snatch at orange peel and pieces of thrown-down fruit as he walks past, rattling his stringed drum; there is a patter of goats driven by; crooning pigeons, crows, miaowing cats—and people, people, people.

In the early morning the food shops are a hubbub. The shopper, when he or she has bought all the things on his list, will not carry them back; a coolie boy will bring them in a round basket that he carries on his head. What will be in the basket? Only fresh food: at the beginning of each month or in the right season household stores are bought: sugar, rice, oil, ata—flour—spices, and grain; in the market basket will be vegetables: young sweet carrots, glossy purple knobs of brinjals—eggplant—ladies' fingers—a sort of zucchini—onions. There will be a papaya or perhaps a pomelo that opens like a big pink-fleshed orange, or plantains—small bananas—and, in season, litchis or mangoes; there will be curd—the dahi that is like yogurt—bought in an earthenware pot, as is ghee—Indian butter—and, unless it is an orthodox brahmin household, once or twice a week the basket will hold eggs, fish, meat—except beef.

Only well-off people can afford curds and ghee, so that most of the cooking is done in groundnut, sunflower, or sesame oil or the mustard oil that has such a pungent smell. Spices are expensive too, but chillis grow easily, and the small bushes of bright leaves, gay green and red fruit, are planted behind many poor village huts; the ripe scarlet fruit spread out to dry in the sunlight on courtyard floors or town window sills makes patches of brilliant colour.

Strict brahmins will not eat spices or strong-tasting vegetables such as garlic or onions, saying these coarsen taste and spoil the refinement of the body, necessary for the refinement of the soul.

The kitchen, or kitchen part of a Hindu house, is immaculately clean, though most of the work is done on the floor or on short-legged tables; no one in outdoor clothes or wearing shoes may come into the kitchen; hands are continually washed. The stove may be gas or electric or a chula—a stove of baked clay—its oven filled with hot charcoal, which is then raked out as in an old-fashioned European bakehouse—or it may have a small tin oven. The pans are dekchis—handleless saucepans or else two-handled iron cooking bowls; the physical fitness of a bride is good if she can pour, without splashing, the water out from the rice pot, often about fifteen seers—approximately thirty pounds—in weight; her patience is seen in how finely she can grind her grain and spices and how she manages her fires; to ignite her coal or charcoal, she uses dried leaves or cow dung, and the best firewood is mango because it does not smoke. Cooking utensils must be scoured, always under running water, with ashes and sand, though nowadays Indian-made scouring powder is sometimes afforded; tamarind has an acid action on brass that will make it shine.

In really orthodox kitchens, on the last day of the month, all the pots and pans are scoured, set clean on freshly papered shelves—often brightly coloured paper cut into patterns; then they are hung with flowers and are given the tribute of a puja; as with the mechanic's tools, it seems fitting— every cook everywhere knows the value of a trusted knife or well-balanced wooden spoon or a pan that never sticks or burns.

Rich houses serve food on thalis and in katoris—small round trays and bowls of silver—but in most homes everyone helps himself from a common platter set on the floor, mixes the food on a banana leaf, and eats with the hand—which is not as easy as it sounds.

In his novel *Too Long in the West*, Balachandra Rajan, one of the best of contemporary Indian writers, has a description of a girl just back from three years at Columbia University, New York, eating her first meal at home:

. . . Nalini looked at the food in neat piles on her plantain leaf, the avial, the sambhar, the curling snake coils laced with shredded coconut, the rich tan of the dal nestling beside the incredibly white, soft rice, and the backs of the brinjals glistening with melted butter. She mixed them together expertly and ardently with the true fervour of the returning exile. Her hand scooped up a portion of the nectar. Then her wrist flicked backwards and upwards gracefully, her tongue meeting her palm unhesitatingly at the precise moment when the food would otherwise have cascaded down her forearm. There was the delicate sucking sound that accompanied the operation when perfectly performed. The hand went down in a continuation of the same fluent, wristy motion and came up again, smooth and certain as a conveyor belt.

Lakshmi [the mother] watched her daughter admiringly, delighted that her right hand had lost none of its ancient skill.

To Nalini the food tasted like nectar; anyone who has lived long in India feels at times a yen, a real nostalgia, for Indian food—cooked by an Indian.

> I rolled them in turmeric, cumin, and spice,
> With masses of pepper to make them taste nice:
> In lashings of sesamum oil I then fried 'em—
> The pungency curled up my tongue when I tried 'em:
> I neglected to wash, and got down to the dish,
> And I swallowed that curry of nice little fish.[8]

That comes from the *Subhasitaratnakosa—A Treasury of Fine Verses—* compiled at the end of the eleventh century, so that Nalini's was indeed an ancient skill. Some of India's most used and famous recipes too are centuries old:

Koftas: Meat Balls

¼ green pepper
1 medium onion
1 lb. finely minced meat
2½ tablespoons dahi
1½ teaspoons salt

2 tablespoons coriander or water-
cress leaves
1 teaspoon garam masala (see
page 203)
fat for deep-frying

Chop the green pepper and onion very finely. Mix all the ingredients except the fat in a bowl. Shape the mixture into tiny balls the size of marbles. Heat the fat in a frying pan and deep-fry the meat balls. These koftas can be served with drinks or added to fried rice.

Prawn Koftas

½ lb. prawns or shrimps, cooked
and shelled
2 medium onions
¼ teaspoon sugar
2 teaspoons vinegar
½ bunch coriander or watercress
leaves

½ green pepper
3 cloves garlic
¼ teaspoon turmeric
2 teaspoons besan (lentil flour)
¼ teaspoon ground chilli
1 teaspoon salt
½ cup cooking fat

Mince prawns. Chop onion finely. Mix sugar and vinegar. Chop coriander leaves, green pepper, and garlic. Mix onion with prawns in a bowl. Add all other ingredients (except fat) and mix well with the hand. Make into walnut-sized balls and fry in very hot deep cooking fat till reddish-brown. The koftas must be well cooked; if necessary, sauté them gently afterwards for a few minutes.

8. Bhavabhuti, translated by John Brough.

Tandoori Chicken

1 2-lb. roasting chicken
1 large onion
4 cloves garlic
1–inch piece fresh ginger or ½
    teaspoon powdered ginger
1 teaspoon coriander powder
1 teaspoon cumin powder

½ teaspoon chilli powder
2 teaspoons salt
½ cup dahi
1 tablespoon vinegar
juice of 2 lemons
2 tablespoons melted butter
1 teaspoon garam masala (see
    page 203)

The word *tandoor* means oven. A large, long earthenware pot is embedded in clay and earth; charcoal is put inside, and the oven is made red-hot. The chicken or meat is put inside on skewers, and the oven embedded again. The meats cooked in these ovens are superb; no other can give the delicious flavour.

Clean the chicken, keep whole but do not truss. Make 3 or 4 cuts on each side of the bird. Grind the onion, garlic, and ginger to a paste; add to it the coriander, cumin, chilli, and salt. Beat the dahi in a bowl and add the paste, vinegar, and the juice of 1 lemon. Mix thoroughly and rub on the chicken. Marinate the chicken for 4 to 5 hours. Roast in the tandoor for 20 minutes or till the chicken is tender. Brush with melted butter, sprinkle with garam masala and lemon juice, and serve.

Macher Jhol: Bengali Fish Curry

1 lb. fish fillets
1 teaspoon mustard seed
1 medium onion
3 green chillis

3 tablespoons mustard oil or any
    other cooking oil
salt to taste
½ teaspoon turmeric

Wash and dry the fish. Grind the mustard seed into a paste. Chop onion and green chillis. Heat the oil and sauté the fish briefly. Add onion and chillis and salt. Sauté for 3 minutes. Mix the mustard paste and turmeric in 1¼ cups water and add to the fish. Cook till fish is tender. Serve with rice.

Macher Mauli

1 lb. rahu fish
2 onions
green chillis to taste

1 cup thick coconut milk
salt to taste
juice of 1 lemon
3 tablespoons fat

Heat fat. Clean fish and cut into pieces; sauté lightly in fat; set aside. Slice onions and chillis and sauté till golden brown. Add 4 tablespoons coconut milk and cook a little while. Add fish and the remaining coconut milk. Add salt. Cover and let it simmer till fish is cooked. Add lemon juice.

Green Peppers Stuffed with Shrimps

4 large green peppers
5 cloves garlic
1 tablespoon cooking fat
¼ teaspoon ground ginger
¼ teaspoon chilli powder
½ teaspoon paprika

1 teaspoon salt
½ teaspoon cumin
¼ teaspoon turmeric
1 lb. shrimps, shelled
6 large onions, chopped

Preheat oven to 375°. Cut the green peppers in half. Take out the seeds and the knob of flesh near the top. Scald in hot water and put aside. Chop the garlic very fine. Heat the cooking fat in a frying pan and sauté the garlic, ginger, chilli powder, paprika, salt, cumin, turmeric, shrimps, and onions, stirring the mixture now and again so that it does not burn. Turn the flame low and cover pan. Simmer until shrimps are soft. Stuff into the prepared green peppers. Place the peppers carefully in a greased ovenproof dish. Place the dish in a roasting pan containing hot water. Put in preheated oven for 30 minutes.

Matar Panir

½ lb. panir or cream cheese (it must be firm)
1 large onion
½ lb. tomatoes
½ cup butter, ghee, or margarine
1 teaspoon turmeric

2 teaspoons coriander powder
1 teaspoon chilli powder
1 teaspoon ground ginger
1 lb. peas, shelled
salt to taste
1¼ cups whey

Cut the cheese into 1-inch pieces. Slice the onion finely and chop the tomatoes. Heat the fat and sauté the pieces of cheese till pale golden; remove and set aside. In the same fat, sauté the onion till pale golden. Add the spices and sauté for a minute or so, then add the tomatoes, peas, whey, and salt. Cook over low fire till the peas are tender, and add the cheese. Simmer for 15 minutes.

Samosas

Pastry:

3½ cups plain flour
½ teaspoon baking powder
1 teaspoon salt

2 tablespoons melted ghee or butter
4 tablespoons dahi

Filling:

¼ cup ghee or butter
1 small onion, chopped
1 lb. potatoes, boiled
2 green chillis

salt to taste
1 teaspoon garam masala (see
    page 203)
vegetable fat for deep-frying

To make the pastry, sift the flour, baking powder, and salt into a bowl. Add the melted butter or ghee and the dahi and make into a pliable dough. Knead thoroughly so that the dough is smooth.

To make filling, heat the ¼ cup ghee and sauté the chopped onion for 2 minutes. Cut the potatoes and chillis into small pieces, add, and sauté for 5 minutes. Add salt and garam masala and mix thoroughly. Take off the fire and cool.

Knead dough again. Take small, walnut-sized pieces of the dough and make into round balls. Flatten and roll out on a floured board. Make thin rounds the size of a saucer. Cut in half. Make each half into a cone, seal with water, and fill with the potato mixture. Wet open edges with water and press together. When all the samosas are ready, fry them in deep fat till they are crisp and golden.

Kachauri: Stuffed Puri

½ cup masoor dal (a species of
    lentil)
1 teaspoon cumin seeds
1 teaspoon anardana (pomegran-
    ate seeds)
salt to taste

1 teaspoon chilli powder
3½ cups whole-wheat flour
pinch bicarbonate of soda
1 cup ghee or butter
vegetable fat for frying

Put the dal in a saucepan with 2½ cups water. Bring to the boil, then simmer till the dal is soft and the water has evaporated. Roast the cumin seeds in a dry frying pan. In a mortar, grind the cumin, anardana, and dal to a paste; add salt and chilli powder and set aside.

Sift flour, bicarbonate of soda and salt. Rub in the ghee with fingertips and knead to form a soft dough. Make round balls the size of an egg and form each into a cup. In this put a teaspoonful of the dal and close. Do not roll out but flatten with hand till the pastry is 3 inches in diameter. Deep-fry in hot fat.

The lentils can be bought from Indian grocers.

Dahi Baras or Bhalle

1 cup urad dal (a species of lentil)
1 cup ghee or vegetable fat
¾ pint dahi
1 teaspoon cumin seeds, roasted and ground in a mortar

salt to taste
1 teaspoon garam masala (see page 203)
1 teaspoon chilli powder

Soak dal overnight. Drain, then grind on a grinding stone or in a mortar to a fine paste. Beat this paste till frothy. If too dry, add a little warm water. Heat the fat in a deep-frying pan. Take a cup and wet a small piece of muslin with water. Pull the muslin tightly over the top of the cup; on this put a small piece of dal paste and pat it into a small round cake. Make a hole in the centre and slip the cake into the fat. Make as many as you can out of the paste and fry golden brown over a medium flame. Drain. Soak the fried baras in boiling salted water for 5 minutes, then remove and squeeze the baras between your hands so that all the water is removed. Beat up the dahi and add the cumin and salt. Put the baras in a serving dish and pour the dahi over. Sprinkle with the garam masala and chilli powder.

Kulfi

Kulfi is the Indian version of ice cream. It is quite easy to make and is delicious. The traditional kulfi moulds are cone-shaped tins with tight-fitting lids. Thickened milk is poured into the moulds, which are sealed with a paste of flour and water. They are then packed in a round earthenware vessel with ice and salt and shaken constantly till the kulfi is frozen. To make the milk mixture, take as much rich Jersey or unpasteurized milk as is required, bring to the boil, and simmer gently till thick and creamy. Add sugar to taste and chopped pistachio nuts, and flavour with rose water.

Watermelon Sherbet

watermelon
sugar

lemon

Scoop out the pink pulp of the melon and mash it in a bowl. Add sugar to taste, thin with water, and chill. Serve in tall glasses with a slice of lemon if desired.

Indian cooking is light and crisp; when an Indian cook boils or fries rice, each grain emerges separately, but again, ask how it is done and a dozen different recipes will be given. Different kinds of rice have different cooking characteristics. "You cannot learn to cook them from a recipe," says Maji—which is true. "You must study rice," says Maji severely.

Rice is so important that, in Bengal, it gives its name to a ceremony, the Annaprasanna—First Taste of Rice—when a baby has its first solid food; this used to be in the eighth or ninth month, but probably, like most modern babies, Hindu ones are more precocious now. The rice is made into a soft, extremely sweet pudding.

Note: recipe for

Garam Masala

1 cup coriander seeds
½ cup cumin seeds
½ cup large cardamom seeds
¼ cup cinnamon

¼ cup cloves
½ cup peppercorns
1 teaspoon powdered nutmeg

Roast the coriander and cumin seeds separately. Peel the cardamom seeds. Grind all the spices in a mortar or on a grinding stone and store in an airtight container. Use as directed in recipes. Ready-made garam masala can be bought from shops selling Indian foodstuffs.

Garam means hot—and the masala is hot! The spices and lentils can be bought from Indian grocers, or in specialty food shops.

Those dishes are as luscious as they sound, but perhaps the utmost pleasure from eating comes to those who have a frugal ration; for a peasant, a bowl of rice with a few spoonfuls of vegetable curry, perhaps a fried cake on top and a little dal, is a banquet.

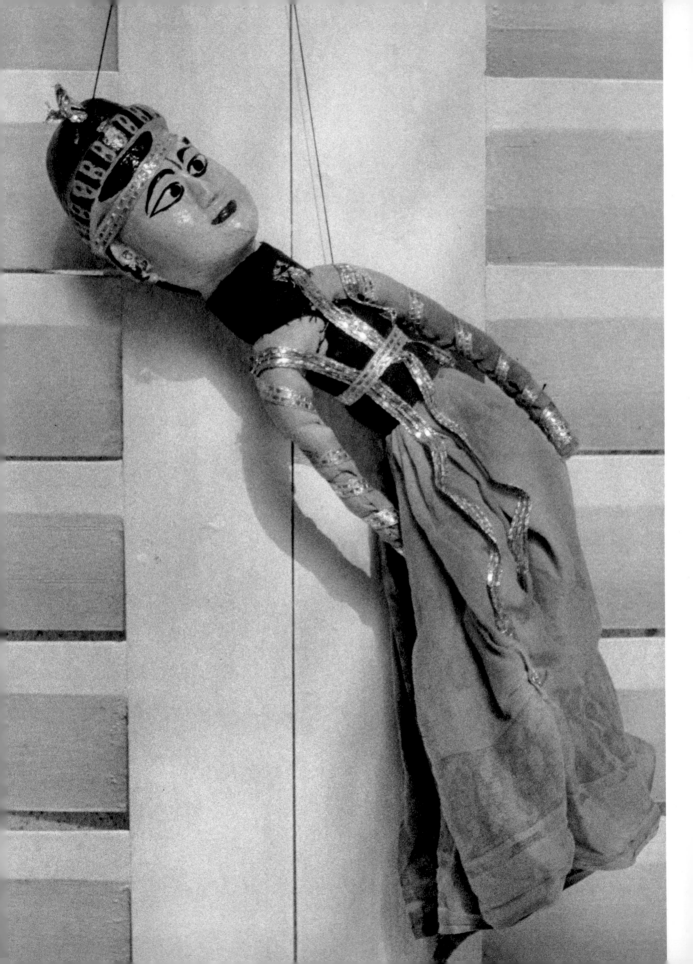

A sweeper woman thinks more of her nose ring or toe ring of cheapest alloyed silver than does a maharani of her pearls. The visit of a storyteller is enough to hold a village audience thrilled and amused for hours; even more so the tawdry little travelling puppet shows.

A puppet theatre, made of bamboo, hung with bright patchwork and ornamented with silver stars, is set up in the village square; the first thing the puppeteers do is to borrow a charpoy—a string bed; up-ended on its long side, it makes a base for the stage, and charpoys can be found anywhere. The puppeteers are shabby; one may be a young man with the refined face and long hair of an actor; there is usually a boy who beats a drum or tiny cymbals, whipping up emotion by playing louder and faster when the drama heightens. A gnarled old woman in a dirty sari, warts on her lip, perhaps owns the troupe. The wooden puppets—only torsos with a weight below wrapped in soft cloth to deaden the noise—have glossy paint and much better clothes than the troupe. Their robes and coats are bright with tinsel, beads, colours of silk and cotton. They are worked from a small wooden triangle, and occasionally a slim brown hand has to come down to disentangle the strings, but that does not matter to the audience. It is too caught up in the epic or purana[9] that is being acted—the story of Rama and Sita, or of the birth of Krishna, or of the battles of the Sons of Pandu, of the old loves and feuds and wars.

9. Puranas: Hindu scriptures.

The world likes to think of India as a land of serenity, philosophical acceptance, peace—at most Gandhiji's passive resistance—but India has always loved a fight and has bred magnificent soldiers: the Dogras, Rajputs, Sikhs, whose hereditary weapon is the quoit of polished steel—the inner ring where the hand holds it is blunt, the outside razor-sharp; when spun at an enemy it can cut him in half or sever his head. The bloodthirsty little Gurkha uses a kukri—a wicked wide-bladed knife like a short scimitar.

It is the same in the cinema; there must be battles. Every town has at least one cinema; it is still often called the "bioscope" and is popular. Amar's children are always wheedling him to let them go, "Just eight annas each, Baba, only eight annas." The seats are cheap, and there is the satisfaction of getting value for money because the performance goes on for hour after hour. The auditorium will be cool after the dust and glare of the streets, perhaps even air-conditioned, or with punkas—electric fans—turning overhead. Smoking is not allowed in any Indian cinema, but the soda-water and lemonade vendors will come round with their bottles, each with an opener tied to the cloth hanging over his shoulder; it is pleasant to relax, to let shoes drop off, feet be tucked comfortably up, but the unsophisticated public does not go to see Indian films such as Satyajit Ray's masterpieces, the *Pather Panchali* trilogy, which have become classics overseas; those are about poor people, strugglers like most of the audience, and who wants to see their own miseries? American or European films are not popular either, not even Westerns or slapstick comedies. India's huge film industry, the second largest in the world, knows that it must make the most melodramatic of highly coloured melodramas for its mass audience; the scripts might have been written by an Indian Amanda Ros: heroic heroes and villainous villains—the villain is always dark—heroines dying of love, enduring horrors for love, unrequited, spurned, but, of course, winning in the end; Patient Griselda mothers sacrificing everything for errant sons; it will all probably finish with reunion in Krishna's heaven, pink and blue and gold—but on the way there must be plenty of dances and songs.

Modern European composers such as Holst and Roussel have been influenced by the East, so that Indian music is not difficult now for a western musician to understand; but to ordinary Occidental ears, brought up on several scales and combinations of sounds, listening to a melody in terms of a fixed drone is hard work. An Indian finds European music easier—perhaps too easy. "How does it sound?" a Hindu can be asked and, "Meaningless," might be the blunt reply; complex Hindus are often blunt where the Moslem of simple faith is politic.

Indian music is infinitely subtle, so subtle that western ears often cannot hear the infinitesimal changes in tone and mood of the stringed instruments, the intricacies of percussion played on drums or silver cymbals no bigger than a rupee. Though one sees large so-called orchestras, especially with dance companies, they are a modern innovation. Indian classical music properly has no orchestras, only one stringed instrument—maybe a sarangi, the violin of India, or a vina or a sitar—the tambura, graceful as a swan, is used for a background, accompanied by percussion and perhaps a woodwind, usually a flute. Nor are there orchestral scores as we know them; the melody is taken by the main stringed instrument, the others blending in with extemporary skill.

Elaborate melodies are played by running a stick over a number of small metal bowls filled with different levels of water; percussion varies from those miniature cymbals to gongs, but always, everywhere, there will be

drums. The Indian kettledrum was used by princes going into battle; the army has it still; it was sounded at palace entrance gates when the king went in or out. There is the village tom-tom; the monkey man has a small drum hung with weighted strings that rattle on it as he walks or chants for his monkey play. The pakhawaj, that has a clay body and two drumheads, is

the drum used for the most classical form of north Indian music, but more universal are tabla, a pair of drums for right and left hands; for tuning, these drums have braces and wedges. The drummer sits cross-legged on the ground and plays with his fingers and the bases of his palms; it can take a lifetime to make a good drummer.

In an Indian school of music the children sit on the floor or on a day-bed, opposite their master, who has his seat of honour on a mat as, with tabla or a pair of cymbals, he gently marks the rhythm.

The children will have heard singing since they were born; Indians cannot live, work, worship, or celebrate without music; women sing as they work in the ricefields or about the home; the boatman sings at his oar; workers heaving a steel girder will use a chanted rhythm, as do the fishermen when they pull in their nets; from a village hut comes a croon as a mother sings her baby to sleep and, at the same time, a priest offering puja sings from the temple; a bullock-driver sings as he drives through the night; but this, in the music school, is serious singing. As often in Indian houses, all the rooms open onto a central courtyard; no doors are shut, so the noise is piercing, but it disturbs the children not at all; with their great brown eyes on their master, they listen dutifully . . . .

. . . . and then sing!

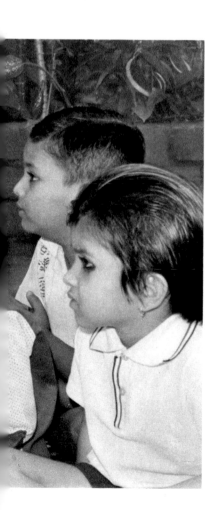

And in what language will they sing?

When he was a child, Sudhin Ghose, the novelist, lived in a tiny estate on the outskirts of Calcutta; the estate was like a village in its compactness and interdependence, but as it was near the city its inhabitants came from many parts and spoke totally different languages. "How many scripts do you know?" Sudhin once asked the estate washerwoman, Moti-Didi.

"I am not a learned woman," Moti-Didi sighed. "I know only Bengali and Persian,[10] but you will have to learn many more, my little brother."

Sudhin knew that already; in the estate school, Bheem wrote in Devnagiri, which is the script of Hindi, Ram Chand in Gujerati, Ayesha in Ooriya, he, Sudhin—like Moti-Didi—in Bengali; five scripts in one small school.

The present government is trying to make Hindi the official all-binding language of India, but this has brought riots, almost mutiny in the South, where Tamil, Telugu, and a dozen other languages are a heritage. Hindi is difficult for many people. "Sushila is doing well at school except for Hindi," a young mother will moan; "she is terribly backward in Hindi"—and the parents cannot help Sushila because, as is so often the case, they cannot speak Hindi themselves. English is universal and, in spite of the turn against it in the agitations for independence, for an Indian to speak English is a sign of culture; but there are still fourteen major languages—more than two hundred if dialects are counted.

"But which language is best?" the small Sudhin asked Moti-Didi.

"A garden is beautiful, my little brother, because there are many varieties of flowers." Moti-Didi was something of a philosopher. "But who will tell if the champak is better than the hasnuhana or the red rose better than the frail jasmine? It is the same with languages."[11]

Indian languages are unusually expressive, often onomatopoeic: "ulta-pulta," the "u" pronounced "oo," for "upside-down," and "nanga-panga," pronounced almost "nunga-punga" for "naked," are Bengali-Hindi slightly Anglicised, but "chup" for "be quiet" and the stronger "chup-rao" for "shut up" are more idiomatic, as is "chup-chap" for "very quiet," "phut-a-phut" for "as fast as possible" or "get a move on," and "adal-badl" for someone or something all mixed up (Urdu).

Sanskrit was the language of learning, of literature, which reached its

10. A washerwoman would be unlikely to know Persian, which was introduced by the Moguls first as a court, then as the official, language; from this Urdu derived and became the language of the army. Moti-Didi probably meant she spoke Bengali with a smattering of Urdu.
11. *And Gazelles Leaping* by Sudhin Ghose.

peak in the poetic dramas of Kalidasa, the Indian Shakespeare of the fourth century A.D., but poets often broke away to write in their own regional languages; the most popular poems are song-poems, and the singers of kirtans, or "songs of praise," gather their audiences in every village or town under the banyan tree, on the steps of the river, in temple courtyards, or, often, in the temple itself, because kirtans are religious, the song-poems of bhakti—devotion to a particular god.

When the sage Shankaracharya brought Hinduism back to the exalted teaching of the Vedas, his philosophy seemed to forget the yearnings and needs of the common people: he taught that God was not to be anthropomorphized; the Trinity should be worshipped only as the One, Brahman, but this seemed impersonal and austere—and comfortless—and gradually, through three centuries, a less intellectual, more intimate belief arose, bhakti.

Particular devotion, love, especially of Rama or Krishna, appeals to ordinary people, yet one of bhakti's known votaries was a princess, Mirabai, a sixteenth-century Rajput royal lady and the embodiment of bhakti, who for love of Krishna left her family and palace, wandering over the land; to the horror of her relations she sang and danced before images of the god wherever she could find him—no lady of rank had ever done such a thing—and it was in one of Krishna's temples that she died. Mirabai's song-poems are as much a part of worship as are the psalms of David, but true kirtans are of a less emotional calibre; they might be by Chandidas and his namesakes, Badu Chandidas and Dvija Chandidas, who wrote in Bengali, as did their modern follower, Rabindranath Tagore; fourteenth-century Vidyapati wrote in Maithili, a language of eastern India, and Thyagraja in Telugu; Thyagraja's kirtans, the most exquisite of the South, are in praise of Rama, but most kirtans tell of Krishna and Radha.

Some describe Radha as a young girl, quivering at the god's touch:

> .   .   .
> She cries: Oh no, no, no! and tears are pouring from her eyes
> She lies outstretched upon the margin of the bed,
> His close embrace has not unloosed her zone,—
> Even of handling of her breasts has been but little.
>
> .   .   .   .   .
> When Kanu[12] lifts her to his lap, she bends her body back,
> Like a young snake, untamed by spells.[13]

12. Kanu: another name for Krishna.
13. Vidyapati, translated by A. Coomaraswamy and Aran Sen.

Part of the kirtan's appeal is its realism; love is seldom bliss; it brings disillusionment and pain; the poets say it can be poison:

He was black,[14]
He had poison-eyes.
A glance from him brought death to my side,
Life lay open to love's five arrows.[15]
Nothing else mattered—
Food or rest.
I disowned all decorative dress.
My heart raced for the kadamba wood.[16]
Having abandoned
Fear and shame,
Like a wild woman I begged for the jewel.[17,18]

These celestial lovers go through every emotion, delicious and bitter, known to their human echoes; their divinity does not manifest itself until their final union, when they disappear in one another and become simply a pair of names, still Krishna and Radha but veiled under pairs of images:

14. Krishna is shown sometimes as blue-skinned, sometimes black.
15. Five arrows of Madan, the god of love.
16. Kadamba: a tree with small yellow fuzzballs of flowers, often seen in religious paintings (*Anthocephalus Indicus*).
17. The jewel or ratna represents love. Often love is described as priti ratna, the love-jewel.
18. From *The Love Songs of Chandidas*.

lightning and cloud, moon and darkness; this is how modern poets prefer to see them—the dark gay god has disappeared and become a force—but simple people like them best as lovers.

Kirtan-singers add their own commentary, and it is in the beauty, wit, and power of these, as it were, cadenzas, that their reputation lies. They will be accompanied by a drummer, but seldom by the group of musicians who accompany concert singers, with the voice taking the place of, or blending with, the sitar or vina; a good singer is often a master of the sitar himself, playing his own accompaniment.

In Indian music, more importance is given to melody than to harmony: the saptak, equivalent to the western octave, has twelve chief notes; seven are sharp, and from these the five flat or half-notes are derived; from these twelve come the seventy-two parent scales. There are several ways of classifying ragas or melody modes, but one that is revelational defines six chief ragas as male, and "marries" them to five raginis, female melody modes, whose musical offspring are the still more subtle melodies called putras, which means sons. Even the greatest of singers is not expected to sing in more than a hundred modes of this vast family.

Concerts go on not for an hour or two, but all day, perhaps all night, while the contests to which the different provinces send their musicians may continue without a break for three, four, five days and nights—the whole of each night. At least twenty-four hours are needed because Indian songs often match the times at which they are sung: the morning is for praise, the evening for merriment, midnight for calm and mystery. The audience catches the mood—and not only the audience; when the "Megha Raga" is sung with outstanding artistry it is said to help bring rain. These musical modes have often been subjects for painters; it seems odd to paint music, but the painters match the mood, it may be in crude bazaar art or in the elaborate miniatures of the Rajputs, which the court painters gathered into albums called "Ragamala"—Garlands of Modes.

It is told that the first painting in the whole world was Hindu; as with most Indians' tales, the story begins "In ancient days . . ."

In ancient days there lived a king named Bhayajit who prided himself that his kingdom was prosperous and pious, but one day a brahmin came before him and complained, "O king, there is certainly sin in your kingdom. Otherwise, why should my son have died an untimely death?"

The king was much disturbed and demanded the return of the brahmin's son from Yama, God of Death. Yama refused and there was a battle in which the king defeated Yama, but then the Creator[19] himself appeared and said, "O king, this is not the way. Yama is not to blame because life and death must accord with man's karma."

The king was abashed and asked what he should do.

"Draw a picture of the brahmin's son."

The king obeyed, and the Creator breathed life into the picture and once again spoke to the king. "You were made capable of drawing this picture only by My grace. If I had not breathed into it, it could not have lived. It is the first picture in the world, but all the others will need to be made the same way."

Over the slow centuries, Hindu artists learned how to adapt the far-away skills of Ajanta's enormous painted frescoes to what became miniature-painting and the even smaller illuminating of manuscripts. When the Mogul Emperor Humayun came back to India in 1555 after his exile in Persia, he brought Persian artists with him; they obviously thought they were coming to barbarian country, but they found flourishing schools of painting in Rajputana, Jammu, and Kangra. It was Humayun's son, Akbar, who merged the two styles, Persian and Hindu, together, and founded the Mogul school of court painting.

Because figures and animals were in these exquisite little paintings, orthodox Moslems condemned them as idolatrous, but Akbar held the same view as Brahma; "An artist," he said, "has a unique means of recognizing God; when he comes to paint anything that has life, sketching limbs and heads, he also comes to know that he alone cannot bestow personality and so has recourse to God, giver of life." Perhaps this is why we have the term "creative artist." If a painting is God-given it cannot be idolatrous, and Akbar continued to encourage his artists, Hindu and Moslem. He loved to visit their studios. The workshop of a painter is a fascinating place and, though many Indian artists have westernized studios, there are still some like the Bengali Jamini Roy, whose workshop, with its apprentices, is like the *bottega* of an Italian Renaissance painter—except that, while some painters work at easels, others work cross-legged on daybeds, holding the

19. The Creator: Brahma.

218

canvas on one knee, or have foot-high tables, or simply a reed mat on the
floor. They mix their colours in chattis—earthenware bowls—unless they
too use oil or acrylic paint from tubes.

One of the remarkable things about Indian painting, ancient or modern, court or folk, is that it always depicts pleasure, whereas in the West, where there is far less suffering, art seems to specialize in torment, misery, and death; think of all the crucifixions, the war scenes of Goya, the stark realism and agony. In India, all art is for pleasure, and the greatest pleasure is dancing. Shiva, as Nataraja, Lord of the Dance, is always shown standing with one foot raised, the other pressing down the dwarf of evil; but again it was Brahma who created dancing to lighten the world, an art meant for everyone, in which everyone can join.

Shiva's dance is not an empty myth, but an image of the Energy which science must postulate behind all phenomena . . . its significance is threefold: first, it is the image of his rhythmic play as the source of all movement within the cosmos, which is represented by the arch: secondly, the purpose of his dance is to release the countless souls of men from the snare of illusion: thirdly, the place of the Dance, Chidambaram, the centre of the Universe, is within the heart.[20]

20. *Dance of Shiva* by Ananda Coomaraswamy.

Bharata Natyam, one of the four classical dancing styles, comes from the temple dancing of southern India and has a strong religious background; temples used to keep hereditary dancing girls, earthly counterparts of the apsaras who dance in the celestial court of Indra; the typical movement, advancing and retreating, of these dances was to make sure the dancer never turned her back on the god.

A dancer of Bharata Natyam is not at all the western concept of a dancing girl, but has the standing of a ballerina—she may even be a Doctor of Sanskrit—and she has a great reverence for her art. Before she begins to dance she will make deep obeisance with folded hands from the ground upwards to the four corners of the earth, then to her guru, the natwanar—dance teacher.

The natwanar, usually long-haired, often elderly, sitting upright, cross-legged on a mat, keeps the rhythm, as did the music teacher, with his tabla or a pair of miniature cymbals.

The extraordinary control over the muscles, especially of the face and eyes, takes years of training, expensive training; if Amar's daughter yearns to be a dancer of Bharata Natyam, it may cost him two or three thousand rupees a year. Every gesture, too, has a specific meaning; the movements of the face have to correspond, and the traditional mudras, or hand and finger gestures, and those expressive thumb movements, have names such as "lotus-bud," "deer's head," "swan's neck."

If the dancer smiles, it is not at the audience, but for the god in the scene she is dancing.

Pure Kathakali, the dance of Kerala, is danced only by men, boys taking
the women's parts; it is always a story dance, with a chorus and strange stiff
costumes, the faces masked in stiff rice paste; this make-up is so heavy that
it takes six hours to put on, and the dancers have to lie motionless all the
time. Gods and noble characters have green faces, except for Hanuman, the
Monkey God, who is red; villains are black or picked out with white knobs
on cheeks and noses, while the "women" have a simple gold make-up.

Kathak, the North Indian style, was once danced at the court of the
Moguls by men and women, yet much of it is based on the Radha/Krishna
theme, the rhythm emphasized by anklets of bells. A degenerate form of
Kathak is the well-known nautch that tourists hope to see, but even here the
suggestiveness is subtle; nautch has none of the open lewdness of the belly
dance that belongs to Egypt. The last of the classics is Manipur, folk and
happy dancing, full of leaps, skips, and spins; it is usually danced by boys
and unmarried girls, who wear full-hooped skirts embroidered with silver,
black velvet blouses, and bright vermilion gauze veils hung from topknots
circled with flowers.

Hill people have their own dancing: near Shillong in the Assam hills, the
men have an annual betrothal dance, in which they posture and show off, as
male birds do their plumage, until they are chosen by their brides.

In Chamba, the men put on wonderful hats with aigrettes of feathers, bright-coloured scarves over their everyday white woven coats, and dance in the temple courtyards while women and children watch from the balconies.

Is art, are dancing, acting, music, sculpture, painting, poems, grown-ups' toys?

Money, real money, is spent on the arts—thousands, lakhs of rupees. Some children have expensive toys too, pedal cars that can be sat in, tricycles, big plastic dolls; some toys are not expensive, the little baskets of cooking pots or wooden animals sold on the railway station platform, or tinsel balls, but still too costly for most families.

It does not matter; toys, like art, can be made of anything—or anything can become a toy. A stick is a bat, and a good ball can be wound of coir, or grass, and shaped with fibres, to play guli-danda, the game that has trained India's famous hockey players; no others are as nimble and quick. Pebbles make marbles; an empty tin turns into a toy drum, while a bamboo is a natural fishing rod. A doll can be made from clay, only it crumbles; far better is an old-fashioned soda-water bottle that is much the shape of a papoose, but it has to be wrapped in the skirt of its small owner's frock; if there are any rags, even scraps of silk or tinsel, they will be kept to dress another kind of doll, the little image of the god that stands in the household niche. Many Indian toys are airy, paper and wind-blown: windmills on sticks, beloved of babies; and at certain times of the year the sky is filled with an army of kites, an army because they are out to do battle. Though Indian kites are made of thinnest paper, stretched on slivers of bamboo, their strings are glassed by being run through a mixture of glue and powdered glass, then hung to dry in the sun. "Bhitu, bhitukya—coward," comes the taunt from some Bengali rooftop, answered by another invisible boy on another roof. The two kites are made to bob in acknowledgment of the challenge; then there is dipping and manœuvring as the strings cross, cutting until one is severed. "Bhon kattya!" shouts the winner and, as the vanquished kite falls down and down, "Dharo dharo dharo—catch it, catch it!" comes from all sides as the boys race to claim it.

Kite-flying is for boys, but girls have a festival, Guria Panchmi, a Festival of Dolls when little girls invite each other to bring their dolls, in new clothes if possible, and the bangle-seller will come, working the unbelievably small bangles over small hands onto small wrists. A bangle-seller is, oddly enough, the only male outside the family who can touch women, holding their hands, kneading the bones until they go through the hoop. There are even bangles for dolls.

Sometimes the peddler comes round too; he is always there at fairs, and in the streets on festival days; from him, for perhaps a paisa, paper windmills, paper fans, a firework can be bought; he may have little jointed wooden figures; they have paper faces but, unlike the soda-water bottle, they can move their arms and legs. Move their arms and legs!

PART V

A "householder" has certain ceremonial duties that he must carry out for his children; the last of these is, for each, a properly arranged marriage. After that they or, if they are girls, their bridegrooms should enter on this stage of "householder" and so release their father. "But are they old enough?" asks Amar.

"What shall I bring you from the mela—fair? The burra bazaar—big bazaar? From the city?" he asks his youngest daughter, Aruna.

Aruna blushes—she always blushes nowadays—and whispers, "Please, Baba, a bottle of perfume."

Baba—Amar—stares. Surely it was only the other day that Aruna, his pet, his baby, began going to school, walking along with the other girls and boys; the girls wore astonishingly clean cotton dresses; each had a heavy plait, well-oiled, hanging down her back or had her hair cropped short; almost all of them had gold rings in their ears—Amar remembers how he opposed Aruna's mother over that but, "The ears must be pierced," Maji said calmly. Aruna carried her books in a strap, and he remembers how she teased him for a satchel. "Some children have only heavy wooden slates," he told her, "some have to write in the dust," but she got her satchel.

Coming of a traditional Hindu family, Aruna was not supposed to start writing until, when she was four or five years old, a small ceremony was held on the feast of the Goddess Saraswati. Sometimes this first and solemn baby attempt at writing is done on a banana leaf with a quill dipped in milk, sometimes on a mango-wood tablet with Ganges clay, nowadays probably on a slate, but long before any ceremony could be held, Aruna was teasing him for coloured pencils. "Precocious! She has always been precocious," he grumbles.

"Just normal," says Maji.

When, obediently, he brings the scent back from Calcutta, he can tell by Aruna's face she is not pleased. "It is rat-ki-rani—queen of the night."

"But, Baba, Grandmother uses that, every hot weather."

"Well?"

The whisper comes, "It is only attar, not proper perfume. Vimala Dutta's father brought her Night in Paris."

"That is black market." And he explodes. "French scent for a little girl!" But is Aruna a little girl?

When she makes a group with other girls there is whispering now instead of games and laughter. Small brothers are told to go away. Vimala Dutta is the ringleader. How he dislikes that girl! It is she who has taught Aruna to paint her nails, read trashy magazines—*Madhuri, Filmi Dunya*. "They're not trashy. They're about *films*." She says it as if films were sacred. He had wanted her to go to college, but schoolbooks are no longer taken seriously.

He hears Aruna arguing with her mother about a border on a sari, the length of a bodice; she is always peeping out of the courtyard or out of a window or, if the house has a flat roof, giggling over the parapet, but he still insists, "She *is* a little girl. Why, she ought to be playing with dolls."

Maji seems not at all perturbed. Men, she could have said, always need to play, need toys; why else will they spend half their days under a car or tinkering with its engine, or pulling a motorbike to pieces or playing with a boat, or a ball, or fishing, shooting? Women exchange toys for husbands and babies. It is the same whether they are daughters of a raja or his, Amar's, daughter . . . or a little village girl.

Outsiders begin coming to the house; nowadays they may even be young men, "Buzzing like mosquitoes," says irate Amar; but most likely it will be a go-between for an arranged marriage—perhaps the aunt of a cousin of an aunt, or, in a village, the barber, who may be a Moslem. In an arranged marriage, adding to the family's status or wealth, particularly wealth, plays an important part, but it is rarely, as told in sensational tales, that a young girl is given to an old man, however rich; the couple are usually "matched" in the sensible use of the word, matched in family background, suitability of accomplishments and interests, in physical aspects and health and in their birth papers—horoscopes; even a strictly orthodox family usually al-

lows the boy and girl to meet at least once nowadays if they do not already know each other, and the girl is given the final chance to accept or reject; usually she accepts and in no time at all, it seems to Amar, a pandal is being set up in front of his house, his pockets and his bank account have mysteriously emptied, and a young man—to Baba he seems a mere boy—comes riding to fetch Aruna away.

All young men ride to their weddings; these days it may be in a be-tinselled, decorated car or a cycle rickshaw, but it could still be on a horse—which must be a white one—and in northwestern or central India it could be on a camel.

Another man, a brother or uncle or cousin, the "best man," rides with him and, if there is enough money, the car, cycle rickshaw, horse, or camel will move to the sound of music, cymbals, drums, perhaps a whole brass band, and following and surrounding the young bridegroom is a crowd of male relations because this is the barat, the procession to the bride's house; the groom's mother, sisters, girl cousins, aunts, do not come but wait in the family house to welcome the bride when she is brought to her new home. For a rich wedding, servants carrying gifts will follow the musicians, perhaps a bevy of maidservants, looking as if they came from the *Arabian Nights*, dressed in brilliant colours and bearing trays on their heads, each tray loaded with presents and flowers; the colours are enhanced by flaming torches—the barat is usually at night.

The children, wide awake and in their wedding clothes, run out to meet the procession.

At a wedding no one rebukes children or tells them to go to bed. They fall asleep when they want, wake up when they want, gorge themselves on the wedding food and meet all the related children, often a big tribe. For children and guests a wedding is wonderful, but poor Baba will be exhausted in more ways than one. For the groom's family the marriage costs some money, but the bride's father may run into serious debt; a clerk, working

quite humbly in an office, may spend five thousand rupees on his daughter's wedding—a sweeper might spend a thousand.

To begin with, there is the dowry; once this far outweighed a girl's attractions and attainments but young men nowadays want a wife to be a companion, an interesting one, not merely a satisfaction for sex and a mother for their children; the old "knows music and knitting" of those matrimonial advertisements is not enough. The dowry may even be dispensed with—it is legally forbidden[1]—but even so most weddings are shatteringly expensive; the "arranger" has to be paid; the young man's mother has to be entertained when she comes to see the girl—"look her over," Aruna may think resentfully, and there are no eyes more sharp than those of a mother when she first sees her son's future wife.

The classic ideal of Hindu womanhood used to be taken from the marvellous carved stone figures of goddesses, apsaras, or gopis in the Hindu temples; their hips are like an elephant's—wine-jar hips—their slow walk like a swan's—useful when a girl is heavy with child. That, though, is a hope for the future, to ensure which the pandits want money for studying the horoscopes of the pair. If the two sets of stars make a match, a day is fixed for the betrothal, when the girl's male relations go to the prospective father-in-law's house, taking coconuts, sweets, almonds, and gifts of money which must always be in odd figures: twenty-one rupees, a hundred and one rupees, a thousand and eleven; even numbers are inauspicious.

In the days following the betrothal the flow of gifts goes on, chiefly from the bride's family—jewellery has to be given to the in-laws, the mother and all the sisters. The pandits must be consulted again for an auspicious day for the wedding and, when this is settled, invitations will be sent, and the girls of the house settle down to making the phul-khana, the wedding veil or shawl, which must be so covered with embroidered or stitched-on flowers that no material can be seen. Mother and bride, though, are immersed in the serious business of the trousseau.

Maji probably began collecting Aruna's trousseau when she was a baby; saris do not date. "It was my grandmother's," a girl may say at a dance when her green and gold embroidered sari is admired, but there can be fashion in saris: there have been mini-saris or one can be worn as a hipster, tied below the navel, with a short bodice, giving a long bare back and midriff which look alluring; during the fight for India's independence many

1. The Dowry Act was passed in 1961, but to pass an act is one thing, to implement it another, and there are still many parents, like Aruna's, who feel they must keep face by endowing their daughters; the prohibition, too, does not extend to jewellery.

of even the richest women, following Gandhi's dictum, wore saris made of the heavy plain handspun cotton—khadi—they had woven; but saris woven or embroidered with gold and silver can be priceless and are still handed down from one generation to another; Indian women are too wise to discard them for European dress. A sari looks dignified and beautiful in wind or sun, on the dance floor, even riding sidesaddle; it conceals pregnancy, makes a stout woman look slimmer, can be worn for any occasion, and is easy to pack or iron. "But doesn't it fall off?" a western girl might ask. "You simply knot it round you, then loop and pleat it in—no fastenings. Doesn't it ever fall off?"

"It hasn't for thousands of years," might be the answer.

Rajputani peasant women do not wear saris but have enormously wide swinging skirts and jackets; Punjabi women have muslin tunics and pantaloons, and in the North women like the baggy trousers and loose shirt known as punjabis or salwar-kameeze, which are even more comfortable than a sari. With these goes a dopatta, a gold-bordered light scarf for the head and shoulders; at fashion shows, the models show modernized punjabis with trousers slimmed and made in a heavy silk the same colour as the gauze dopattas. Young women love them, and Aruna will beg for some in her trousseau—to her grandmother's disapproval. Caste Hindus used to have a taboo against seams: "Only a straight piece of cloth can be properly washed and dried in the sun," says Grandmother, but Aruna will not listen. She will probably want underclothes, even brassières. "*We* never wore them," said Grandmother. Perhaps she did not wear a choli—bodice—either; in South India high-born women knot their saris round their waists without a bodice, but Aruna will have many tight-fitting bodices, short-sleeved and showing her enticing slim brown waist. "A plump one would be more enticing," says Grandfather.

The true Indian shoe is the juti of soft kid or suede or velvet, often shaped with a curve at the toe and sometimes embroidered; or else sandals, which are made now in fashionable French or Italian styles, but poor women prize the hideous plastic sandals because they never wear out.

Traditional and beautiful outdoor wear is a shawl of thick silk or soft fine wool with fringed and embroidered ends; coats or jackets look quite wrong over saris but most Indian women wear them, chiefly raincoats.

For a bride all these must be new, with new pots and pans, bedding, every kind of household goods; often there will be clothes for the bridegroom as well, and Maji has it sharply in mind that everything will have to be displayed and looked over by the guests, admired or criticized, especially by the in-law relatives—especially the jewellery.

Indians have always had a passion for jewellery, such a passion that it amounts to a mania. It is understandable; conquerors have so often come razing houses, looting, or confiscating, that it seemed safest to have what fortune the family possessed where it could be quickly snatched up, run away with, and hidden, and it was kept on a man's person, or rather his wife's person, who often became a walking bank.

Some of the necklaces are of actual coins threaded together—sometimes valuable old coins: a seventeenth-century gold mohur or a William IV sovereign—and it does not seem to matter how heavy an ornament is; nose-rings can be so large that a woman will bring a few strands of hair down across her forehead and thread them through the ring to take some of the weight —she would not dream of taking the nose-ring off; she is its custodian. This feeling of responsibility for their jewellery runs from rich to poor; if a pearl necklace needs restringing, its owner will not take it to a jeweller's shop or to the bazaar; the pearl-threader comes to her. Seated in front of her on the floor of the veranda, he puts down his box of needles and thread, rolls up his shirt sleeves to show that there is nowhere for anything to be hidden, and spreads out a red cloth on which the necklace—each pearl having been counted—is laid, while she watches every move he makes. She will stay there until every pearl has been slipped down the new string, every knot fastened. Pearls are not as valuable as they once were, but even a small one can be sold for something in the bazaar, and what a disgrace it would be for her if, at some future date, a cultured pearl, carefully secreted and inserted while she looked away for a moment, was found, perhaps by her daughter-in-law or her granddaughter-in-law, among the real heirloom pearls!

It may be difficult for a middle-class woman to stretch the family income so that everyone has enough to eat, but she will still possess at least a pair of earrings, a nose-stud or nose-ring, all with precious stones; she will have necklaces and chains, bangles, anklets, and sets of rings for her fingers and toes. Her poor sister will wear bone or shell or the glass that has the colours of the jewels she envies—but when her husband dies, her glass bangles will be broken; she may have to do with hooks of iron for her ears, an iron stud for her nose, and her toe-rings may be only twists of wire.

It is not only women and girls who wear jewellery; baby boys have their ears pierced at the same age as baby girls and, as they grow up, often wear earrings and bangles as well as charms, chains, and rings. It is said that if all the privately owned gold in India were given up it would be enough to finance several Five Year Plans—but it will never be given up.

Gold is so honoured that in some provinces lower castes are forbidden to wear it, while the higher castes may wear it only above the waist; to wear gold on the feet is an insult to the metal unless the wearer is royal or a deity. The ornaments of feathers and shells and woven grass that is suitably gold in colour, still worn by some of the tribal people, have a mystical meaning, and jewels are important in astrology, each stone having its planetary influence and attraction. "You should always keep an amethyst or a ruby or a pearl somewhere about you," an astrologer will tell his client. "If you can't afford a pearl, a chip of mother-of-pearl will do. Wearing the wrong stone can be dangerous."

Gold is a must for a wedding, and now a sonar—goldsmith—will be called; perhaps some of the family jewels are to be reset for the new bride, or else new bangles, necklaces, and earrings ordered.

The sonar's shop may be small but he belongs, by tradition, to the skilled jewel-workers who still today cut precious stones by hand in Jaipur, city of jewellers, as they cut them in the time of the Moguls; then they used to inlay jade and ivory with emeralds, pearls, and rubies; the fabulous Peacock Throne was made for Shah Jehan by the court jeweller Bebadal Khan, a Mogul Fabergé on a giant scale; its enamelled canopy with an eleven-inch fringe of pearls was supported by twelve golden pillars inlaid with emeralds; between the pillars were pairs of peacocks, their bodies crusted with jewels. The throne took seven years to finish, and even then was valued at ten million rupees.[2]

The town sonar may have a jewel-cutter or setter to help him, or he may call in a polisher, but in the villages he will still make every part of each ornament himself, using no machinery, only a few crude tools, tiny bellows over a fire—and his sensitive hands, the precise, delicate hands of the Indian craftsman. He can make filigree so fine it looks as if it were spun of silver or golden spiderweb-thread, in shapes of flower petals, shells, flying birds. Indian silver is alloyed and has a delicate pale look, but the gold is bright. When a piece is sold it is wrapped in thin pink paper, and every time there will be vigorous bargaining.

Southern Indian women have an uncanny flair for diamonds—no jeweller could unload a flawed stone on them—and there is always that question of good and bad luck which is why it is the custom, when buying jewellery, not to pay cash but to take the piece away and wear it for a while to see what good or evil it attracts; the jeweller quite concurs. Especial care must be taken when buying sapphires: one with red lights can be dangerous, as can a diamond with black specks; but now the sonar is in a strong position because he knows, and his customers know, that for a wedding jewellery is a necessity; certain pieces must be given to a girl at the time of her marriage, and these become stri-dhan, her inviolable property, and in Bengal there must be the wedding bangle, as necessary as the ring in a Christian wedding; the bangle must be made of iron.

2. It is now in Teheran, having been carried off in the Persian sack of Delhi, 1739.

. . . But no matter what caste she is or what part of India she comes from, for her wedding the bride will be as resplendent as her family can make her.

As the wedding day draws near, the house, whether a village hut or a mansion, is furbished and refurbished, and the expenses really begin to pile up on Baba. Often something like a large camp is set up, or houses are rented, even furnished, for guests who must stay; relatives coming from far away probably demand travelling money. If possible, a pandal is put up over the entrance, lucky banana trees at its corners; garlands of mango leaves are hung; hired cooks appear because not only relations—and relations of relations of relations—and friends have to be feasted, but brahmins and beggars as well; it is lucky to feast the holy and the poor. There must be musicians. In South India, rich parents sometimes arrange for a stage to be set up right across the road—traffic has to be diverted; chairs are arranged and a famous singer or dancer is engaged, to entertain not the guests but the public. It is the family's gift to the town. In the house carpets or

mats are spread, daybeds set with cushions, and floors decorated with those
rangoli patterns.

"But how does your hand know where to go?" Aruna may ask, watching
her mother.

"My mother knew, and her mother, even my mother's mother's mother.
Now I am teaching you," says Maji.

When the barat arrives at the bride's house, all its women go out to meet the bridegroom with songs. He is king for this night and day—or three days and nights, it used to be ten—but this does not prevent the girls, perhaps, after the ceremony, from using their privilege of teasing him, hiding his shoes, his turban or headdress, his sword, extorting money from him, while the old women look on and sing bawdy songs. Even if he is the son of a poor peasant or is an artisan, he will be dressed in a new white dhoti, shirt, and scarf, be garlanded; but he will probably have silk charidar—pyjamas—a brocaded achkan; his wound turban may be the shrill pink that looks so well against the blue Indian sky; and it will be stuck with at least a tinsel aigrette or he may wear a headdress modelled on Krishna's when he danced Rasa Lila with the gopis.

In a traditional wedding, the little bride must stay hidden in a back room until it is time for the actual ceremony and she must fast all during the wedding, even if it does last three days—though her mother often brings her milk and food secretly at night. "I can't have you going to them looking peaky"—"them" being the new in-laws. On the day itself, she will be bathed, anointed with oils and scent, then made up; her eyes will be rimmed with kajal or kohl, which is often made by holding a spoon over a burning almond; the black sediment is taken off with a little pure butter and delicately put on the eyelids; it is supposed to be soothing and is even put on babies' eyes. Then the soles of the feet and palms of hands or tips of fingers must be painted scarlet with the henna which is so prized.

> A kokila[3] called from a henna-spray:
> Lira! liree! Lira! liree!
> Hasten, maidens, hasten away
> To gather the leaves of the henna tree.
> The tilka's red for the brow of a bride,
> And betel-nut's red for lips that are sweet;
> But, for lily-like fingers and feet,
> The red, the red of the henna tree.[4]

Her sari is red too, the colour of life, but it may be of tissue made richer with jewelled embroidery. Her hair, if it is long, will be braided with gold and coiled in a knot held by jewelled pins, the centre parting threaded perhaps with pearls or a pendant hung on her forehead, and she is often so laden with jewellery that she can hardly walk.

The *Ramayana* describes Sita on her wedding day: "Her ears and nose are resplendent with jewels, her wrists and arms are adorned with bracelets;

3. Kokila: a cuckoo.
4. From a poem by Sarojini Naidu.

her slender ankles are circled round with golden rings, while little golden bells tinkle upon her toes as she walks with naked feet over the carpeted floor."⁵

5. Sita could wear gold on her feet because she was royal and a goddess.

251

The ceremony begins in the presence of all the guests while music beats softly in the background. Whether it is a prince's wedding or a peasant's it must be witnessed by Agni, God of Fire—so that a place will have been cleared for the small firepit where the fire will be kept burning with ghee, which the priest will pour on the flame. He sits on one side of it; the couple face him on the other after the veiled bride has been led to her place by her maternal uncle.

The priest has with him flowers, ghee, rice, honey, red powder, and Ganges water, but he begins by tying bride and bridegroom, perhaps by their clothes, together in the sacred knot, symbolizing that this is a joining for life. He recites mantras, scatters powder and Ganges water, joins the young couple's hands, covering them with a cloth or heaping flowers on them; they throw rice on the fire when he tells them to, but otherwise sit perfectly still, passive and obedient as his voice drones on and on, though now and again they steal glances at one another, she very shyly from under her lashes. At last the priest finishes, tells them to stand, and, knotted to her, the bridegroom leads his bride twice round the sacred fire; then they take the "seven steps": one for prosperity, one for good health, another for children, and so on, and this time it is the bridegroom who has to recite the seven sacred texts.

The ceremony is over now and they sit in a bower of jasmine flowers while everyone comes to congratulate them. Again and again they make namaskar, the bride joining her slim henna-decorated hands together. Then there is a feast, the men sitting in rows on the ground, the women eating apart; the feasting and music go on until it is time for the groom and his retinue to take the bride away.

In the old traditional return, behind the bridegroom's horse, camel, or car, there would have been a swaying palanquin carried on long poles.

The moment of entering her doli—the bridal palanquin—was once a terrifying one for an Indian bride; very young, perhaps in her early teens, she was leaving her parents and her home, everything she knew and loved, for a life among strangers, perhaps never coming back. She was allowed to take an old maidservant, perhaps her nurse or the midwife who had brought her into the world, to comfort and support her. Nowadays the bride is older and usually knows her husband a little, as well as his mother, perhaps his sisters, but even so it is a poignant parting. "Beti—daughter—you must leave us now," Baba says as he blesses her. "Be a dutiful wife. Think only of your husband," while a grandmother or aunt is sure to tell her to be a "proper little Sita."[6]

The bride used to be taken to her father-in-law's house, where she would become, at least for some years, part of a large joint family, and when she was helped from her palanquin would be confronted by a crowd of strange women; they would greet her kindly, even lovingly, but their eyes would be appraising her, alive with curiosity. Now she may simply be going to a flat or small house made ready for her, and the welcoming relatives will soon go away but, joint family house or simple flat, sooner or later she will be alone with this man who, even if she has seen him before they sat together by the sacred fire, has suddenly become a stranger with an even more strange right or power over her.

6. When Rama, with the help of his host of monkeys and bears, defeated the demon who had stolen his wife, Sita, Hanuman, the Monkey God, was sent to bring her back to Rama, bathed, scented, and adorned with jewels. When she saw Rama she was "radiant as the moon" but, as Rama sorrowfully spoke, she looked at him sadly "like a doe with tear-filled eyes." His victory, said Rama, had wiped out the insult to his family but she was stained by "dwelling with another than myself and I am forced by honour to renounce you." "Stained," cried Sita. "It was not by my consent that another touched me. My body is not in my power but my heart, that is under my own sway, was yours alone," but gently, with inexpressible grief, Rama told her this was the law and she must choose a palace—"any you like, take it for your own and go away."

"No," said Sita and proudly called for a funeral pyre to be built. The people wept as the logs were piled, ghee poured on, and fire leapt up; they wept still more as, praying, Sita entered the flames. The gods came down and rebuked Rama, saying he should not be held by the codes of ordinary men: he was a god, the avatar of Vishnu, and now Rama wept bitterly. Then Agni, God of Fire, rose up, bearing Sita untouched; even the purity of his fire could not match the purity of her; indeed she was unstained, and so Rama took her back and "his heart was glad." As for Sita's heart, even though Rama sent her away again, yet, when she finally won her vindication and, blameless and pure, was taken to the "abode of the nagas," she waited for him in heaven.

An Indian girl has plenty of spirit, but she has usually been schooled by her mother, whose husband is so sacred to her that in all her married life she has never allowed herself to pronounce his name; yet, schooled or not, Indians have an instinctive feeling against personal touch: they do not like to shake hands; a grown-up does not even hold a child by its hand but leads it lightly by the wrist with his finger and thumb; few girls have gone further than flirting with eyes; they have not known caresses except for family ones and, for all the erotica of stories, statues, and paintings, in cinema love scenes there are no kisses; actresses prefer not to kiss. Now suddenly the young girl is faced with the unknown God of Love, Kama, who has his bow strung with bees because love can sting—hurt. Will it hurt? Sita, of course, made no murmur, yet Sita was so submissive she was almost boring. Krishna . . .

But this officer or clerk or graduate in spectacles is not at all like Krishna, full of fun and mischief: the groom may even seem to be a man much like the girl's father; to nineteen or twenty, thirty-five years old or even thirty seems much the same as fifty, so that she feels she should kneel and press his feet rather than . . .

He may be greedy, seize her; worse than that, the groom may be timid. Then she will have to play the minx, remembering things that have been whispered to her—in case . . . And all the time that old servant or midwife will be hovering, not inside the room, of course, but near. With an old servant's deadly knowledge, she will know if her charge has been made properly sore, her lip bruised. She will look at the sheets. . . . Suddenly the girl hates her.

But perhaps Krishna really is in this young man. Perhaps she loves him already; he may even be the boy to whom, long ago, she gave that tasselled bracelet, her raksha bandan. The night may be spent in shy delicious play, and there is nothing wrong in this. "I am the lust that procreates." Krishna himself said that. "This is a holy thing."

Something holy can be fun, warm and tender:

> When his mouth faced my mouth, I turned aside
> And steadfastly gazed only at the ground;
> I stopped my ears, when at each coaxing word
> They tingled more; I used both hands to hide
> My blushing, sweating cheeks. Indeed I tried.
> But oh, what could I do, then, when I found
> My bodice splitting of its own accord?

> "Look, darling, how we've disarranged the bed:
> Now it's too hard with rubbed-off sandal-paste,
>   Too rough for your soft skin," he said,
>   "Come, lie on me instead."
> While he distracted me with kisses sweet,
>   All of a sudden, with his feet
>   In pincer-fashion then he caught
>   My sari firmly by the hem:
> And so the sly rogue forced me then
>   To move the way he ought.

Those nights may grow into passion:

> Last night in private, while the household slept,
> With passion unrestrained, Love's feast they kept:
> And when, this morning, at the breakfast table,
> Their glances meet in joy, they do their best
> To guard their secret from the older people,
> And hide the merry laughter in their breast.[7]

An Indian bride and bridegroom seldom have a honeymoon; that bedroom may be their only privacy—if they are lucky enough to have a bedroom; in a family hut or a tenement flat there may be only a corner with a charpoy up-ended to close them off; a cloth will be hung over the charpoy, but inquisitive small brothers and sisters peep, grandmothers peer; the bride knows, too, that all eyes are quietly watching the new "bow"—bride—and not so quiet tongues remarking, whispering. . . .

---

7. All these poems are from the Sanskrit *Amaru* collection or anthology, circa fifth and sixth centuries. The experts say they may be by several different poets, but one cannot help feeling that the same hand wrote these unique and delicately provocative love poems, which are just as applicable today as they were fifteen centuries ago.

"Beti, you are a woman now," says Maji when they meet.

Twashtri—a form of the Creator, Brahma—tells how He made woman.

When I, Twashtri, came to the creation of woman, I found that I had exhausted my materials in the making of man, and that no solid elements were left. . . . In this dilemma I did as follows: I took the rotundity of the moon, and the curves of creepers, and the clinging of tendrils, and the trembling of grass, and the slenderness of the reed, and the bloom of flowers, and the lightness of leaves, and the tapering of the elephant's trunk, and the glances of deer, and the clustering of rows of bees,[8] and the joyous gaiety of sunbeams, and the weeping of clouds, and the fickleness of the winds, and the timidity of the hare, and the vanity of the peacock, and the softness of the parrot's bosom, and the hardness of adamant, and the sweetness of honey, and the cruelty of the tiger, and the warm glow of fire, and the coldness of snow, and the chattering of jays, and the cooing of the kokila, and the hypocrisy of the crane,[9] and the fidelity of the chakrawaka[10] and compounding all these together I made woman, and gave her to man."

Sometimes the new husband wonders why Twashtri did:

"After one week," says Twashtri, "man came to me: 'Lord, this creature that you have given to me makes my life miserable. She chatters incessantly, and teases me beyond endurance, never leaving me alone; she requires incessant attention, and takes all my time up, and cries about nothing, and is always idle; and so I have come to give her back again, as I cannot live with her.'"

"Very well," Twashtri took her back. Then after another week, man came again. "Lord, I find that my life is very lonely since I gave you back that creature. I remember how she used to dance and sing to me, and look at me out of the corner of her eye, and play with me, and cling to me; and her laughter was music, and she was beautiful to look at, and soft to touch; so give her back to me again."

"Very well," Twashtri gave her back again but, after only three days:

"Lord, I know not how it is, but after all I have come to the conclusion that she is more of a trouble than a pleasure to me, so please take her back again."

"Out on you! Be off! I will have no more of this. You must manage how you can."

"But I cannot live with her."

8. Hindu poets see a resemblance between rows of bees and eye-glances.
9. The crane is a byword for inward villainy and sanctimonious exterior.
10. The chakrawaka, or brahmany drake, is fabled to pass the night sorrowing for the absence of his mate and she for him.

"Neither could you live without her." And Twashtri turned His back
on man and went on with His work.[11]

11. From *The Digit of the Moon* by Professor Bain.

Yet a marriage has more chance of being successful in India than perhaps in any other country because anything else is scarcely to be thought of—there are divorces but they are rare. The newest husband and wife know that marriage cannot be all love; dharma—duty and obedience to the ultimate law—is something much bigger than people, and duty is instilled into all Hindus from childhood; it is far more important than romantic love. Even in a joint family house a bride has to care for her husband; she must meet him when he comes home, be always suitably dressed, ready to press those tired feet and legs, no matter how tired her own may be from endless duties done for her mother-in-law; she will always go that extra mile, not because it is imposed on her but for love and concern; it is her pride to serve her husband's food, be ready to attend him if he goes out, or uncomplainingly be left at home if he does not choose to take her.

If they have their own small flat or house she has much to learn: how to keep it spotless, perhaps with only one sweeper boy to help her; how to cook—if only she had paid more attention at home! She has to endure loneliness after the chatter of her friends and sisters, and learn the perpetual battle of making ends meet, which means resisting the blandishments of the bangle and earring-seller—how else is the electricity bill to be paid?

"Don't you know what electricity costs?" the husband will storm.

"How could I? Baba always paid it."

"Turn off that light—*now*."

"If I do I can't see to serve you."

As with any new marriage, bills lead to quarrels, hurt, and tears. "Mango goes out of season! And to make into achar—oil pickle!"

"It is your favourite."

"But out of *season*, when they are so costly."

"What is the season?"

"What? You don't know *that*!"

And, quite forgetting Sita, she sends the flashing answer back, "I'll never, never make it for you again."

But she will, and he will eat it—in fact, come to boast about it: "Her mango achar!" It will all settle down and sooner or later, if all goes well, there will come a moment when the girl will know that she may no longer spend her days alone, and will take a very different position in the joint household.

At first she may try to hide her secret within herself, but those acute eyes will notice certain signs; probably too she goes more often to pray, taking small offerings, food or incense, a handful of marigolds or red oleander blossoms, whispering, "Let it be a son."

Very beautiful is the way that flowers enter into all ceremonies in India—have always entered. In the fifteenth century an ambassador from the Sultan of Herat came to the court of the Hindu king of Vijayanagar; when he described the splendours of the capital of this southern empire, the City of Victory, with its seven walls and seven citadels, its jewellers, horses, riches, and the magnificence of its bazaars, he also wrote: "Roses are sold everywhere. These people could not live without roses, and they look upon them as quite as necessary as food."

Perhaps those roses of Vijayanagar were the small, fragile pale ones, pinkish-white and sweet-smelling, growing in humble gardens and near temples, springing up in the most unlikely places—their petals are scattered at weddings and are laid on altars. White flowers belong to Shiva; especially his is the bhant,[12] the small white, clustered flower with pink stamens that grows wild; when the sun warms the ground in early spring, every patch of open ground, each mango grove, is filled with its scent; it is suitable for Shiva as it has a bitter taste.

Vishnu loves all flowers: roses, jasmine, the fragrant champa or temple flower, and the perpetual humble marigold, but he must not be offered hibiscus or he will be offended; the scarlet hibiscus—jaba—is the flower of Kali and must never be given to anyone else. The most sacred of flowers is the lotus—padma—pink-petalled, long-stemmed, that floats on village pools and tanks in full summer. A lotus is kept at the feet of the gods to show that divine beings do not touch the earth, except in their earthly manifestations. Lakshmi, the darling goddess, sits in a lotus.

The flower scents that haunt the memory for anyone who has been in India are marigold, jasmine, and tuberoses, the fuzzy yellow flower puffs of the kadamba tree, and, oddly, sweet peas, a legacy of the gardening taught by the English to their malis[13]—sweet peas and the smell of the evening watering on hot earth and dust, the early sound of lawns being swished with long bamboo rods to brush off the dew before the sun can make it so hot that it scalds the grass.

Every winter flower shows are held in cities, and the fashionable ladies of Bombay, Delhi, and Calcutta have taken to flower-arranging classes, European or Japanese. Most Indian girls, though, are content with the making of garlands for the house images or sacred pictures and for their own hair. The flowers are threaded, without a needle, on a fibre pulled from a banana stem, which is stiff but, dipped in water, becomes soft and does not cut into the stalks as silk or cotton thread would. The flower heads are caught, or looped, in a fisherman's knot and strung close together. For a fillet to wear

12. Bhant: *Clerodendron fragrans.*
13. Mali: gardener.

262

round a hair-knot, they are strung singly, for a pigtail strung double, the heads lying in opposite directions; in the first case it will automatically curve, in the second it remains straight.

If the baby turns out to be a little girl it may wear small copies of its mother's fillet of tuberose heads.

When the Buddha was born he was "unsmeared by any impurity from his mother's womb, emerging pure and spotless, flashing as a jewel." Ordinary women can be delivered of a child three weeks earlier or three weeks later than the ten lunar months of pregnancy, but for the mother of a Buddha the time is exactly ten months. Nor does she give birth lying down or sitting as do other women; the mother of a Buddha gives birth standing up, and Queen Maha Maya, mother of Siddhartha, at the requisite time, insisted on going on a journey until she came to a grove of sal trees and decided to stay awhile there; she wished to take hold of one of the branches of a monarch sal tree and the branch, "like the tip of a well-stemmed reed," bent itself down within reach of her hand. She seized hold of it and immediately her pains came upon her. Thereupon her people hung a curtain round her and retired. Standing proudly erect, she gave birth to the Buddha, who was received by angels into a golden net.

Buddha's followers greet their newborn with prayer flags put up outside the house, and lamas say prayers on three days for a boy, two for a girl. Relations come, bringing white scarves, presents of honour for the child, and guests are given halva, other delicacies, and chang—home-brewed beer. The baby son is given the name of an important lama, perhaps Karma Tashi—Tashi means fortunate—but will be known by a pet name until the lama has given his approval.

Immediately after a Moslem child is born, a maulvi is asked to call out the "azaan" close to the child, so that the first sound the baby hears is this call to prayer. For forty days mother and child are not supposed to leave the house; then they are taken out to the courtyard to be formally "shown the stars." Both mother and baby are bathed on the sixth or seventh day; then, or sometimes a month or two later, the aqiqa, or tonsure, ceremony is held; a boy, later still, when he is perhaps four years old, will be circumcised. At the aqiqa a goat will probably be sacrificed and the child's name chosen: a boy may be Mahomet, Abdul, Subhan, Mahmud; a girl, Ayesha—name of the Prophet's wife—Farida, Laila, Taj.

For a Hindu baby, religion begins before it is born. In the fifth or seventh month—it must be an odd-numbered one—there is a ceremony in which the mother-to-be is given a sari, perhaps ornaments, and was usually offered the five holy products of the cow: ghee, milk, curds, cow dung, and cow's urine; now it is only the first three, with sugar, honey, sweets, and fruit. Sometimes relatives come, bringing presents, so that it is like the American baby shower, but blessed with holiness; also, the presents must not be for the baby—that might bring bad luck.

Omens are suddenly of great importance—not that they have not always been taken seriously. For a Hindu, what is seen first thing in the morning will influence a whole day; it is inauspicious to see a broom, or to sneeze, on getting up. A crow seen on the left is inauspicious, so is a man with a big nose or a widow; the sight of a pitcher full of water, a fire, a calf drinking its mother's milk, a lizard on an eastern wall, a cow, a horse, or an elephant, are all lucky and will make a lucky day, as will the sight of a dwarf—maharajas used to keep dwarfs for luck in their courts. A woman expecting a child needs an amulet to protect her against the evil eye. If she has lost a child, the right nostril of the next baby is bored for a nose-ring so that, if it is a boy, it may look like a girl; if it is a girl the left nostril is bored so that it may look ugly—all to avert the evil eye. That and the asuric forces are so feared for a baby that when Amar's father was born he was sold to the family sweeper for a few cowries, so that the gods would think he was a nobody and would not bother about him. To say a baby is gaining weight is to invite evil. "No, no. He has lost at least three ounces," the mother will protest.

If possible the birth should take place in a separate room, preferably in an outhouse, because, in orthodox thought, the mother is unclean; she has to stay apart from the family, for ten days if she is a brahmin, twelve as a kshatriya, sixteen as a vaisya, twenty-nine as a sudra; after which the priest comes to purify her; then comes the Name-Giving Ceremony. The sixth night after a birth is a dangerous time for the newborn; a fire should burn in front of the room where the baby is, and a barrier of thorns made so that Yama, God of Death, cannot come in. It is on this sixth day that the child is dedicated, with gifts of nuts and rice, to Shasti, the Goddess of Children, who rides on a cat.

All this will be carefully seen to, but a doctor's care in childbirth, a maternity hospital, even a clinic, is still only for a few; most Indian babies are brought into the world by the dai—midwife—though nowadays she probably is trained; missionary women doctors have done wonders here, as have Indian women doctors.

There is no need for a layette; indeed it would be positively baleful to get one ready, and when the child is born it is wrapped in old clean rags. An ordinary baby, unless it is left naked, oil being rubbed into the skin for warmth, will wear only a shirt or jacket coming down to the waist; these tiny jackets hung up in gaudy rows on the open-fronted bazaar shops look like cut-out paper jackets meant for dolls. An Indian baby does not wear diapers; from the waist down he is simply oiled and never seems to get sore, but every Hindu baby is given a charm-string to wear as an amulet, and his proud father may buy him socks or an embroidered cap.

Often, when a baby is born, particularly if this is in a village, a conch is sounded outside the house—three times for a daughter, five for that longed-for son.

PART VI

Dadaji—grandfather: most men are content to end their days as that, surrounded by their families—it is a rare being who goes beyond the "householder" stage—but for a few the sound of the conch is a mystical one, a call, and gradually their thoughts turn away from material cares and loves; religion takes on a deeper, more pervasive meaning; pilgrimages are no longer family jaunts but to be taken in prayer and silence; festivals, which were an excuse for a holiday, have a new spirituality, while images become transparent, because eyes look through them now to the eternal One.

Is this the beginning of the rishis' third stage, of vanaprastha, of relinquishment? Amar does not know, but there is a reverberation, a note within him that matches the sound he hears.

In the churning of the celestial Sea of Milk, when the legendary mountain of Mandara had to be split to make a churning stick, the huge serpent Vasuki allowed himself to be used as the rope—Indian churning is still done by pulling a rope attached to a stick which stands upright in the churn. As Vasuki churned there began to appear on the surface of the sea, one by one, fourteen precious things: the moon, which Shiva took; the mythological parijati tree and the elephant, claimed by Indra: the cow: a wine, sura which the gods drank: the apsaras—dancing girls: the white horse: the Ayurvedic system of medicine: a draught of deadly poison: the Goddess Lakshmi: the mace, symbol of sovereignty: a jewel and the conch which calls to holy battle or to prayer; finally came the ambrosia called amrita. Vishnu, for his share, took Lakshmi, the mace, the jewel, and the conch; when his spiral conch shell is sounded it reverberates through the universe.

There is a description in the *Bhagavad Gita,* of the different conchs used by the Pandavas, the five mighty sons of King Pandu but begot not by him but by the gods. They were entering on the battle against the misguided Kauravas. Krishna himself drove the chariot of one of the Pandavas, Arjuna. All blew their battle shells:

> Krishna with knotted locks, blew his great conch
> Carved of the "Giant's bone"; Arjuna blew
> Indra's loud gift; Bhima, the terrible—
> Wolf-bellied Bhima—blew a long reed conch; and Yudhisthira . . .
> Winded a mighty shell, "Victory's Voice . . ."
> . . . Nakula blew shrill upon his conch
> Named the "Sweet-sounding," Sahadev on his
> Called "Gem-bedecked." . . .[1]

1. From the *Mahabharata,* translated by Sir Edwin Arnold.

Conchs are sold in the bazaar because homes, as well as temples, often have them; they are blown after earthquakes and thunder and at evening to evoke the Goddess of Dusk. The conch is also sounded in honour to any passing god-image procession or raja or important person; women can make an echo of it by ululating with their hands vibrating over their mouths. It is the temple call to prayer.

Thousands of years ago a Hindu place of worship was the Vedic bare brick altar under the open sky, but this simplicity gave way to the magnificent temples built by early emperors and kings. Some are in ruins; the Moslem iconoclasts razed and burnt every temple they could find, looted, and cast down the images that seem to Moslem minds so profane—their

own mosques are bare of everything but lamps and carpets. Still, in remote and unlikely places from which all sign of human habitation has disappeared, enormous granite blocks, carved and incised, can be found when the encroaching jungle is cut away, with hewn stone figures lying swathed in creepers, crawled over by red jungle ants.

The early temples of the South were saved by that chain of the Vindhya mountains joining the East and Western Ghats, which for centuries acted as a barrier against the invaders. Many temples, too, were made in caves—all caves are sacred to Hindus; the huge cave at Elephanta stretches over a hundred and thirty feet into the rock and holds the statue of the brooding three-headed Shiva, the Trimurti. At Ellora there are thirty-four cave temples, twelve Buddhist, five Jain, and seventeen Hindu, of which the most remarkable is the Kailasa scooped out of the side of a hill; almost twice as wide as the Parthenon and one and a half times as high, it is another shrine to Shiva, cut and sculptured out of rock, of which two hundred thousand tons were displaced as the sculptors worked from the top downwards between the surrounding rock cliffs. The inscription of the maker has been found, perpetuating his words, "O how did I do it?"

Structural temples followed, toweringly solid masses of stone, ornamented with amazing richness. Some of their sculptured figures are serene, still . . . others so vibrant with warm, sensuous rhythm that they seem more alive than anyone or anything living today.

Most joyful of all are the wonderful carvings of the Sun Temple at Konarak, designed as a chariot for Surya, the Sun God. It was built on a ramp of sand which was then taken away, but over the centuries the sand has drifted back so that the temple stands seven miles inland, facing the sea. The sun shines on its twelve statues of Surya, striking them at different times of the day, making a gigantic sundial.

At the eastern door, facing the rising sun, huge stone horses with waving manes and tails used to stand; all but one are fallen now, but the enormous eight-spoked wheels carved with the signs of the zodiac are extant. Other doors are guarded by elephants and lions, while the pyramidical walls are richly covered with sculptured figures, gods, musicians, dancers, and embracing, entwined couples caught in maithuna, the act of love; they are pitted and marked by sun and the sea wind now, but surely as eternal as anything made by man can be.

These vast temples surmount and enclose the innermost sanctuary, usually a small windowless chamber with only one door, which is known as the "womb-house" because the worshipper, beholding the image it enshrines, is born again. When a pilgrim—probably taking all his family—goes on a journey to one of these temples or holy places and, at last, comes face to face with the god—or the symbol of the god—what is it he wishes to do? He does not kneel or pray as a Christian would, or does not pray at once; he simply stands and looks, only looks.

This same gazing happens with famous men; millions of Hindus travelled the length and breadth of India to see Gandhiji, not "see" in the sense that means "meet"—most never met him, or Nehru or Badshah Khan or Rabindranath Tagore or Doctor Ambedkar or Ram Mohum Roy or Sri Aurobindo or Ramakrishna or Swami Vikenanda—they only looked and quietly went away.

If, for instance, the President gives a garden audience in Delhi, a middle-aged couple might be found standing quietly among the flowerbeds of the presidential gardens, not approaching too near, not speaking, asking nothing except to look. This act of "seeing" is called "darshan"—vision—a mixture of silent homage and of satisfaction; the couple go away, having gained a new holiness, a vision of greatness. Having—or taking—darshan makes western jostling for handshakes, autographs, even conversation, seem clamorously vulgar. A quality that has disappeared from the West is awe; in the Hindu it is innate—and it is this that makes every father who can manage it take his family on pilgrimage.

Not that pilgrimages are solemn; like those students of the People's Party, while it is on the way, the family will probably stop off to see the sights. A party of hill nomads may clatter up to the Victoria and Albert Memorial in Calcutta, their tikka gharry—a cheap hired carriage like a box on wheels—with bundles and bedrolls on the roof, children overflowing onto the step. In a touching cultural urge the nomads have come to visit the museum with its miniatures and paintings; their wonder is all the deeper because it is so naïve. Pilgrims will camp, not in tents but in the open, in the streets, on a piece of waste ground, near the Taj Mahal or a palace or a temple and, if they are travelling by rail, on the station platform itself.

Five million passengers travel on India's railroads every day, and for an unsophisticated Hindu this, quite probably, is not the simple operation of catching the right train; although he will, long ago, have asked the price of the ticket, seldom will he ask the time the train leaves but, when the date draws near, moves into the station with his family; they spread their sleeping mats on the platform, cook their food over small braziers, wash under the station tap, while luggage coolies, railway officials, and other passengers step over or round them. Goats, chickens, pai-dogs, pigeons live in the station; quite often there is a sacred bull. There are sellers of curry and savoury hot food; a sweetmeat-seller who also has sherbet and ice cream. The coconut-seller will obligingly hack off the top of a green coconut so that the customer can drink the cool milk. Water-sellers are everywhere with different water for Moslems and for Hindus: the chai[2] wallah—tea-seller—goes up and down the platform with his cry of "Garam chai"—hot tea. There are barrows laden with toys, chip baskets of miniature brass cooking pots, bigger baskets of wooden animals or birds, all painted with crimson daisies, green leaves, yellow roses; there are palm-leaf fans, ice-sellers, book-sellers, unbelievable bustle, noise—drama.

When the right train does come in, it is probably as crowded as western city subways in the rush hour; a compartment may have, for days of travel, one stinking latrine, probably without water, but that does not really matter because when the train stops the passengers swarm out to relieve themselves, to wash—but not, of course, from the dubba or ladies' compartment, distinguished by a large lady in a sari painted on the coach side; many third-class passengers cannot read.

2. Chai: pronounced *char*.

In the dubba no questions are too intimate to ask. "Where are you going?" is usually the first, then: "Why are you going?"

"Are you married?" "When were you married?"

"How many children have you?" "Only two?" "Why haven't you got more?" "Is anything the matter with you?" "The matter with your husband?" "Who is your husband?" "What does he do?" "How much does he earn?"

A mother with an ailing baby has to bear the brunt of advice from the whole compartment; "Give him to me and I'll cure him in a couple of weeks," says a buxom matron. "Why, you should see my sons brought up on milk and butter."

A married daughter is taking her baby back to her mother's home. Glad faces welcome her at the station and kiss the baby in his spangled hat. A bride wrapped in her gay silks weeps a furtive tear, and at the next station the solicitous young husband rushes up with sweetmeats and puris hot from the pan; but sometimes real chatter is impossible, except by signs, because again there is that problem of language—the women cannot understand one another.

The talkative matron pours out her advice in Tamil because she lives and was born on the coast near Madras; the shy little bride is from Burnpur and speaks Bengali. A beautiful fair woman and her companion are dressed with so much jewellery they look as if they were going to a party, but it is simply that, as pilgrims on a long pilgrimage, they must take their valuables with them. The other women admire the silver and stones but the two wearers can only smile and nod because, coming from Chamba, they speak Paharia or a Paharia dialect.

It is by going on pilgrimage, by this pilgrim travel, that the Indian begins to think of his country as a nation. The rich, too, are beginning to discover their own land: their houses now are filled not with English or French furniture but with Indian treasures; instead of holidaying in Europe they will go to Kashmir, Kulu, or Nepal, to their own beaches, to Ajanta, but north, south, east, or west, they will discover different looks . . . .

. . . . other customs, different festivals, rituals, and processions.

The same sound of a conch, of a gong, or of music, wafts of incense, can come from a huge stone edifice or a tiny bazaar temple, its roof of kerosene tins shining like silver; it may come from a conical whitewashed spire in a village, or from one of twenty temples clustered on an islet in the Ganges, or from a solitary pavilion in the hills. A temple may not even have the ap-

pearance of a temple, being perhaps one of those tiny shrines, a slab of inscribed rock set in the roots of a pipul tree or a tree-stump decorated with a few flower heads; a piece of rag waving in the wind at the mouth of a cave, or an iron trident stuck in a cleft in the rock, is all that is needed, "Shiva is there."

People go in and out of the temples all day long, beginning at dawn. The warm temple air smells of burnt oil, sweat, incense. The ornaments of polished brass catch gleams from countless tiny lights. There are heaped flowers wound with gold and silver thread, little bowls of rice, dal, chopped sugar cane, curds—homely food. The priest offers these to the god who stares above them over the lights and incense smoke. As the priest says the evening mantras he waves a tray of miniature lights before those unmoving eyes, sprinkles water; then, when he goes, men and women can come nearer and, with their own hands, arrange their offerings just as they like.

Sometimes the temples are horrifying; Kalighat in Calcutta is notorious for the number of animals and birds, goats, cocks, pigeons, sacrificed to Kali, the bloodthirsty; it is a shambles of blood and avariciousness and, at the entrance gate, the beggars cluster with their bowls, waiting for the evening distribution of food, or some spare crumbs from the worshippers who picnic in the temple grounds, or a coin or two dropped into an outstretched hand. If even one paisa cannot be spared, it is wise to give something else, a piece of fruit, half a chapati, because who knows who a beggar may be?

Perhaps he is Amar, on pilgrimage alone, perhaps disguised. A mendicant may be a prince, a sage, a saint.

Some holy men believe they may find release by the paradox of submitting their bodies to terrible discipline and torments, lying on a bed of nails, sitting unmoving for years with one arm uplifted until it almost withers. Nobody interferes, takes them away, locks them up, any more than they would lock up a harmless lunatic—the mad, too, have been touched by the gods. Besides, if a holy man chooses to sit on the banks of the Ganges or under a tree in the Himalayas on a deerskin in the open, or takes a cave or a corner of a derelict building as his hermitage, it is a privilege for the people near at hand to provide for him, bring him food or wood for his fire, fresh water, flowers; often they will come to sit with him, seldom talking, simply taking darshan.

Shiva, when he disguised himself as an ascetic, wore a snake for his sacred thread but, for all India's snake stories, anyone who comes to visit her is unlikely to see a snake, unless it is a snake-charmer's. Snakes are quiet and shy and, except for the hamadryad or king cobra, they will not attack unless they are disturbed.

In Rudyard Kipling's *Kim*, the Lama and the boy Kim were walking along the bank of a canal when,

"Look! Look!" Kim sprang to the Lama's side and dragged him back. A yellow-and-brown streak glided from the purple rustling stems to the bank, stretched its neck to the water, drank, and lay still—a big cobra with fixed, lidless eyes.

"I have no stick—I have no stick," said Kim. "I will get me one and break his back."

"Why?" asked the Lama. "He is upon the Wheel as we are—a life ascending or descending—very far from deliverance. Great evil must the soul have done that is cast into this shape. . . . Let him live out his life." The coiled thing hissed and half opened its hood. "May thy release come soon, brother!" the Lama continued placidly.

"Never have I seen such a man as thou art," Kim whispered, overwhelmed. "Do the very snakes understand thy talk?"

"Who knows?" [The Lama] passed within a foot of the cobra's poised head. It flattened itself among the dusty coils.

"Come thou!" he called over his shoulder.

"Not I," said Kim. "I go round."

"Come. He does no hurt."

Kim hesitated for a moment. The Lama backed his order by some droned Chinese quotation which Kim took for a charm. He obeyed and bounded across the rivulet, and the snake, indeed, made no sign.

There are cobras all over India, but they keep themselves hidden in gardens, sometimes in roofs; occasionally they come into houses, especially into an old-fashioned bathroom with a hole in the wall through which the water runs out; they are attracted by the coolness. Their strike is of lightning speed and power, but before the snake can inject its poison, it has to take a bite and close its jaws. Then the victim, after violent convulsions, asphyxia, and paralysis, turns blue and is dead—perhaps in thirty minutes, perhaps not for thirty hours.

The giant python of the jungles kills by suffocating and crushing, but first it too has to strike and bite to get a firm hold; it then winds around its prey and, each time another panting breath is taken, tightens its coils. It is a myth that pythons slime their victims to swallow them, and it is seldom that they will attack a human being—they know the shoulders are too wide for their long gullets; nor are snakes slimy and cold; they are cool and dry. Many are harmless—the big rat snake, the pretty grass snakes—but most dreaded of all is the dark little krait because it is so difficult to see; it may be only a foot or eighteen inches long. Tread on one in the dark, and it will act like a deadly whiplash; a krait can fall out of the thatch of a stable on to a racehorse's back and in half an hour kill a beast worth half a lakh of rupees.

Because snakes slough their skins they are thought to be immortal, and temples are sometimes dedicated to them; there are snake-shrines, even in private gardens, perhaps at the foot of a pipul tree between whose roots a cobra has made his hole: it lives there undisturbed, fed with milk and fruit, becoming almost a household pet. On the fifth day of Shravan—July/August—the Snake Goddess Manasa is worshipped, especially in Bengal, and legends are told of the nagas and naginis who appear in paintings and sculptures as creatures with men's and women's heads and torsos but with snakes' tails from the waist down—the naginis are as beautiful as sirens. The great snake gods, many-hooded, do not live on earth but down in the nether world in a magnificent city built of jewels whose brilliance lights the darkness.

Some of the mythical serpents are well disposed, such as Ananta, on whose coils Vishnu sleeps, and who protected the infant Krishna as the newborn baby was carried secretly away through floods and darkness to the safety of his foster parents' home; other snakes keep their natural evil dispositions. Kaliya was a serpent whose venom poisoned everyone who came near the River Jumna, especially the cowherd boys, Krishna's friends; even the cows, when brought down to drink, were overcome by the venom. Krishna was only a little boy, playing on the bank, but one day he dropped his ball into the Jumna and daringly dived in after it, whereupon Kaliya rose with all his hundred and ten hoods vomiting poison and engulfed him. Krishna's friends wept and cried, the cows ran about lowing and snorting, but Krishna, though wrapped in the hideous coils, made himself so huge that Kaliya had to release him; the boy sprang onto the snake's head and, taking on himself the whole weight of the universe, danced on the hoods, beating time with his feet.

Kaliya began to die, dashing his hoods about, putting out his forked tongues, streams of blood pouring from his mouth; then he thought, "This must be the Primal Male; no other could escape my venom," and he gave up hope and lay still. Now came his beautiful nagini wives and prayed Krishna to spare him. "It is the nature of a snake to be venomous," they pleaded. "Pardon him, pardon him," and so Krishna stepped from Kaliya's head, forgave him, and told him to go to his proper home among the gods; but Kaliya was afraid because of Garuda the vulture, enemy of all serpents. Then Krishna said, "When Garuda sees the mark of my feet on your head he will not touch you."[3]

Snakes are not India's only poisoners. Outsize spiders, some grey and hideously spotted with orange, leave a poisonous rash; a scorpion bite can kill a child and cause hours of agonizing pain to a grown-up.

> I remember the night my mother
> was stung by a scorpion. Ten hours
> of steady rain had driven him
> to crawl beneath a sack of rice.
> Parting with his poison—flash
> of diabolic tail in the dark room—
> he risked the rain again.
> The peasants came like swarms of flies
> and buzzed the Name of God a hundred times
> to paralyse the Evil One.

3. Adapted from *Myths of the Hindus and Buddhists*, the Sister Nivedita and Ananda Coomaraswamy.

With candles and with lanterns
throwing giant scorpion shadows
on the sun-baked walls
they searched for him: he was not found.
They clicked their tongues.
With every movement that the scorpion made
his poison moved in Mother's blood, they said.
May he sit still, they said.
May the sins of your previous birth
be burned away tonight, they said.
May your suffering decrease
the misfortunes of your next birth, they said.
May the sum of evil
balanced in this unreal world
against the sum of good
become diminished by your pain.
May the poison purify your flesh
of desire, and your spirit of ambition,
they said, and they sat around
on the floor with my mother in the centre,
the peace of understanding on each face.

More candles, more lanterns, more neighbours,
more insects, and the endless rain.
My mother twisted through and through
groaning on a mat.
My father, sceptic, rationalist,
trying every curse and blessing,
powder, mixture, herb and hybrid.
He even poured a little paraffin
upon the bitten toe and put a match to it.
I watched the flame feeding on my mother.
I watched the holy man perform his rites
to tame the poison with an incantation.
After twenty hours
it lost its sting.

My mother only said
Thank God the scorpion picked on me
and spared my children.[4]

4. *Night of the Scorpion* by Nissim Ezekiel.

This idea of expiation—the human attempt at atonement for sin by sacrifice, courage, and acceptance of suffering—is found in all mystical religion, but the Hindu acceptance extends to an almost-brotherhood felt even for poisonous reptiles and arachnids, in spite of a natural fear of them. Like the naginis, "It is the scorpion's nature," those villagers would have said—or the spider's, or the cobra's.

Through this Hindu sense of brotherhood, kinship, with all creatures, it is possible to glimpse, as nowhere else in the world, that long-ago time when animals were not man's servants, drudges, or victims, but friends and equals, often gods venerated with awe and love.

When Hindu children see monkeys they think of the five great monkeys who, from their mountaintop, watched the demon Ravana carry Sita away to Lanka; their monkey chief was Hanuman, now a Monkey God.[5] The animal statue in the temple forecourt on page 282 is Nandi, the bull whose name means "That which gives happiness." He is being worshipped on page 261 because he is Shiva's steed. Most of the gods have vehicles. Durga, the goddess, rides on a lion: Garuda, the vulture, of whom Kaliya was so afraid, carries Vishnu: Ganesh has a rat, and Kartikeya rides on a peacock.

5. From the *Ramayana,* which has been called the best tale of the love of creatures ever told.

The tolerance seems a complete contradiction to the cruelty and callousness towards animals that is so dismaying in India: the starvation thinness of the tonga ponies, the sores rubbed by the yoke on the bullock humps, kittens thrown out to die—but a Hindu must not take life, not even to put an end to hopeless pain, and if he is poor his own life is lived in conditions not much higher than these. His may be the hand that twists the bullock's acutely sensitive tail, but he has to drive his own spent body as hard as he drives his team. How can he feed a kitten when he can hardly feed his child? To him it is their common lot and, in his simple way, he has found the same truth as the pandits: creation is all one.

When Swami Ramakrishna, as a young priest, tended Kali, the Goddess Mother, he was reproved for giving her food offerings to the temple cat; afterwards he used to tell this story:

> The war god Kartikeya, son of the Great Goddess, happened once to scratch a cat with his nail. On going home he saw there was the mark of a scratch on the cheek of his Mother. Seeing this, he asked of her, "Mother, dear, how have you got that ugly scratch on your cheek?" The Goddess replied: "Child, this is your own handiwork—the mark scratched by your own nail." Kartikeya asked in wonder, "Mother, how is it? I never remember to have scratched you!" The Mother replied, "Darling, have you forgotten having scratched a cat this morning?" Kartikeya said, "Yes, I did scratch a cat; but how did your cheek get marked?" The Mother replied, "Dear child, nothing exists in this world but myself. I am all creation. Whomsoever you hurt, you hurt me."[6]

And so a Jain[7] will not give the death slap to a mosquito that has bitten him, not even kill a rabid dog.

Hindus feed snakes, monkeys, stray bulls; a woman will bow her forehead to the ground before an elephant and ask it to protect her children.

---

6. *Ramakrishna: Prophet of New India*, translated by Swami Nikhilananda.
7. Because of this absolutely uncompromising rule against killing—and its severe asceticism—the Jain religion has never been a popular one; there are only two million Jains in India but they have a profound influence on Hindu thought.

"For sale, quiet, docile she-elephant, well-grown and used to walking in processions; ears ready pierced for ornaments, all four legs fitted with anklets of bells." Just as a western birthday party is not a real one without a cake and candles and a wedding lacks sparkle without champagne, so an Indian festival or procession is not really festive without at least one elephant.

For a procession, elephants are bathed, then painted with elaborate flower patterns, white, pink, blue, that form a tracery against their grey mottled hides; they really come into their old glory during Dasara, the longest festival of the year, which is celebrated everywhere but with special pomp and magnificence in Mysore. Here, in the capital of this southern state, on every morning of the holiday, the palace elephants are "dressed," then lined up in rows in the palace courtyard and at a given signal raise their trunks in salute. The state elephant that used to carry the maharaja, and now carries the governor in the procession to the temple, is so richly caparisoned with brocaded cloths, ropes of pearls, a jewelled and embossed cap on its forehead, gold ornaments on the sawn-off tips of its tusks, that it looks like an enormous moving jewel-case.

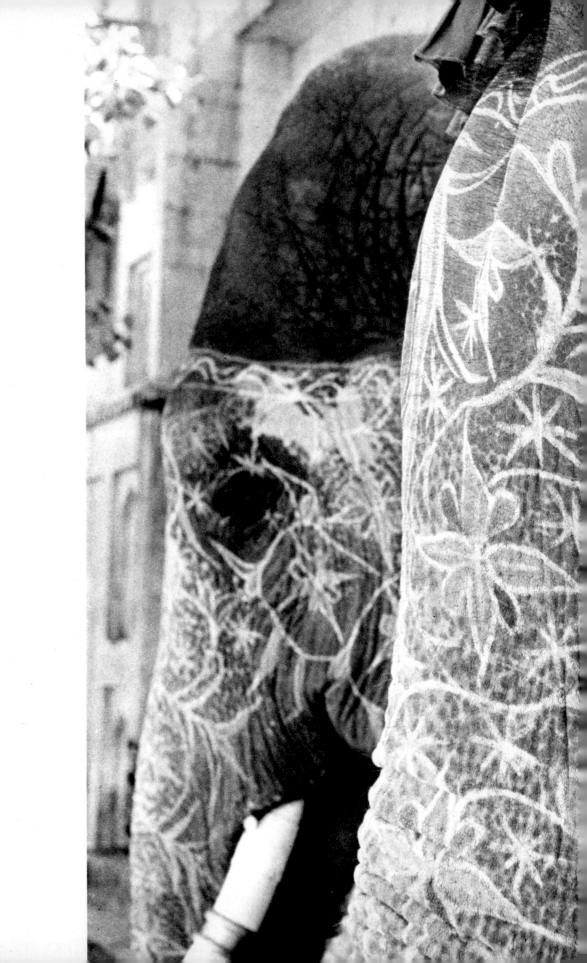

Elephants are part of Indian history. Chandragupta Maurya, grandfather of Asoka, the first Indian Emperor—or the first known to history—relied on phalanxes of armed elephants when he went into battle and with their aid defeated the armies of the famous Greek general Seleucus. War elephants must have been terrifying; made fighting drunk with wine, they were heavily armoured, sometimes with scythes fastened to their trunks, and carried howdahs of armed men; they filled the enemy with terror, but they were no match for the archers and trained cavalry of Alexander the Great when he came with his armies; fleeing, the war elephants trampled down the infantry of their own side as, many centuries later, they stampeded from the firearms of the Mogul Babur's army.

In their own jungles, the herds move like huge grey shadows between the trees; sometimes the presence of a moving, feeding herd can be detected by an agitation in the treetops, a cracking of branches, and perhaps a distant rumbling and trumpeting or a shrill squeal; sometimes an elephant can be glimpsed as it crosses one of the many open forest rides where at night they often stroll, leaving large round heaps of elephant dung, over which, as the sun rises and warms the dew-soaked jungle, yellow butterflies hover, rising together in a yellow cloud and settling again.

Elephants are tamed by being driven into a keddah, a high, strong stockade, then are broken in with the help of tamed elephants; they work in the forests, hauling timber, excavating, acting as live bulldozers, and are still used for shooting; an elephant "staunch to tiger" is worth a price that almost matches its size.

The reverence in which they are held is understandable. "No one told me they were *big*," a small boy said, stunned with surprise, when he first saw one in the zoo. A bull elephant can stand ten feet tall and weigh six tons, will eat five hundred pounds of food a day, yet, in a way, elephants are delicately formed; Krishna's beautiful gopi Radha is often compared to a she-elephant, and this is meant to be flattering. To Indian-trained eyes, African elephants with their great flapping ears are monstrosities; Indian elephants look shapely and sagacious; indeed the great domed foreheads seem to be reflecting; a tall elephant passing under jungle trees will lift its trunk to find out if branches are so low that they may hit the humans on the carrying pad; a huge foot will come out to test a treacherous-looking patch of ground. An elephant crossing a shallow river may blow bubbles to amuse itself, its trunk held just below the surface, the delicate pale pink tip sensitive as a sea anemone; and, unless they are enraged, elephants will never, never hurry; competitive ways of humans are not for them. A "bright" person, bright in our modern sense, once thought of organizing an elephant race:

> . . . when the pistol went, the elephants moved forward in a perfect row, taking no notice of the babel of shrieks, the proddings on their necks. Keeping one another in line with their trunks they moved majestically up the track; in a perfect row they breasted the tape at the other end.[8]

No wonder Ganesha, elephant-headed, is the God of Good Judgement and Prudence.

The Hindu week has no day set apart as a day of rest or a sabbath, as Friday is kept for Moslems, Saturday for the Jews, Sunday for Christians, but every day is holy because it is dedicated to the sun, the moon, or one of the planets. Some days are beneficent, some are not; Friday, Sukra, is the luckiest and belongs to Venus, who in India is not a lovely goddess but a wise and ancient brahmin. Women who fast usually fast on Tuesday, because it is dedicated to Mars, who is malefic. Saturday is Saturn's, most malicious of the planets, and so is auspicious for anyone of evil bent— thieves and murderers.

There are new all-India holidays now: Independence Day, when patriots are honoured; Republic Day, when, in Delhi, a huge parade of troops, guns, tanks, all the armed forces, files past the President with floats showing tableaux of industry, folk art, agriculture, schoolgirl and boy activities, an echo of the Lord Mayor's Day in London and the May Day parade in Moscow. Gandhiji's birthday, Gandhi Jayanti, is a public holiday when people gather to remember him, spin with the charka, and pray; but all through the year, strung like flowers on a garland, are religious festival days or weeks, Hindu, Moslem, Buddhist, Christian, Jain, Parsee, in which other faiths and communities may join.

8. From *The Little World* by Stella Benson.

Tahira, Fahmeeda,
Shameen Khatoon
All dance together for
The little Id moon

Dance in a circle
In the lit room
Dance all together for
The little Id moon.

This way
That way
Three in a line,
Three feet
Beating
All in time.

Noodles this evening
Pulao at noon
Sweet yellow rice
For you, little moon.

Bibiji fasted[9]
A whole month long
Now it's all over
Let's sing a song!

"O, thread of silver
Night's precious boon
Rising within us
Little Id moon!"[10]

9. Bibiji: grandmother.
10. *Rhymes for Ranga* by Freda Bedi.

Ramazan, the Moslem month of fasting, comes once a year when, from sunrise to sunset, nothing, not even a sip of water, must pass the lips; this can be cruel when Ramazan falls in the hot weather. There must, too, be abstinence from sexual intercourse; the Prophet knew that women need a rest. Ramazan ends with the first sight of the new moon, the Id moon, when there will be a feast; Tahira, Fahmeeda, Shameen will be given sweetmeats, gay little caps, gauzy new dopattas, perhaps toys. The weeks of denial are over, but for the faithful of Islam there is still the Haj; at least once in a lifetime a Moslem, no matter how far away in India he lives, must make the tremendous pilgrimage to the shrine of the Ka'ba in Mecca and, if possible, pass through Jerusalem because this is where the mosque of Al Aqsa rose on the spot where Mahomet stopped on his night journey before, riding his winged horse Al Buraq, he ascended to heaven from the sacred Dome of the Rock. He saw the delights of paradise and Allah gave him instructions for the faithful; then the Prophet came down again and rode on to Medina that

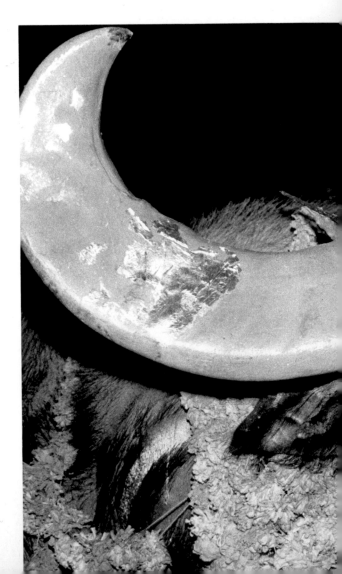

night. After making the effort of the Haj, a Moslem may dye his beard red.

The Buddhists have their Buddha Jayanti—Buddha's birthday—a national holiday; in March, at the vernal equinox, the Parsees keep Nowruz, their New Year. Hill people have their own festivals; the Minjar Mela is held at Chamba, when, as a culmination to days of feasting and carnival, everyone goes to a high cliff above the River Ravi to propitiate the river goddess, at one time by the drowning of a young buffalo, but now by throwing tassels made of silk and silver into the torrent. An unlucky bullock or buffalo is still led garlanded to the sacrifice at the festival of Dasara in Nepal, or anywhere that a Gurkha regiment is stationed; a Gurkha will show his prowess by cutting off its head with one clean and tremendous blow of his kukri, but in Nasik for Divali there is another and more gentle buffalo festival, in which the biggest and finest male buffaloes are taken in procession with music and dancing to make obeisance at the buffalo shrine on the edge of the town.

At the opposite end of India, in the South, the people of Kerala keep their own four-day festival of Onam, with singing and dancing, boat races and fireworks, to show their ancient legendary king, who is supposed to visit them for these few days, that all is well and his people are still prosperous and happy.

In January or February comes Vasanta Panchami, when students bring their books to Saraswati, the white-armed Goddess of the vina and peacock. Some Hindus say no writing or studying should be done on this day; others that it is the luckiest on which to start a book or thesis; the mustard is in flower for Vasanta Panchami and everyone who can wears yellow clothes, but for the spring festival of Vaisakhi—the beginning of the Hindu new year—clothes should be new.

In Kashmir, by early morning, hundreds of picnic boats will be tied up under the willows below the Mogul garden of Nishat, each boat swept and tidied after the night, quilts and pillows stacked, carpets laid down in the compartments for the coming feast, hookahs put ready and bunches of lilac hung from the roof, while a hired cook is busy in the galley. The rest of the people are ashore; the Hindus at the temple making their ablutions, the men immersing their naked little boys in the lake, the women in the women's pool, while, on the grass outside, priests will be waiting to make the tikka mark in sandalwood paste that shows the ritual has been done.

Moslems and Christians who have come to watch are already in the garden where once Shah Jehan and Jehangir sat and dreamed; whole families will sit in a circle on the grass round the samovar, drinking salt tea and eating kulchas—ringed sesame-seed-sprinkled bread; along the waterfront are sweet stalls and cookshops with savoury hot food; there may be a few paise to spare for these and for jilibis—toffee rings—or barfi—a kind of nougat stuck with silver paper—far more beautiful to the children than the terraces of chenar trees and roses, the water channels and the fountains playing.

But there were, once, fateful years when spring failed to come to India. Long, long ago a wicked demon held sway over the whole world—which, of course, was India—and so perverted the seasons that they forgot to do their work; this harassed even the gods, because they were beset by the anguished prayers of men for cold weather or hot weather, rain, and above all, the absent spring's fertility. The Council of the Gods appealed to Brahma but, ethically, Brahma could not help because it was he who, mistakenly, had given the demon those powers. "I can't very well take them back," said Brahma, "but, if you can persuade Shiva, my equal in the Trinity, to marry again, I promise you he will have a warrior son who will destroy the demon."

This was easier said than done. Shiva's wife, Sati, had died and Shiva had been so maddened with grief that he had danced round the world seven times with her body, but now he had retired into the remote Himalayas for deep meditation, and marriage was far from his mind. No one dared disturb him.

The gods finally deputed Kama, God of Love, to go to Shiva, taking Uma—Parvati—as a possible wife; Brahma had thoughtfully re-created her from Sati. Kama was so frightened that he also took his own wife, Rati—Desire—and with her, Spring.

The story is told in a long poem, *Kumara Sambhava* or *Birth of the War God,* by the master poet and dramatist Kalidasa, most brilliant of the Nine Gems of literature of the Gupta kings. Kalidasa was at the court of Chandragupta II, circa 380 A.D. The poem was finished by lesser poets but the matchless third canto is his; it tells how Spring and her companions stole through the Himalayan groves on their way to Shiva's hermitage and woke the whole forest to love:

> When, in the forest of their meditation,
> The holy hermits saw the untimely Spring,
> Their minds were hard-pressed to resist temptation,
> To keep their thoughts from Love's imagining.
>
> When Love came there, his flower-bow ready stringing,
> With fair Desire, his consort, at his side,
> The forest creatures showed the passion springing
> In every bridegroom's heart towards his bride.
>
> From the same flower-cup which his love had savoured
> The black bee sipped the nectar as a kiss;
> While the black doe, by her own consort favoured,
> Scratched by his antlers, closed her eyes in bliss.

The elephant with water lotus-scented
Sprayed her own lord, giving of love a token;
The wheel-drakc, honouring his wife, presented
A half-chewed lotus-stalk which he had broken.

. . .

When trembling petal-lips made laughing faces,
And blossom-breasts the slender stems were bending,
Even the forest-trees received embraces
Of creeper-wives, from their bough-arms depending. . . .[11]

Spring, though, had no effect on Shiva; as Kama, standing near Uma, stretched his bow of stinging bees to shoot the love arrow, Shiva caught sight of him and, with a glance from his third eye, turned Kama to ashes, since when the god has been bodiless and so, all the better, can steal into men's and women's hearts.

In the end Shiva married Uma, after, for love of him, she had undergone those "countless austerities" that are a natural part of Hindu mythology, and Kartikeya, God of War, was born to them. As Brahma had promised, Kartikeya defeated the demon, and spring has come at the proper time ever since.

11. Extract from Third Canto, *Kumara-sambhava of Kalidasa,* translated by John Brough.

But the most popular spring festival for the people, the sudras and pan-chamas, is Holi; the excitement in the air seems to presage the colours that will soon be brilliant on the flowering trees, scarlet, shrill yellow, purple, pink—Holi is a festival of colours.

Groups of exhilarated people, sometimes carrying phallic symbols, romp through the streets; drums sound all day and night and a man dressed as Hanuman, the Monkey God, clowns and dances—uninhibitedly suggestive dances.

There are, of course, a dozen different explanations for Holi: it celebrates the birth of Krishna, or the red powder thrown symbolizes the menstrual flow of the great Goddess, the breaking of her virginity, but it is quite clear that it is a fertility festival, a saturnalia, an April Fool's Day, Fun Festival.

Anyone, everyone, can "play Holi": a servant or clerk pinches or slaps or tickles his master; friends—and enemies—daub one another's foreheads with thumbs dipped in the red powder; the powder may be thrown at

anyone. Crowds of men and boys roam the streets, filling the air with red; hair and clothes are dyed every shade of scarlet, red, and violet; children are free to play any pranks they like, and are given water squirts for jetting coloured water.

At the beginning of winter comes the most beautiful of all festivals, Divali, the Feast of Lights, chiefly in honour of Lakshmi, Goddess of Wealth and Prosperity; to welcome her, thousands of little lights, divas—traditionally a wick burning in a small earthenware saucer of oil—are placed under trees, at crossroads and shrines and, because the goddess may overlook an unlit house, they are set along rooftops, on window ledges, and on steps, so that every building, every home and temple, even every boat on the rivers, is outlined in small twinkling points of light; firework displays go on until dawn, rockets soaring into the night sky.

Yet perhaps the most important festival to a Hindu, particularly in Bengal, is the one that comes before Divali, the ten days of Dasara, the Durga puja, when sons and daughters, even if they are grown up and middle-aged, should go back and visit the elders of their families, because Durga, though she is Goddess of War and the feast celebrates her victory over demons, is still an aspect of that Mother of the whole universe who some believe is the supreme deity, who reveals Herself to Her children under those scores of aspects, among them—Durga, Sati, Parvati, Uma, and black, black Kali.

The young Ramakrishna, her priest who told the story of the cat, is still called the prophet of new India—the nineteenth century is young for India; his Ramakrishna Missions, founded to perpetuate his teachings, are not ashrams in the sense of simple spiritual camps, but places of learning and Hindu theology, modern as American universities, with lofty halls, libraries, and lecture rooms. The orange-robed swamis of his order are ready to talk, instruct, read, or meditate with souls in every stage of advancement, from sight-seeing tourists to deep initiates. It seems a far cry from these centres to the little temple above the river, not far from Calcutta, where the Master used to tend the black goddess.

The priests care for their images as if they were alive; they must be fed, dressed, soothed, entertained; sometimes they are carried or wheeled on great wooden carts called juggernauts in procession through the streets on festival days; in the mighty temple of Jagannath at Puri, the god, after being ceremoniously washed in public, always catches cold and is put to bed for a fortnight.

Ramakrishna knew "the absurdity of putting on a pedestal That which cannot be limited by space; of feeding That which is disembodied and incorporeal, singing before That whose glory the music of the spheres tries vainly to proclaim," but as long as a man is bound by his human limitations —and in those days even Ramakrishna was so bound—he can only worship God through human symbols; and so the image-makers in the town bazaars and villages make humble replicas of Ramakrishna's black basalt goddess, and of Saraswati, Lakshmi, Ganesha, for household or festival use when big

images of the particular god of the feast are set up under pandals in streets and courtyards. Some of the images are beautifully painted and decorated, but if there is no image-maker the potter is often deft in this work of straw and clay plastered over a wire frame.

In the clatter and turmoil of the bazaar, the cacophony of the radio, car horns, clang of tools, machines, is a sound even older and more homely than the softly humming charka—the drone of the potter's wheel that, for the West, used to be the symbol of the East. Plastics, aluminum, enamel have invaded India but the potter, with his skilled thumb, still makes pots of every size and shape from the huge storage jars, several feet high, in which a family hoards its grain and pulses, to the tiny cheap chattis or tea-bowls that, in the tea-shops—rough open stalls equivalent to cafés—are used by one customer, then thrown down and smashed; if a Hindu has to drink from a glass or a china cup he will often not let it touch his lips but tilts the liquid down his throat.

The potter makes painted clay animals too for festival days, or, if a family
cow or horse is sick, he will make a little replica to be placed as a visible
prayer, at a shrine.

In the evening of the festival, or on the last day, the figures are lifted down from their pandal and taken in procession, pulled on a bullock cart perhaps or, nowadays, driven in a decorated lorry, to be immersed in the river or the sea, where the image soon disintegrates and melts away. Vasanta Panchami, Dasara, Divali are over for another year. Tomorrow is an ordinary day.

But, even on ordinary days, on some warm summer evenings men, women, and children gather in the open to sit on the ground, still hot from the sun, while they listen to some learned pandit, engaged very likely by a rich man of the neighbourhood for katha, which is story-telling. Once again the tales will be taken from the familiar dear epics and puranas; as with the kirtan-singer, the pandit tells them with his own commentaries, such gestures and modulations of voice, such wonderful explanations and detail that the audience calls out with delight, laughs, weeps, groans, forgets itself in a tide of religious feeling, as it sits and listens, often far into the night.

To Westerners the stories often seem pointless, besides going on and on. "Of course they do," says Panditji. "It is really very simple. The West starts from the theory that everything has a beginning and an end, whereas we Orientals believe that life has neither beginning nor end, but evolves in cycles, a process of gradual change. In that unceasing series of transformations we find our purpose in life but behind them is prakriti—nature that will never change. It is for you, your generation," Panditji tells his audience, "to find an interpretation of prakriti to fit this restless age."[12]

12. *My Life with a Brahmin Family* by Lizelle Reymond.

The women, who are always segregated from the men, sit close-packed as a bed of flowers, heads covered with their pallus as a mark of respect, faces, alight with interest, all turned one way, bodies still until, at the words of an inspired story-teller, a ripple of excitement or ecstasy runs through the crowd and sets them swaying; a whole village may resound with chanting: "Hari Hari . . . Hari Hari," or "Hari Rama, Hari," "Ram Rama Nama," "Ram, Ram, Ram," or "Govinda, Govinda"—mystical, unending, each but one of the thousand, thousand, thousand, names of God.

PART VII

Death is a part of life; then why, a Hindu may well wonder, do western people seem so afraid of it, seldom dream of preparing for it? For himself, as he grows older, may come recognition of the meaning in himself of a certain weariness of worldly affairs. His vague longings deepen into mysticism, and now he may calmly decide to commit himself and become a true vanaprastha,[1] "seek the forest" again, but a reverse kind of "forest" from the student's, a withdrawal from the world, hermitage—often a wandering one —in fact, a life of meditation and growing asceticism, gradual relinquishment of all worldly ties. Finally, through this discipline, he hopes to reach the rishis' last stage, of sannyasa—holiness—living on another plane of unselfconsciousness and freedom. A true sannyasa is released from life already —he has deliberately died while still alive—and to him moksha should come naturally: "When an earthen pot is broken the space within is one with the space without."[2]

Humans can interfere with life, stop its begetting; they can nurture and cherish it, or torture and twist it, even cut off life; but death is inexorable.

Indian families do not easily hand over their sick into other people's care; even if the ill one has to go to hospital, the family will want to come too, often making a camp around the bed but, no matter how tenderly he is looked after, the moment may come when the doctor or nurse or senior relative has to say, "It is time to lay him on the ground."

A Hindu should die not in his bed but lying on earth—if it is the floor it must be washed with cow dung mixed with water—earth and, if possible, by a river.

1. The Sanskrit words must be used because there is no exact equivalent in the West: pilgrim, wanderer, holy man, ascetic, monk—none of them will do.
2. Ananda Coomaraswamy.

If possible, too, that river should be the Ganges.

Only a few sick and dying can reach the actual Ganges, but all Indian rivers, by implication, are Herself: the Jumna, the Jhelum, the Godavari, Ravi, Narmada, Krishna, and Kaveri, and, farther east, the Brahmaputra, which rises in Tibet. They leave their ravines, their rapids and jungle gorges, to flow, some of them miles wide, between sandy or mud banks, sometimes changing their courses bewilderingly from year to year.

Although great stretches seem empty, alone under the bowl of the sky, in parts there is a busy river traffic; small boats with wicker shelters on

wooden hulls have eyes painted on their prows; ferry boats are crowded with passengers and, as they cross, the far bank shows as a line of blowing sand across the width of the river. The big country boats are like galleons, laden perhaps with a mountain of terra-cotta-coloured pots or a great load of straw—a floating haystack inside which a whole family lives; they drift majestically downstream under a spread of coloured sails, or their crews, straining in a long line, the towing rope on their sweating shoulders, pull them upstream. Black crescents of fishing boats float in the water with weighted nets stretched between them.

The rivers pass thatch-roofed, mud-walled villages with a background of fields and blue sky that meet the flat horizon. Women come down the bank to fill their water pots; naked children play in the wash thrown up by a passing black-funnelled paddle-wheeled river steamer; herds of cows or buffaloes are driven down to drink; and fishermen wading in the shallows throw fine small nets that bring in finger-length fish shining in the mesh. The large fish are hung between poles to dry in the sun.

And the rivers have an indigenous life of their own; skeins of geese and wild duck pass overhead; in the distance, shining white dots are a family of pelicans; kingfishers, pied or jewel-coloured, dart and swoop; huge crocodiles sun themselves on the sandbanks; porpoises somersault in and out of the water, their hides shining grey, bronze, blue. Deep in the river bed are the mussels whose shells yield pink river pearls.

As the rivers near the coast, the sea flows in to meet them—many of these big rivers are tidal; there are larger fish, small Indian crabs scuttle across the sand on the banks, and the boats change; they are heavier, more clumsy, and their shapes are very different—fishing boats like junks and catamarans.

For aeons the Ganges, Ganga—Mother Ganga—flowed only in heaven. Then an earthly king did everything in his power to induce her to come down to the world and on to the nether regions, where his sixty thousand sons had been reduced to a pile of ashes by an angry sage; only her sacred water, he knew, could revive them. The king did not succeed; probably he did not know that the only way to circumvent a capricious goddess is not by importunity but by silent holiness—do not speak and she may answer. His great-grandson Bhagiratha was wiser and, again by practising those "tremendous austerities," persuaded the river to descend. The gods were afraid that earth would not be able to sustain the shock of her fall, so Shiva agreed to break it on his head. The proud and wilful Ganga imagined that she would be able to sweep the god with her to the nether regions but she found herself lost and wandering in the tangled forest of his hair, and Shiva laughed gently to himself. It was many years before he at last allowed her to find her way to earth, on which she fell in a thunderous torrent and divided into seven streams, of which Bhagiratha led one to the underworld.

The Ganges, as she flows, is joined by many other rivers, the Jumna at Prayag and finally the giant Brahmaputra; then they flow together through the delta of the Sunderbans to the sea but, on her way, the Ganges has watered an immense fertile plain, at least three hundred thousand square miles of northern India, the setting of much of her history and of her antique cities such as Pataliputra, built where the town of Patna now stands. She has always carried a rich, busy traffic of trade but is a river of contrasts, almost of moods; sometimes she sparkles: from some reaches, in certain rare weather, perhaps after a storm has cleared the air, a distant rosy gleaming line can be seen at sunset or sunrise hanging in the sky—the line of the high Himalayan snow peaks, miles and miles away. At other

times she is veiled in mist and is often a lonely river, running her solitary way between low banks of shining silver sand.

Near any of her sacred towns, though, the Ganges is crowded; her wide, flowing stream is starred with islets covered in temples and, in every city, she passes innumerable burning ghats with blue smoke rising from the fires, because the place where a Hindu prays to die is at Hardwar, where the river emerges onto the plains, or at Prayag or, and above all, at Benares; but if the dying cannot come to her, a little of Ganga's blessing can be taken to them. Small brass containers are made for Ganges water, unscrewing from an ornamented lid; when they are antique, they seem to have a patina from being carried with deep reverence for the sacredness they hold; the worn brass has the feeling of many other people's touch. A little of the water is dropped into a dying mouth.

There was once an aristocratic old lady who lived in the "big house" of a Punjabi village and from her matriarchal throne—a string bed in the shade of a ber tree in the courtyard—ruled her large household, sons, daughters-in-law, children, servants, as she thought wise and fit.

In a trunk in her room was a tin of Ganges water to use when her last hour came. She had always kept it there. It was in the same place when the old dog, fifteen years old and a member of the family, died. One morning he had walked round in circles, and then put his head pitifully on her feet, and she realised that the old pet was dying. So she called for his accustomed halva,[3] a full seer of it, and when he refused to touch it, she took out the tin of holy Ganges water and gave it to him to drink. Then she fetched her copy of the Gita and read it over him until he gave her one last look of farewell and died.[4]

3. Halva: a sweetmeat-cum-pudding. For a dog it would probably be sujee—sago—mixed with ghee and sugar into a sweet rich paste.

4. *Behind the Mud Walls* by Freda Bedi, the old lady's English daughter-in-law.

She had a precedent in the *Mahabharata*, the great Hindu epic from which the *Bhagavad Gita* comes; it tells of the battles of the Pandavas, those god-begotten sons of King Pandu. When they were old and at the end of their long reign, they chose a successor and set out on one last journey to find heaven or the abode of the gods. "If we can't reach it," they said, "then let us perish." A lean, dirty dog followed them.

All but one of the five died on the road; that one, Yudhisthira, went on alone, except for the dog, which still followed him. Suddenly there appeared Indra with his celestial chariot; the king of the gods had come himself to take Yudhisthira to heaven, but Yudhisthira had never been known to desert anyone and he told Indra that without his brothers he would not enter heaven. Indra assured him that, though the rest of the Pandavas could not be there in the flesh, their souls were already in the abode of the blest. "Get into the chariot," said Indra.

Then Yudhisthira saw the dog. It was standing near the chariot, looking expectantly at him. Yudhisthira beckoned to it and, wagging its tail, it was approaching when Indra objected.[5] "The dog is an unclean animal and will pollute my chariot, much more so heaven. It cannot possibly come. A dog cannot enter heaven," said Indra.

"King of the Gods," Yudhisthira answered, "this dog has followed me all through my journey and I cannot desert it. Either we get into the chariot together or together stay outside."

It was the final test. The dog now transformed itself into a god, Dharma, God of Righteousness, the very god who had begot Yudhisthira.

---

5. Indra's objection to the dog would be that of most Hindus, and understandable; Indians eat on the floor and a dog might come too close and breathe over the food, even snatch it; gods presumably eat the same way in heaven. This lowly regard of a dog makes Yudhisthira's loyalty to his, the old lady's blessing of hers more remarkable.

Hindus believe that the span of a human life should be a hundred and twenty years[6] but often they do not know how old they are; most Indian birthdays pass unnoticed, yet, if a man does know when he has reached his sixtieth, halfway mark of what the gods can grant, he is entitled to celebrate it as extravagantly as he likes, even though this leaves him penniless. "My children will support me," he says in serenity. They will, and in the family. "What? Put Dadaji into a *home!*" his son and daughter-in-law, or daughter and son-in-law would say, shocked, if such an idea were suggested: Dadaji, or a grandmother or great-grandmother, or a widowed old aunt or troublesome crone of a sister. There are houses for old people, like Aram Ghar, House of Rest, in Hyderabad, or the houses run by the Little Sisters of the Poor—"But those are for people who have no one to look after them," says the family. "*We* are here," and it is amazing how gentle and sweet servants, for instance, are with old people's whims and cantankerousness. "She is old," the little maid will say in a gentle singsong as she bends for the tenth time to pick up the fan that has been thrown at her, takes away the sujee the doctor has prescribed and that has been pronounced uneatable, wipes the dribble off a chin; sings, fans, presses legs and back. "She is old," is a perfectly satisfactory explanation.

Even where there are no servants to help there is an honourable corner in the hut, food stretched to include the old, a little money kept by, now and then, if possible, for the biris or sweets they love; but there are some homes that are too poor to offer even that. It was for these lost ones, the flotsam and jetsam of the cities, that Mother Teresa opened, in a derelict warehouse in Calcutta, the first of her famous homes for the dying.

Mother Teresa, an Albanian nun, has done in Calcutta and Delhi and is beginning to do in Bombay and many other centres what governments and organizations have largely failed to do: work towards clearing streets and gutters, alleys and market-places of their thousands of derelict, diseased, and dying humans, and done it in the only possible way—by becoming almost one of them.

She first came to India to teach in a Loreto convent, but that disciplined

6. A pathetic belief in a country where the average expectation of life is not much more than fifty years; it used to be twenty-four.

life seemed too comfortable and prosperous compared to the misery she saw all around her, and she got permission to leave and found an order of her own, vowed to serve the poorest of the poor and live as they do. At first she was alone with what she calls "a handful of rupees"; now she has a large sisterhood, mostly Indian or Anglo-Indian, Hindu as well as Christian, and money flows through their hands, but none of it is for themselves; they live in bare rooms without fans in summer or warmth in winter, sleeping on native string cots, wear the poorest of cotton saris, their underdress made from gifts of old sheets, or else from flour bags; they are allowed only two pairs of chaplis—cheap native shoes—a year, and must never eat or drink outside one of their own houses, where the food is nearly as cheap and frugal as the poorest peasant's; yet they are in the streets from eight in the morning until late at night, working in their homes for the dying or in their pavement schools where, as Amar told little Aruna, the children write in the dust. They take their ambulances to the leper colonies, where whole families are cured and rehabilitated; they arrange marriages and even provide small dowries for girls they rescue from prostitution. In the chapel of these Missionaries of Charity, the charity which means love, the figure of Christ on the cross has bruised and broken knees.

In 1962 Mother Teresa was given the high Indian honour of the Padma Shri, and Mrs. Pandit, Nehru's sister, described the leveé.

> There were the usual recipients—men and women who were getting various awards and they received recognition in the shape of polite hand-claps. But when this little lady entered that magnificent hall, with its painted ceiling and all the pomp and panoply that attends such functions—the military on parade and the guards on duty, all dressed in splendid colours, a band in attendance—she walked up just as she is every day. She received the award as she would have received a dying man or picked up a child, but the hall went mad. The stamping and the clapping and the cheering was absolutely spontaneous. I looked at the President, there were tears in his eyes. . . .

Mother Teresa was called from that panoply because a poor labourer was dying outside on the road.

But, mercifully, most old people have that place of innate reverence—their own home.

Old men, like old men everywhere, wait quietly for death, but old women like to help with the household chores and the children of the family as long as, and longer than, they can. Grandmothers are popular; they are usually the best story-tellers: "In ancient times . . ." they will begin, and they usually have a private store of sweet things—a handful of puffed rice, a sandesh,[7] or peanuts to slip into a small hand. When the stories get too hazy to be told any more, the children, even a baby, too energetic for a worn-out body to mind, the old women sit, backs to the wall of the hut, warming their bones in the sun, smoking a little, dozing or dreaming, watching without taking part; watching children, grandchildren, great-grandchildren. Which are which?

7. Sandesh: a sweet of curds and sugar, rather like sweetened cream cheese.

There are those few who choose to be lonely, who decide, like the Pandavas, Yudhisthira and his brothers, to leave all that they have and go on a last long wandering journey to the gods.

When the right time comes, his children safely married, a man, and his wife, if she wishes, should be free to leave the management of their affairs, for him of business and money, for her cares of house and dependents, to a son and daughter-in-law, or daughter and son-in-law; the younger ones accept this, no matter how deeply they love them, and let them go.

Perhaps, too, a man like Amar has a graver reason for his decision than a desire for quiet and holy things. He has been a "student," left, as he should, the shelter of his home to fend for himself; for long years as "householder" he has done his duty to his wife and children. These are right things, but what of others? It is unfortunately true that bribery and corruption undermine much effort in India; there is simony when a public man puts his family concerns before his honour, and often it is not the candidate with the best qualifications who gets the best appointment, the grant overseas; not the most honest and able contractor who lands profitable orders; the chosen candidate or contractor will quite likely be a minister's or a chancellor's or committee member's grandson, nephew, niece, or a cousin's cousin's cousin. In everyone's life there are myriad regrets, not big public faults perhaps, but small shameful ones, secret perhaps, but not from oneself—and not, if one believes in them, secret from the gods.

I came out alone on my way to my tryst. But who is this that follows me in
  the silent dark?
I move aside to avoid his presence but I escape him not.
He makes the dust rise from the earth with his swagger; he adds his loud
  voice to every word that I utter.
He is my own little self, my lord, he knows no shame; but I am ashamed to
  come to thy door in his company.[8]

There is only one way to be rid of him and, "Yes, I must go," says Amar.

8. Rabindranath Tagore, *Gitanjali*.

Were Amar's thoughts already turning towards this when he took to going on pilgrimage alone? In tune with his aspirations he may have chosen the high difficult places like the sacred cave of Amarnath, thirteen thousand feet up on the mountainside below a snow peak in the extreme northwest of Kashmir. In this vast cave a five-foot-high ice lingam, emblem of Shiva, forms in the summer months; it rises out of the ice only at times but is supposed to wax and wane with the moon and reach its greatest height when the August moon is full; on that day of full moon comes the yatra, the huge pilgrimage, which must arrive between dawn and dusk, bringing offerings of flowers and incense to lay before the symbol of the god.

The rough stony track is lost most of the year in snow and grows narrower and steeper as it climbs; its last twenty miles can be covered only on foot or on mountain ponies. The path, snaking up two thousand feet of an almost vertical mountainside, is so steep that women are almost tipped out of their dandys[9] and, as a grisly warning, from far down the precipice below comes the stench of dead ponies, fallen over the edge; the bodies of their riders are brought up but the ponies, caught on rocks or rolled to the bottom, left to rot.

The track crosses a high pass, then, still above tree line, comes down to a rocky plain, where pilgrims make a line ten to twenty miles long that presses steadily on, shepherded by police and guides and local Moslem ponymen, and besieged by food-sellers, flower-sellers, beggars, all hoping for a good harvest of paise from these few hectic days.

There are families, the mothers so terrified for their children that they are driven to reproach the father: "I didn't know it would be like this!" Urchins get lost as they scramble far ahead, and there is real danger they may not be found again. Old people are helped along and, in a state of exaltation, seem to forget a hardship that would normally kill them: a Jain millionaire who never travels but by a smoothly running car or first class seat in a plane, plods barefoot. There are adventurous tourists, even a tour with a guide explaining as best as he can in spite of want of breath from altitude and steepness. Saffron-robed, immaculately clean ascetics walk with their companions in holiness, wild-looking naked sannyasis; like the old people they seem lifted out of physical feeling, but a little Bengali clerk who never dreamed it could be so cold shivers, his goosefleshed legs showing below his muslin dhoti, only a thin jersey over his muslin shirt, and he has not brought a blanket.

Even in August the nights, at this height, are bitterly cold, and there are camps now where the pilgrims can shelter, though the tents are too crowded for sleep. One camp is near the sacred lake of Sheshnag and, to add to the sense of confusion and the din, there is a constant roaring from

9. Dandy: an open reclining chair carried on poles by four men.

the crushed ice of the glacier as it crashes into the lake. The blue-green waters are ice-cold—icebergs float in them all summer—but the truly earnest will bathe in them for added merit. When, on the holy day itself, they reach the last slope to the cave, they will bathe again in the clear Amarvati stream.

The queue of pilgrims, on the move before dawn to nightfall, becomes a double one: an ascending file of the freshly bathed and purified, struggling into the mouth of the cave, fighting and pushing for a sight of the lingam, even in danger of pushing one another off the narrow ramp into the gulf below in their frenzy; a descending line passing the first, Hindu men, women, and children shouting the name of Shiva, "Jai Shiva! Jai Shiva!" By the sandalwood paste shining on their foreheads and their look of beatitude, they show that the wish, perhaps of a lifetime, has been fulfilled.

By evening the last pilgrims will have left the cave; many will be far on their way home. Soon every trace of the great trek, the marks made by thousands of feet, the small piles of human excrement left on every rock, under trees, and along the banks of streams and lakes, will vanish into the earth. Clean mountain winds will blow away the trash and litter, the trampled sward take on its true colour and sheen. Soon the only human sound to be heard for days, perhaps for months on end, will be wild, harsh, but sweet and trembling whistles of mountain shepherds and nomads calling to their herds . . .

. . . and the rock pigeons can settle down on the cave ledges again. It was at Amarnath, the legend says, that Shiva condemned those humans who had offended him to live through a span of life as pigeons, but it does not tell what they had done. Had they jostled someone off the path in their haste to see the wondrous lingam? Or, as Shaivite holy men, extorted money—as it is only too easy to do—from some poor superstitious pilgrim? A sannyasa must never ask, or even show, his need for alms, and to do so is a double fault if done in Shiva's name. Or were the pilgrims, having achieved the sight of the god, filled with not holy humility but unholy pride? Nobody knows, except that every year there are plenty of new pigeons to haunt the cave.

But now Amar has set himself to climb higher still, to still lonelier places, trying to find the "mountain" he thirsts for, the "place of peace"; or maybe he will have journeyed towards the even holier river.

A sannyasa, in the rishis' last stage of living, is more removed from life, more indifferent to the world than even the vanaprastha; he neglects his health, eating only once a day and that what is given to him as offerings; if nothing is given it does not matter. He lets his hair and beard grow long, often refrains from washing; it is long years perhaps since he needed a bed or bedding—people who tend him often say they never see him sleep. He used to carry a dhuni—a small earthenware stand for his fire—now he has probably forgotten it. It does not matter if he is cold or what the weather is; he is preparing for death, when there is no weather, no feeling. This is his short twilight before the curtain of night.

Twilight is called "cow-dust time" because then the cattle are going home, driven along the small dust roads to the village.

Twilight is brief; night comes in a few minutes. . . .

In India, stars seem bigger and brighter than stars seem anywhere else, the moon rising behind palm trees, improbably round and gold, a stage moon. Chand, the moon, is masculine, Chandra, the Moon God, a shining young prince with twenty-seven beautiful starry wives, all sisters, the twenty-seven constellations. While the sun rests peacefully at night, his brother the moon is condemned to eternal sleeplessness because he spied on his mother when she was having her bath; but the bold and shameless moon is a favourite with everyone.

> A ray is caught in a bowl,
> And the cat licks it, thinking that it's milk;
> Another threads its way through tree-branches,
> And the elephant thinks he has found a lotus-stalk.
> Half asleep, a girl reaches out
> And tries to rearrange the moonbeams on the bed
> To share the warmth.
>> It is the moon that is drunk with its own light,
>> But the world that is confused.[10]

The Indian night has its own unmistakably Indian sounds: the eerie, unearthly howls and cries, startling to strangers, of the jackals that roam in packs round the outskirts of villages and penetrate even into towns; jackal howls are at their loudest and most bloodcurdling when the moon is full. In the spring and hot weather there are birds that call all night:

> Suddenly a cruel scream from the kokila bird
> Shattered my sleep and dream. . . .[11]

but most maddening and sleep-preventing of all is the hawk-cuckoo, whose piercing and continually repeated call grows more fevered at the approach of the rains; it is translated into English as "brain-fever, brain-fever!" but in Hindi as "prem kahan?"—where is my love? Those birds of ill-omen, the nightjars, give calls that can be heard a long way off although, when flying like large, soft, mottled moths in the dark spaces between the trees, they hawk for insects, their flight is uncannily silent. In the rainy season, frogs croak from every flooded ditch and pond, and there is always, somewhere in the background, music from a bazaar or a distant temple: a loudspeaker, a radio or a gramophone playing into the small hours; a group of kirtan-singers; bells or a conch, and the steady throb of drums.

10. From the *Subhasitaratnakosa*, compiled by Vidyakara, translated by John Brough.
11. From the fifteenth-century Bengali poet, Badu Chandidas, translated by Deben Bhattacharya.

There are Indian night scents too, of night-flowering cactus,[12] which opens its huge white flowers only in the dark, and Chandnee, Moonbeam, whose white, white flowers dazzle against its dark leaves on moonlit nights and can flood a whole garden with sweetness—and drown the ever-present smell of defective drains.

At certain times of the year in town gardens, on the outskirts of villages, and in the jungles, hosts of fireflies gather to dance at night in the under-growth and through the trees, making starry patterns in the darkness.

The fires along the river banks make star patterns too; at Benares they shine all night; small campfires from those who have brought their old or incurably sick to die on the river bank—they may have carried them a hundred miles—and other fires, burning low now, from the pyres on the ghats.

Death is not solemn, quiet, or decorous in India—particularly if it happens at home; brahmins—pandits or priests—loudly intone their mantras while crowds of relations and friends gather, and the loud wailing of women sounds through the house, sometimes going on for days, sometimes extolling the deeds and virtues of the dead, sometimes becoming a high keening. All ornaments are stripped from the dead body—if it is a man, his widow has her jewels taken from her—it is washed and perfumed, wrapped in linen, perhaps covered with white silk—white is the colour of death—and tied onto a bamboo mat and stretcher, so that it can be carried through the streets or the lanes of the village to the burning ghat; the garlanded corpse often looks pitifully small and light. As chief mourner, the eldest son or, for a woman, her husband, walks in front of the bier; relatives and friends follow, chanting "Ram Ram," or "Ram nam sach hain"—God's name is truth—"Aur sab gat hai"—All else is transitory. They may scatter Ganges water from bunches of kusa grass or twigs of the five holy trees, throw coins to beggars, and often there is music. When the funeral procession reaches the entrance to the burning ghat, a pitcher of water is broken to make sure another death shall not visit the family too soon.

Moslems dig graves for their corpses; Parsees expose them to vultures on the Towers of Silence because a corpse must not defile the sacred elements, water, earth, and fire. In some parts of the high hills and in Tibet, where wood is scarce and the frozen ground stone-hard, dead people are left to be disposed of by birds of prey, or by wild animals. It is known from the *Vedas* that the Indo-Aryans buried their dead, and yet their descendants, Buddhist and Hindu, burn them in the open on funeral pyres—by burning the body becomes anonymous, which is what a Hindu would choose his to be. Babies and young children, though, are never burnt; their small bodies, wrapped in

12. *Cereus grandifloras.*

350

scarlet silk or cotton and covered with flowers, are carried to the nearest river and placed on little bamboo rafts in the stream.

The pyre is made of logs carefully arranged; the corpse is covered with sandalwood, more logs, then ghee, if the family can afford it; if not, oil is poured over the whole, incense scattered, then a lighted torch is handed to the eldest son or grandson, who holds it to the pyre—at the feet for a woman, at the head, or even in the mouth, for a man.

As the flames leap up, everyone draws back, but if the skull does not burst in the heat, someone must come forward to break it and let the soul escape. A sannyasi's body has to be burned by the people who have tended him because no one knows where his family may be—he is already anonymous—but, at the moment when the skull cracks or at the moment when his last breath failed, a cry is often raised, "Amar rahain"—Live eternally. Amar: immortal.

After the skull has broken, the mourners turn away, leaving the fire to its attendants; when it has cooled, some of the ashes and bones are collected in a jar, which is covered with a red cloth bound round the neck; it will be put in a special place in the house and kept decorated with fresh flowers.

The family is "unclean" and may not even cook on the first day after the death; some families fast, some eat food sent in by neighbours—a time of death is always, everywhere, a neighbourly time—but the ritual of these days must be carefully kept because the dead man, or woman, has to acquire a "subtle body" in which to start on another life's journey after passing through, or lingering a little, in heaven; for this new body he must have food and gifts which will reach him when the ceremony of the Shraddha is held—on the twelfth day for brahmins, the thirteenth for kshatriyas, the sixteenth for vaisyas, and the twenty-ninth for sudras. The family is then formally cleansed, the husband or eldest son or grandson has his head shaved, and a feast and money are given to brahmins, neighbours, and beggars; it is through this charity that all these necessities will reach the soul that has gone. To help in this, a new set of everything one person uses, a bed and bedding, utensils, clothes, shoes, are given to a brahmin, with fourteen pitchers of water, one for each month of the year and two extra—water is life and there must be no danger of the new body running out of it. When this is done, the time of mourning is over.

But the last duty to the dead has yet to be fulfilled. Months, a year, or even years later, the jar or vase is lifted down and taken by the senior member of the family to Prayag or Hardwar or Gaya, where the ashes or bones are poured, perhaps from a boat in midstream, into the quick water of the Ganges.

Even this is not quite the end; that same evening, as it grows dark, a toy-sized boat, shaped like a cup and made of leaves stitched together, filled with flowers—roses, jasmine—and holding a little earthenware lit lamp, is set adrift on the river with many other little boats just like it, each holding its twinkling point of light that vanishes into the darkness as it floats away.

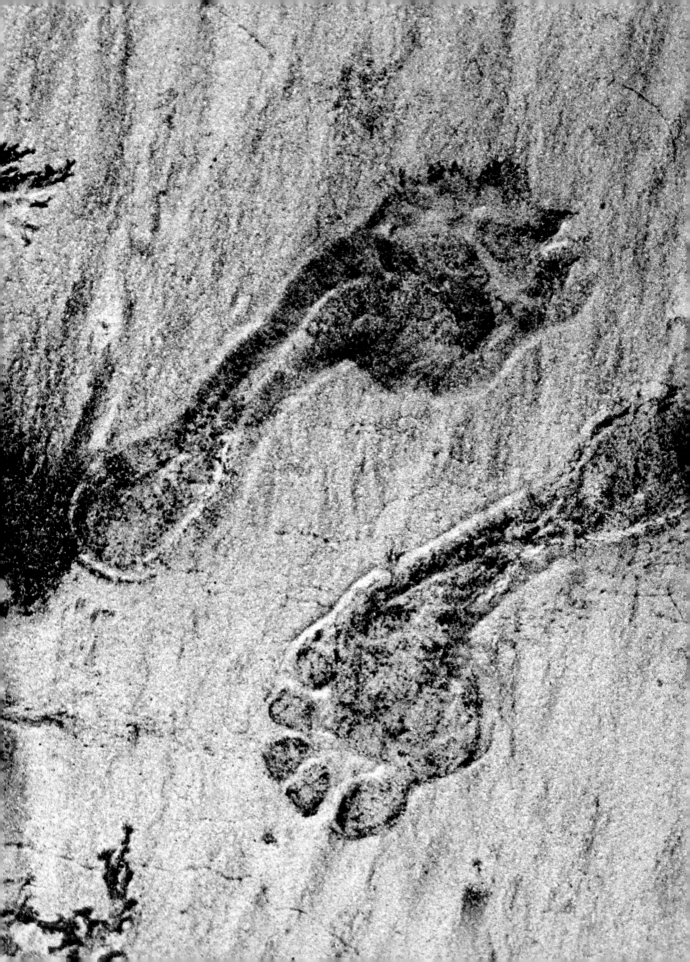

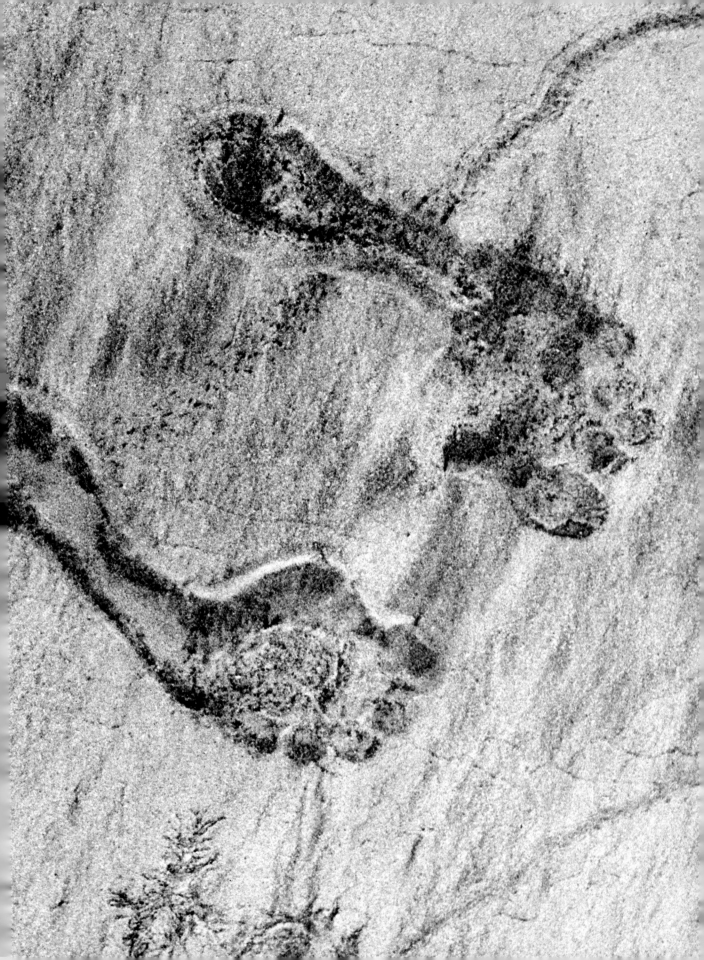

PATTERNS BY SHEILA AUDEN

The large pattern (used as a decoration for the opening of each Part of this book) is alpona, which differs from the rangoli of our text in that alpona is a ritual, not simply a traditional drawing, and has a deep mystical, even magical, meaning; completely freehand, it, too, is done by women with liquid rice paste on the ground, but preferably earthen ground.

The smaller patterns used elsewhere in the book are katha, a kind of quilted patchwork made from rags; again, it has a mystical meaning; what was once in shreds is now whole again, man's "little rag of life is of no account until it has been joined to the Supreme Being and so transformed."

CAPTIONS

PHOTOGRAPHS BY STELLA SNEAD (pages 6-308)

6. Brooding doves.

11. Stone carved balcony with pigeon, Jaisalmer, Rajasthan.

12. Head of Shiva on a lingam. It was hidden behind the solitary temple of Dundeshwar in the forests of the Kumoan Hills.

16–17. Pigeon footprints.

PART 1

19. Astrologer. Fakir Baba was the name we knew him by in Nasik, where he had come to live in his old age. Born a Moslem, he had long ago embraced Hinduism and adopted the life of a mendicant holy man–astrologer. He would come and sit beside us in the garden and talk of the stars as well as the gods.

23. Jantar Manta. This photograph shows the gnomon, the central shaft of the Samrat Yantra or Supreme Instrument at Jaipur.

24–25. Section of marble quadrant from above, Jaipur.

27. Gnomon and part of quadrant, Jaipur.

29. View through an arch of the Samrat Yantra, showing smaller similar constructions which refer to the signs of the Zodiac, and in the distance, a minaret—Jaipur.

31. Child jewellery. Farmer's child in a village, north of Bombay. He is wearing his silver charm belt which he keeps up with his genitals.

35. *Ganesha* dancing on his Vehicle, the rat. Folk painting from Orissa.

37. Marble wall of a shrine beside the lake at Ajmer, Rajasthan.

38–39. A courtyard of the Old Palace at Udaipur. The woman is probably helping with some building work and will return with the basin on her head filled with cement or bricks.

40–41. Toda boy. The Todas are an aboriginal people who live in the Nilgiri Hills in southwest India and, like many aboriginal tribes, are distinctive in appearance. Todas wear their hair covering ears and forehead while the women curl theirs into long ringlets—see the old woman on page 338, PART VII. Their houses are made of mud and bamboo with rounded roofs, very low doors, and no chimneys, so that they are often filled with smoke. They keep buffaloes which only the men and boys are permitted to touch. This particular boy is unusual in that he goes to school and wants to become an engineer.

43. Shadows of a champa tree, known sometimes as frangipani.

44. High-caste young woman of a reasonably well-to-do Hindu family.

47. Spray of wild grass.

49. Hand prints on the mud wall of a village house. Besides their decorative charm, it is believed they will hold back evil from the house and its occupants.

51. Namaskar. Except among the sophisticated and westernized, this greeting is used instead of shaking hands.

52–53. Ablutions, Mylapore tank, Madras.

57. Rajasthani grandmother holding one of her many grandchildren. The pair of trousers hung up on the wall to dry is typical of the kind she wears. These are worn by younger women as well, tight of leg and all too ready for the bulge of pregnancy above.

58–59. Beach pattern. The sand on many Indian beaches is of two kinds, light and dark. When runnels of water uncover the dark which is just below the surface, these patterns are strongly defined. They may look like many things, from wet streaming hair to the growth of trees, but they are sand.

PART II

62. Twig thrown on the sand and lapped by the waves.

64. Launching a fishing boat into the waves on Puri beach, Orissa.

65. Woman and child walking the long straight beach at Puri.

66. Three fisherwomen. They are Maharastrians and typical of the fishing villages around Bombay. Whenever their men bring in the boats, they are there to collect the fish, dry it, and sell it.

69. Squirrel hanging from a leafy branch. From Bharhut, 150 B.C., now in the Indian Museum, Calcutta.

73. Hunger. Woman holding out her begging bowl. Note her bangle, perhaps her iron wedding one, which she will not sell, though she is starving.

74–75. Street sleepers. A usual sight in Indian cities and towns.

77. Old woman. The old are perhaps the most tragic of India's beggars. Her gnarled hands show a lifetime of drudgery, and the empty hole in her nose tells of the day when she sold her nose ring to eat.

81. Tree which seems to have a curve reminiscent of much Indian sculpture. Kangra valley in the Himalayas.

82–83. Line of high peaks seen from near Almora, U.P. Eternally snow-covered and almost as high as the northeastern ranges, they are, from left to right, Trisul, Nanda Kot, and Nanda Devi, the last being 25,645 feet. In the foreground are deodar, cedar, and pine forests, farmhouses and terraced fields.

84–85. Clouds filling a valley. A common sight in the hills at about 5000 feet in the early morning. Later the clouds will disperse.

87. Buddhist monk. He is a Tibetan going on a pilgrimage to the various Buddhist shrines in India. Here he is at Bhaja Caves, near Bombay. Like Ellora, these were carved out of the solid rock by other Buddhist monks in the second century B.C.

89. Laughing Tibetan, at Manali in Kulu, one of the many who escaped into India. His hair is still bound round the head in a plait in the traditional style; his pullover is very likely a gift from abroad.

90. Kashmiri nomad of the Gujar tribe.

93. Pine forest, Manali, Kulu.

95. Kulu youth, wearing typical red velvet hat. He is a fruit grower.

96–97. Dal Lake. The best known of the several lakes in the Vale of Kashmir. It is closest to the capital, Srinagar, and many of the visitors' houseboats are moored nearby.

100. Mullah at the door of the mosque in Char-i-sherif, a pilgrimage place near Srinagar, Kashmir.

103. One of the numerous canals that run through the town of Srinagar and lead into the Jhelum River. Here are tightly assembled the simple houseboats that the local people live on. In the foreground is one of the poles of a shikara. In these small boats visitors are paddled smoothly and slowly around the waterways.

105. Kashmir lake and mountains, from a shikara.

107. Bakriwal matriarch, another nomad of Kashmir. Fierce and hating to be photographed. Typical silver jewellery and hair in tiny plaits.

109. Subsidiary shrines that surround the eighth-century Sun Temple of Bara Adit at Katarmal, near Almora, U.P. Standing on a hill, it commands a splendid view of the high snows. Trisul and Nanda Kot can be seen between the two towers.

PART III

115. Surya, the Sun God, astride a charger. From the Sun Temple at Konarak in Orissa, built in the thirteenth century.

116. Female figure. From Menal, a little-known eleventh-century temple in Rajasthan.

117. From the fort, Jodhpur.

118–119. University students. Many of them go first to an Indian university, then are sent to continue their studies abroad.

123. Portrait of a Scindi girl.

127. Girl carrying a load in the Himalayas. The headband is generally used in the hills instead of carrying things on the head as in the plains.

128. Bullock-cart nomad.

129. Kulu woman wearing a blanket draped in the traditional way, her basket on her back.

130. Tea basket hung on a wall in Kangra. This is the skeleton only; a tighter mesh will be woven in, and soon it will be filled to the brim with freshly picked tea leaves.

132. Hill boy carrying a load, this time not with a headband but with ropes around his shoulders.

133. Bamboo. Many kinds of bamboo grow in India, some as big as trees, as in the Mysore jungles, and some delicate and thin-stemmed. The stem of this particular variety has bright green stripes on a hot yellow ground, the lower part encased in a furry sheath.

134. Old Gypsy (Lambari) woman. Dishevelled but indomitable, she has probably spent her life in work as hard as a man's.

136. Banyan tree in the University gardens at Poona. As the original tree puts down roots from its branches, the effect is as of many trees growing together. Thus one tree can spread almost indefinitely, but as these trees often line the roads of India, their aerial roots have to be cut, and hang like chopped-off hair.

137. Detail of banyan tree, left, showing complicated interplay of branches and roots.

139. Typical village elder, but in actuality the guardian at Sanchi stupa. He is distinguished by his beard, which he wears in the old Rajasthani style, parted in the middle and brushed out at right angles.

141. Truck jewellery. In India jewellery is worn not only by people, but by animals, by horse-drawn tongas, and even by trucks.

144–145. Village well. The meeting place for all country folk, especially the women. If there is no river or pond, they wash clothes there, besides drawing water.

148–149. Tool shop with shopkeeper, Bikaner, Rajasthan.

151. Girl resting on a trail in Chamba in the western Himalayas.

153. Cows wander in the streets of every Indian city, getting mixed up in the traffic, living on whatever they can find, mostly garbage. Although their cowshed is the open street, they belong to someone and, as these in the photograph, are tended and valued.

154. Rajasthani peasant with a fine smile and a jaunty moustache.

156. Child wandering and lonely in the courtyard of a group of temples at Jageshwar in the foothills of the Himalayas. Her black dress, very much worn and turning green with age and damp, must have belonged to her mother or an elder sister.

158. Women fetching water. Looking down on the steps of the big tank in Jaisalmer, Rajasthan, where the women of every household must go for their daily supply of water.

159. Woman returning from the village tank with a full and well-balanced jar.

161. Water spiral at Mandu, the once splendid Moslem city near Indore, where water runs in this decorative manner from one tank or pool to another, travelling part time underground.

PART IV

165. Trellised window. This jali or open screen of stone makes up most of the outside of a room in the seventeenth-century Palace of Amber outside Jaipur, Rajasthan. It looks down on a lake in which a decorative stone platform has been constructed.

167. Miniature painting of Sri Ram Singhji, possibly one of the Maharajas of Jodhpur. Late eighteenth century, Marwar.

171. Four horses. The scene represented is from the *Vessantara Jataka* (ancient Buddhist tales). From Bharhut, second century B.C., in the Allahabad Museum.

173. Miniature painting of a Rajasthani nobleman. Copy of Mogul style, late eighteenth century, Marwar.

175. Domes and walls seen from a higher part of the Palace of Amber. This seventeenth-century building clambers picturesquely up a hillside, affording views on many levels.

177. Opium poppy. Fields of these can be seen in Rajasthan and elsewhere; the flowers look delicately innocent and are pale in colour.

178. Big-turbaned man in Patan, the old capital of Gujerat. In this part of India the horns of the bullocks are particularly ample and so are the turbans—yards and yards of cotton cloth in brilliant colours: orange, red, and magenta.

180–181. Tiger beside a pool. Detail of a Kotah miniature painting, 1790, Victoria and Albert Museum, London.

182. Pipe smoker in Patan, Gujerat. This is the typical peasant way of holding a pipe or a cigarette.

185. Areca palms. They grow best where there is steamy heat and plenty of moisture, their thin, polished trunks rigidly straight, leaves dark at the top, and from among them hang the round, hard areca nuts. This plantation is at the foot of the Nilgiri hills near Coimbatore.

187. Palm leaves—these are cocoanut palms at Juhu beach, Bombay.

189. Spice seller in the Bombay bazaar. His whole shop is in this round basket. He can squat down among the other vendors and start business. If it is slow, he can put the basket on his head and move on. Spices are used so much in India that he probably makes a good living.

191. Bakri Id is a Moslem festival at which goats are killed in celebration of Abraham's sacrifice. People wear new clothes, go to the mosque, and later feast in their homes.

193. Secondhand bottle shop.

204. Puppet. The best ones come from Rajasthan. Some have faces of painted wood, like the one photographed, but he has lost his jointed and stringed limbs and is nothing more than a doll.

207. Cinema posters, in sizes from colossal to modest, are everywhere, often printed in two or three languages.

208. Sitar player. One of the sons of Nikhil Ghosh, well-known tabla player of Bombay, learns the sitar.

209. Playing tambura. The hand of a singer as she accompanies herself on a tambura while her teacher plays tabla (drums).

210–211. Tabla. Nikhil Ghosh in action.

212–213. Children paying rapt attention.

213. Children during a singing lesson.

219. Artist at work repairing a mosaic-covered wall at the Lake Palace (now a hotel) at Udaipur, Rajasthan.

221. Nataraj or Dancing Shiva, thirteenth-century Chola bronze, Indian Museum, Calcutta.

222. Dancer's hands. One of the many mudras, or hand poses, that are an important part of Bharata Natyam. The dancer had just performed one of these strenuous and exacting dances when the photograph was taken—note the sweat on her neck and the disarray of her necklace.

225. Bharata Natyam dancer in a typical attitude.

226 Autumn festival in Chhatrari, Chamba (western Himalayas). Every year most of the people of Chamba move down from their high summer pastures to lower winter ones. In the larger villages they stop for two or three days while the men dance in the temple courtyard and the women and children watch from every balcony and hillside. The men wear handsome white wool coats wrapped around by yards of brown cord, a bright scarf added for the occasion. The women are particularly gay in many colours and much jewellery.

227. Dance hat. Certain of the men in Chamba, the leaders of the dancing, wear these hats during a festival. The hat is of wool, practically buried in gold braid, and topped with a bunch of feathers.

228–229. Children watching through a lattice.

231. Toy seller. He carries a wooden pole bound with straw, stuck with paper windmills and cardboard figures which, when twisted, will fling out their arms and legs in gay abandon. He strolls along the beach or from house to house and sells his wares for next to nothing.

PART V

235. Village girl, from Rajasthan. She wears earrings that hang from the top of her ears as well as the lobes.

236–237. Wedding by camel in the desert country toward the Pakistan border in Rajasthan. The young bridegroom, in ornamental turban and brocaded coat, sits in front, his uncle behind. The camel cloth or malra is in appliqué of bright colours; ordinary buttons effectively decorate the bridle.

239. Children dressed for a wedding, Rajasthan. Everyone enjoys such festivities, except, possibly, the bride's father because of the expense.

243. Arm with jewellery. This is everyday wear in certain parts of India. Curiously, the women who do the hardest physical work often load their limbs the most heavily with bangles and bracelets.

244. Jewellery for men is not at all uncommon, particularly among the peasants of Kathiawar and Gujerat. Note the ear caps.

247. Girl with jewellery met at a bus station in Kangra. Judging by the amount of jewellery—amber beads over a wide necklace of silver, two gold nose rings—she is going to a wedding; maybe she is the bride.

248. Rangoli—those patterns that are made by women on the stone or mud floors of houses, and on steps and thresholds at the time of weddings and other festivities.

249. Rangoli—coloured powders are sometimes popular and, deftly dribbled through the fingers, form an endless number of patterns, or, as here, a paste of rice water is used which allows the pattern to last longer.

251. Two mannequin dolls, dressed as bride and bridegroom, in a shop window in Bombay's bazaar.

255. Krishna holding a lotus. Detail from a Basholi painting, 1680, Krishna from the Rasamanjam of Bhanudatta, Victoria and Albert Museum, London.

257. Lingams and Yoni, symbols of male and female genital organs, carved on a flat rock beside the Tungabhadra River at Hampi where are the extensive ruins of the capital of the Vijayanagar empire.

259. Young bride of Jaisalmer, handsomely decorated with gold, silver, enamel, and ivory; she seems to have her new husband already well in hand.

261. Woman bowing before Nandi, Shiva's bull, at Mahakuteshwara temple, near Badami, Mysore state.

263. Hair wreaths. Women and girls, even the smallest, frequently wear flowers in their hair; some of them do so every day. Throughout the north white flowers are used—jasmine, champa, tuberoses—the photograph shows the last—but in the south the flowers are of many colours—bright bunches on the black hair. Or, perhaps, a fishergirl will wear a single blossom which she has just stolen from your garden.

267. Blowing a conch shell. This earliest of musical instruments is still blown by Hindu priests during puja—religious ceremony or worship. Behind the priest in this photograph is the base of a giant seated figure, a decoratively painted village guardian. The small standing figure is an attendant.

PART VI

271. Conch-seller. In addition to the four large white shells, this pavement salesman offers the kind of beads holy men wear and framed pictures of the gods.

272–273. Pieces of sculpture lying among vegetation near Bajinath village, U.P. The head could be Vishnu—eleventh or twelfth century.

274. Buddha's attendant, in Cave 2 at Bagh, fifth century A.D.

275. Detail of a lion, collar, mane, and tail. From the Sun Temple at Konarak, thirteenth century.

279. A woman of Chamba, now a part of Himachal Pradesh.

280. Festival procession in Trivellore, south India.

281. Boy holding staff and taking part in a temple procession in south India. Painted on his forehead is the sign of Vishnu.

282–283. Temple at Baijnath, Kangra—twelfth or thirteenth century. This Shiva temple has the usual seated Nandi—bull—under the canopy facing the entrance, and there is also a standing Nandi, which is uncommon.

285. A wandering holy man. Taken beside a temple in Trimbuk, above which is the source of the Godavari River. A few miles downstream is Nasik, which every twelve years sees a vast gathering of holy men from all over India. This one has come at such a time, carrying his small bundle, probably with his only possessions.

286. A Sadhu makes a rangoli pattern round his fire at the time of Divali.

289. Snake shrine. At this small open-air shrine on the edge of the Maidan in Calcutta, the image of a hooded cobra is garlanded and worshipped.

293. Kartikeya, one of the sons of Shiva, riding on his Vehicle, a peacock. From Bihar, twelfth century. Indian Museum, Calcutta.

295. Cat mystery.

297. Back of an elephant's ear, showing also the leg of the mahout with his bare foot in a stirrup of rope.

298–299. Decorated elephants, painted for ceremonial occasion or temple processions. These are painted for tourists who may ride them up to the Palace of Amber, near Jaipur.

303. Id. The main festival of Id is celebrated, usually for three days when the moon is new after Ramazan, the month of fasting which all orthodox Moslems observe.

304–305. Garlanded buffalo. Buffalo are sacrificed by Ghurkas at Dasera, but there is another and more gentle buffalo festival in Nasik for Divali.

310. Boy at Holi. His clothes are bespattered with coloured water and red powder; he himself very likely added the moustache. At Puskha, near Ajmer, Rajasthan.

311. Gypsy road worker. They do the hardest work and wear the heaviest jewellery, skirts instead of saris, and bodices with colourful appliqué and mirror work.

313. Images in the making. Such headless clay images are sometimes seen out in the streets, where they are placed to dry in the sun.

314–315. Potter in Orissa. The wheel is always on the ground and is turned with a stick.

316. Clay horse with groom—more than life size. Part of a group of village guardians in a temple courtyard near Madras.

317. Horse with branches of Singapore cherry. Pottery horses and cows may be found in groups in the fields south of Madras, made and put there by the peasants for superstitious reasons.

318. Image of Lakshmi, generously garlanded, outside a temple in Assam during the celebration of Shivratri, Shiva's birthday.

321. A guru or teacher. He was in charge of the Ramakrishna Mission, Nasik.

322–323. Women devotees listening to the guru at the Dera, an ashram at Beas, Punjab. On these occasions it is customary for men and women to be segregated.

323. Water hyacinths.

PART VII

327. Iron rods in water at Sewri, Bombay.

328–329. Boat with nets. Method of fishing on the Brahmaputra River in Assam.

330. Drying fish on bamboo racks. The beach areas around fishing villages are filled with these; often the racks are on high platforms to allow the tide to come in beneath. At Varsova, near Bombay.

331. Prow of a boat with paddle, Colva Beach, Goa.

333. Fishing boat with outrigger.

338. Toda woman with hair in typical long ringlets. The Todas live in the Nilgiri hills at about 7000 feet and are usually to be seen wrapped in blankets or hand-embroidered shawls.

341. Simul tree (Bombax Ceiba) in the forest near Lake Periyar, southwest India.

343. Jagged mountain. It rears from the forest on the way up to the snows from the Srinagar valley.

345. Shepherd carrying a kid, at about 9000 feet.

347. A sage who was present at a Kumbha Mela (meeting of holy men) in Nasik. Note his three kinds of hair—head hair long and matted, beard combed, clean and very white, while that on his chest is grey and curly.

348. Small lamps or divas used at shrines or at Divali, the festival of lights.

351. Funeral pyre.

353. Rippling sands.

354–355. Footprints—going away.

CHRONOLOGY

*As even the most learned sources differ about
the early dates of Indian history, those quoted
here should be taken only as approximate.*

J.G. R.G.

B.C.

Circa	2500	The Indus valley civilization with its city communities of Mohen-jo-daro and Harappa.
Circa	1500	The Indo-"Aryan" infiltration from the northwest.
Circa	1200–800	The *Vedas*.
		Caste system evolves.
		Early Hinduism.
	599–527	Mahavira, founder of Jainism.
	563	Birth of the Buddha, Siddhartha Gautama.
	519	First incursions of the Persians under King Cyrus.
	327	Alexander invades India.
	322	Chandragupta Maurya founds the Maurian dynasty, under which India, except for the South, is united for the first time.
	268–231	Reign of Asoka.
		Buddhism spreads through India.
	185	Maurian dynasty ends: the empire is broken up into many short-lived kingdoms.
Circa	200	Greek kings reign in the Punjab.

A.D.

	20–48	The Indo-Parthian king, Gondophares, reigns at Taxila, a centre of culture and learning.
Circa	48–220	The Kushan empire, a period of growing art and spread of different religions. Buddhism becomes Asia-wide, Christianity and the old Persian religions are practised in India, and in Hinduism the gods are given human-like personalities. When this empire disintegrates, it seems there is a "hidden" time of darkness and disorder.
	320	Chandragupta I and the Gupta dynasty. } India's "golden age" of prosperity
	375–415	Chandragupta II.
	480–490	Break-up of the Gupta empire.
Circa	500	Huns subdue northern India.
	606–647	King Harsha, who reunites India as far as the Vindhya mountains.

	620	King Pulikesa II of the southern Chalukyan empire repulses Harsha.
Circa	800	Shankaracharya, the south Indian philosopher, almost banishes Buddhism from India and gives Hinduism a renaissance.
	985–1014	Rajaraja the Great of the southern Chola dynasty, whose navy invades Ceylon.
	997–1030	Mahmud of Ghazni. With other Moslem invaders he makes annual raids into India and fights the Rajput kings of the north.
	1206–1526	Moslems settle for the first time in India and become Sultans of Delhi.
	1336–1565	The southern empire of Vijayanagar, which virtually ends with the battle of Talikot.
	1469	Guru Nanak makes the Sikhs into a separate sect.
	1498	The Portuguese arrive as traders, nearly two hundred years before the Dutch, French, and British.
	1524	Babur comes to India and in 1526 founds the Mogul Empire.
	1542	Birth of Akbar the Great. Under him the Mogul dynasty begins its heyday. As it declines, Hinduism once again surges into new power.
	1627	Birth of Sivaji, the Maratha leader who fought the Mogul Emperor Aurangzeb.
	1639	The English East India Company granted land for a factory in Madras.
	1712	Decline of the Mogul Empire begins with the death of its Emperor Bahadur Shah I.
	1780–1839	Maharaja Ranjit Singh, lion of the Punjab.
	1857	Indian mutiny against the British, who, after Ranjit Singh's death, gained control of the whole subcontinent.
	1858	Queen Victoria proclaimed Empress of India.
	1869	Mahatma Gandhi born.
	1947	Independence. Pandit Jawaharlal Nehru becomes Prime Minister.
	1948	Assassination of Gandhi.
January 26,	1950	India's new constitution comes into force and she is declared a republic.

Chief Mogul Emperors

The Moguls, though latecomers by Indian standards, left an imprint out of all proportion to the time—not three hundred years—during which they ruled.

From Babur, they were:

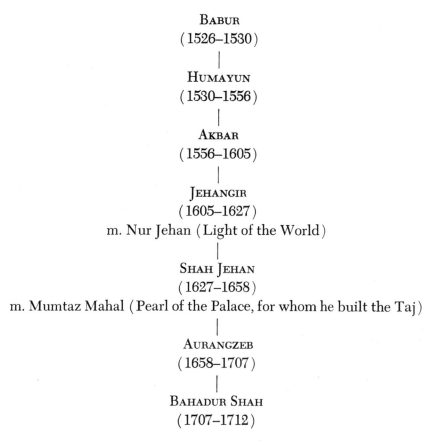

BABUR
(1526–1530)
|
HUMAYUN
(1530–1556)
|
AKBAR
(1556–1605)
|
JEHANGIR
(1605–1627)
m. Nur Jehan (Light of the World)
|
SHAH JEHAN
(1627–1658)
m. Mumtaz Mahal (Pearl of the Palace, for whom he built the Taj)
|
AURANGZEB
(1658–1707)
|
BAHADUR SHAH
(1707–1712)

The last Moslem king, another Bahadur Shah, no longer emperor, old and blind, was expelled by the British after the mutiny; in October 1858, the old king with his wives and children was exiled to Rangoon.

It was ironic that Babur's dynasty should be called the Moguls because he detested them. "Mogul" was originally the same word as "Mongol," and it was his Mongol relations who stole the little kingdom of Ferghana he inherited when he was twelve years old; he never ceased to mourn its fertile valleys. "Mongol," or "Mogul," was used in India to describe all invading foreigners from the north until, with the British, the word "Mogul" came to designate an Indian emperor or king.

ACKNOWLEDGMENTS

Atheneum Publishers, William Heinemann Ltd., London, and Balachandra Rajan: From *Too Long in the West* by Balachandra Rajan. Freda Bedi: From *Behind the Mud Walls* and *Rhymes for Ranga.* Thomas Y. Crowell Company and Nissim Ezekiel: "Night of the Scorpion" from *Poems from India.* The John Day Company, Inc., John Farquharson Ltd., London, and Kamala Markandaya: From *Nectar in a Sieve* by Kamala Markandaya. Copyright © 1954 by The John Day Company. The John Day Company Inc., The Bodley Head, London, and Allied Publishers, India: From *Toward Freedom* by Jawaharlal Nehru. Copyright © 1941 by The John Day Company; Copyright renewed 1968 by Indira Gandhi. Reprinted by permission of the publishers. Doubleday & Company, Inc., Macmillan & Co., Ltd., London, and Mrs. George Bambridge: From *Kim* by Rudyard Kipling. Grove Press, Inc., George Allen and Unwin Ltd., London, and Deben Bhattacharya: From *Love Songs of Chandidas,* translated by Deben Bhattacharya. Copyright © 1967, 1969 UNESCO. Reprinted by permission of Grove Press, Inc. The Hamlyn Publishing Group Limited, Attia Hosain and Sita Pasricha: From *Cooking the Indian Way* by Attia Hosain and Sita Pasricha. Reprinted by permission of The Hamlyn Publishing Group Limited. George G. Harrap & Company Ltd., The Sister Nivedita and Ananda Coomaraswamy: From *Myths of the Hindus and Buddhists* by Ananda Coomaraswamy. Reprinted by permission. Harvard University Press, Yogesvara, and Daniel H. H. Ingalls: From *An Anthology of Sanskrit Court Poetry* by Daniel H. H. Ingalls. Indiana University Press and Vidya Niwas Misra: From "Evening at the Seashore" by Nalin Vilochan Sharma from *Modern Hindi Poetry* by Vidya Niwas Misra. The Macmillan Company, Curtis Brown Ltd., London, and Sudhin Ghose: From *And Gazelles Leaping* by Sudhin Ghose. Copyright 1949 by Sudhindra Nath Ghose, The Macmillan Company, New York, The Macmillan Co., Ltd., London and Basingstoke. The Trustees of the Rabindranath Tagore Estate: from *The Crescent Moon* by Rabindranath Tagore, Copyright 1913 by The Macmillan Company, renewed 1941 by Rabindranath Tagore, from *Collected Poems & Plays* by Rabindranath Tagore. Reprinted by permission. Lillian Morrison: "The Street Sleepers," reprinted by permission of the author. John Murray Ltd. and Sarojini Naidu: From *An Anthology of Modern Indian Poetry,* Wisdom of the East Series, by Sarojini Naidu. Swami Nikhilananda: From *Ramakrishna, Prophet of New India.* Orient Longmans Ltd., Delhi, and Shanta Rameshwar Rao: From *Ancient Tales of India* by Shanta Rameshwar Rao. Penguin Books Ltd. and John Brough: From *Poems from the Sanskrit,* extracts from "The Subhasitartnakosa," "Bhavabhuti," "Amaru," and "Kumara-Sambhava." Copyright © John Brough, 1968. P. Thomas: From "Vidypathi" translated by Ananda Coomaraswamy and Aran Sen.

We would like to offer our apologies to those literary heirs whom we have been unable to trace. We hope they will accept this general acknowledgment for material we have quoted.